CUNNINGHAM SECURITY

BETRAYED

A.K. EVANS

Betrayed
Copyright 2019 by A.K. Evans
All rights reserved.

ISBN: 978-1-951441-04-3

No part of this book may be reproduced, distributer, or transmitted in any form or by any means including photocopying, recording, or other electronic or mechanical methods, without the prior written permission of the author except in the case of brief quotations in a book review.

This is a work of fiction. Names, characters, places, and incidents are the product of the author's imagination or are used fictitiously. Any resemblance to actual events, locales, or persons, living or dead, is coincidental.

Cover Artist
cover artwork © Sarah Hansen, Okay Creations
www.okaycreations.com

Editing & Proofreading
Ellie McLove, My Brother's Editor
www.grayinkonline.com

Formatting
Stacey Blake at Champagne Book Design
www.champagnebookdesign.com

BETRAYED

PROLOGUE

Quinn

If there was one thing in this world I never wanted to be, it was *that woman*. The one that was too blind to see what was happening right in front of her face.

But now I was starting to understand just how easy it was to become that woman. Because what did it say about me if I'd made all the wrong choices that put me in this position to begin with?

Was oblivion the smarter choice?

Logically, I knew that it wasn't.

But it at least wouldn't have forced me to see my own failures and bad decisions. The ones that I made because I trusted and believed in someone.

Admitting the truth meant admitting that I was wrong. I took a chance on someone, chose to have people in my life, and was now convinced I was being betrayed. How would I ever recover from that? Was it even possible?

For the last few months, I'm not sure if it was naivety or an unwillingness to really look at and believe the signs. The red flags. Everything that was screaming at me to wake up and take notice of what was happening right under my nose.

I didn't know how to respond or react when I was left

with that dreadful feeling of emptiness in the pit of my stomach. The one that told me I knew what was happening. The one that wouldn't let me ignore warning signs.

I didn't want to believe that it could happen to me. Nobody does. Especially when it comes to something like love.

But now it was too obvious to disregard.

I couldn't continue to pretend anymore. I couldn't continue to fool myself into believing it was just in my mind or that it could never happen to me.

I couldn't continue to be *that woman.*

It was happening to me.

I knew it deep down in my heart.

The final piece of evidence came to me in the form of a text message only minutes ago and all but confirmed it.

My best friend, Alicia, and I had been working together for the last eight months on a new business venture.

Jewelry making.

The two of us had always been lovers of accessories with an eye for fashion, so I proposed the idea to her one day. We could start taking classes together to learn how to make those accessories and turn it into a business.

Alicia was all about it.

So, we did our research and found a few places that offered the training. We settled on one that was being offered in the evenings at a local college campus.

It fit perfectly into my schedule, since I didn't exactly have a job. I made money, a good deal of it, in fact. But I didn't have a typical nine to five. My husband, Chris, and I owned several pieces of property that we rented out, which provided us with an income that was more than healthy. My husband handled most of the management of our properties, while I took care of the business side of it. So, when he had something to tend to in one of the rentals, I was searching for new properties for us to get at a steal, fix up, and rent.

It worked for us.

And I loved the freedom it gave the both of us to explore other things in our lives that would bring us happiness.

For him, it was coming and going as he pleased or meeting up with his buddies to head to a ball game, whether football, baseball, or basketball. For me, it was a new business that allowed me to merge my love for jewelry with my business-driven mind. Being able to bring my best friend on board was icing on the cake.

But I should have heeded the age-old advice: never mix business with pleasure.

Or, at least, never mix business with family. Because that's what Alicia was. She was like a sister to me. And I knew what it meant to have that because I already had one sister—a blood relative—with whom I was very close, save for the fact that she didn't live nearby.

I glanced down at my phone again and reread Alicia's text.

I can't make it tonight. I got called in to work an extra shift again. You'll fill me in tomorrow afternoon?

Sure, it seemed like a completely plausible excuse. Alicia worked as a bartender, so it was certainly possible that she got called in to work the occasional extra shift. But this was the fourth class I'd attended without her in as many weeks.

I probably would have accepted her excuse at face value; however, she wasn't the only one with them.

Nope.

Over the last four or five weeks, my husband had them, too. The biggest of which was that he was suddenly too tired to ever make love. For someone who had a healthy sex drive and frequently made love to his wife, this was too out of character.

I could have possibly been foolish enough to accept that excuse if he was doing something that would cause him to be tired. Occasionally, our properties needed more than just routine maintenance, and sometimes, he'd need to do hard, physical labor. Chris was handy and didn't seem to mind it, so instead of hiring someone to do the job, he did it himself.

But for weeks, I started feeling like I was the butt of a cruel, practical joke.

One where my husband and my best friend tried to pull the wool over my eyes.

Because the biggest eye opener came when I was doing laundry two days ago. It was Sunday afternoon. I'd stripped our bed earlier that morning and put the sheets in the wash. After transferring them to the dryer, I sorted the clothes. When I checked the pockets of my husband's jeans, I found a receipt from a restaurant. It shouldn't have caused me any concern because he had told me that he was going out with his friends for dinner before they went back to one of the guys' homes to watch a game. Chris and I were well off, so he frequently picked up the tab. Not always, but often enough.

The receipt I held in my hand that afternoon was not nearly enough to cover the cost of meals for five grown men. No. It was just enough to cover the cost of a meal for my husband and one other person. A person I was beginning to worry was not one of his buddies at all.

It was time for me to put an end to this madness. So, I tapped out a quick response to Alicia.

Bummer. And yes, we can meet up tomorrow.

She responded almost immediately.

Alicia: Perfect. Thanks so much! And I'm sorry I've been so absent lately.

Me: No worries. Class is about to start, so I've got to go. I'll reach out later.

Alicia: Have fun without me! xx

I slipped my phone back inside my bag, gathered my things, and saw my instructor entering as I was leaving.

"I'm so sorry, but I can't stay today," I lamented. "Suddenly, I'm just not feeling well."

"Oh, gosh. Okay, well, I can email you some materials about today's class if you'd like," she offered.

"That would be perfect."

With a nod, she returned, "Great. I'll send them over later tonight then. Hope you feel better, Quinn."

"Thank you."

With that, I turned and walked out. Then I hustled across the campus to my car.

On my drive home, I tried to come up with a plan. Because if I walked through the door and found that I was wrong, I didn't want to seem like I was paranoid. And a big part of me really hoped that I'd gotten this all wrong. Part of me was praying that all the signs really were just coincidences.

When I pulled into my driveway twenty-five minutes after I'd walked out of my class, I decided not to open the garage door. I didn't want to do anything that would alert anyone that I was home. There were no other cars in the driveway, which made me wonder if I was, in fact, just being overly suspicious for no good reason.

I exited my SUV, closed the door as quietly as possible, and pulled out my key that would open my front door.

I went in, half-expecting to see my husband sitting on the

couch watching a game on television, but knew that wasn't rational. Not with the proof I believed I had.

Stupidly, I moved through the first floor of our home, knowing I wouldn't find anyone. I think in some small part of my mind, I was trying to delay the inevitable. When I made it out to my kitchen, that's when I saw them.

Her keys.

Alicia's.

Sitting in the middle of our massive island countertop.

I was instantly sick.

My body flew to the bathroom just off the kitchen, where I heaved over the toilet. The sight of those keys was going to be burned into my brain for the rest of my days. I had no doubt about that.

Deciding I needed to face the music and get this over with so I could move on, I walked back through the house toward the stairs. As I climbed them, I struggled not to get sick again.

You deserve the truth, Quinn, I told myself.

I made it to the top of the stairs and walked down the long hall toward the bedroom I shared with my husband. And the closer I got, the clearer it became because I heard it.

I heard them.

I didn't need to go in to confirm it, but something pushed me to keep going. Maybe it was my need to make sure they knew that I knew what they were doing.

So, I pushed the door open and wished I hadn't.

Because I found my best friend's legs spread and wrapped around my husband's waist as he fucked her in the middle of our bed.

They didn't know I was there.

At least, not until I slammed the door and ran out.

CHAPTER 1

Quinn
One year later

IT WAS ONE BOX.

One little box.

And yet it held so much meaning.

I took the pen and positioned it. Then, I took in a deep breath as I moved it over the paper, making a check mark in that box. When I finished, I looked down at it and smiled.

Never did I imagine I'd ever be in a position to have to do that. But things happened, and life threw a wrench in all the plans I had.

So much so that I now had the honor of doing something I hadn't expected I would. Because now my marital status had changed. And I had the privilege of being able to check the box that indicated I was divorced.

Normally, I wouldn't have thought of being able to do that as a privilege. The last year taught me differently.

Divorced.

That single word really just signified that I'd reached the end. It was confirmation that everything I'd gone through was finally over, and I'd taken that last step in what had been a very long process for me.

Over the last twelve months, I'd gone through all the stages of grief. At first, denying that it had become my reality before moving to anger. I sat there for a long time, feeling so much anger that two people I'd loved and trusted could betray me the way they did. But somehow I moved beyond that anger into bargaining, wondering what I could have or should have done differently so that I didn't end up right where I was. Eventually, depression took over, and that was another place I spent a long time. Ultimately, though, I got to the point where I was ready to accept what had happened and move on from it.

The minute my divorce was final, which was a lengthy process for us considering the assets we owned, I took steps to start over. Chris and I split the rental properties, transferring ownership of some into just his name and others into just mine. Monthly, we would have a relatively even split in income, which was fair, but I requested the properties that I knew were going to need the least amount of maintenance over the next few years.

Chris didn't fight it.

In fact, it was sad how much he didn't fight me.

Of course, I should have been grateful to get through the divorce without the hassle, but some small part of me was hurt by how easily he was willing to let everything between us go. Maybe I shouldn't have been surprised. He'd managed to let me go long before attorneys got involved, and he seemed to do it rather easily, too.

Once I took the time to reflect, though, I realized it was all for the better. If I was that easily disposed of, it was evident that I didn't really know the man I'd married.

As for Alicia, I believed she'd get what was coming to her. I wholeheartedly believed that life wouldn't just come and knock me down, while allowing her toxic behavior to go unpunished.

Losing her hurt.

When I was going through the worst time in my life, I should have had my best friend there by my side to help me through it. Instead, she was on the other side. She was a big part of the reason I was getting divorced.

I didn't blame Chris or Alicia solely. They were both equally at fault. Maybe it was just a bit worse in Chris' case since we'd taken vows; otherwise, I held them both responsible for the mess they'd made of my life.

But it was over now.

Officially.

To the point that I had just signed the paperwork for the purchase of my new house. Chris had been willing to let me keep our old house, but I didn't want it. I didn't want to walk into the bedroom for the rest of my life and have the vision of the two of them play over and over in my head.

So, he kept the house, bought me out, and I'd stashed the money aside. Until now. When I used it as the down payment on my new place.

My fabulous new place.

One that I deserved. One that I had no doubt would serve me for years to come. One that was all mine to make a boatload of new memories in. Good memories. Memories that included checking one little box.

"Here are your keys," the mortgage broker declared.

I looked up and held my hand out to receive my keys. After she placed them in my hand, she smiled and said, "Congratulations."

I returned her smile and stood. "Thank you."

Then, I walked out of the room and went outside. The

minute I took in the frigid February air, I felt something come over me. It felt like I had officially reached the end of the worst experience in my life and this was the start of something new, exciting, and wonderful.

This feeling was the one thing that had been missing the day my divorce had become official. I waited that day to feel this, but it never came. It was almost… anticlimactic. That day had been such a long time in the making; yet, other than being happy that it was over, it didn't feel good.

But this?

Today?

This felt *good*.

I marched over, got in my vehicle, turned it on, and gave it a minute to warm up before I pulled out. By the time I drove out of the parking lot, making a turn toward my new home, my sister's voice filled the cabin of the car.

"Hey! How did it go?" she asked.

"The house is officially mine," I announced.

"I'm so proud of you, Quinn. As much as I wish you would have relocated back here so we could be there for you, I've got to give you credit for being strong enough to stay in the place you've called home all these years."

My sister always knew what to say to make me feel good. "Thanks, Cassie. You know I love you and will always need you, but this was something I needed to do for me. I built a life here in Wyoming, and I wasn't about to let those two push me out. So, while you don't have me there, you can rest assured that I'm doing my best to put the Jacobs family mark on this place."

The truth was, I had briefly considered going back home to Montana. My whole family and a lot of my friends were there. But part of me believed that if I went back home, I'd be admitting defeat. And I wasn't about to let the fact that I'd been betrayed by my husband and my best friend make me leave a place I'd grown to love. As much as I missed my family, the little town of Windsor, Wyoming was my home now.

"I don't doubt that for a second," my sister responded. "But just to be sure, I'll be out there at the end of the week to confirm it."

"I can't wait to see you, Cass. It feels like it's been a lifetime since I last saw you," I said.

It really had been, since the last time my sister and I had time alone together was less than twenty-four hours after I called her when I was a blubbering mess because I'd walked in on my husband cheating on me. I had no doubt that the only reason I survived those first few days after I learned the truth was because my sister was there to get me through them. She dropped everything for me, and I'd be forever thankful that I had her in my life. I'd seen her again at Christmas, but I'd gone back to Montana for that. And with all the holiday festivities, there wasn't a lot of time for one-on-one sisterly bonding.

"Well, this time I'm expecting to have some fun added into the mix," she started. "You know I won't mind lounging around and hanging out at your new house with you, but I also want at least one night out on the town."

I laughed. Cassie liked to have a good time; that's who she was. But *she* didn't need a night out on the town. She just thought that was what I needed; so, she'd use her trip here to make it happen.

I couldn't say she was wrong in her assessment. Since things ended with Chris and me, I hadn't gone out much. If I was being honest, I hadn't gone out at all. The last eleven months had been spent with me finalizing a divorce, finishing my jewelry-making classes, enrolling in some new classes, officially opening my new business, and searching for my dream home.

So, I had been busy.

But I hadn't gone out.

And while I missed the company of a man, I wasn't certain I was ready to hop back into something serious either. I often wondered if a real relationship was something I could even handle again.

Knowing my sister wasn't going to take no for an answer, I promised, "We'll be sure that you get at least one night out."

The second the words were out of my mouth, Cassie started celebrating. Halfway through her revelry, I got a notification of an incoming call. My eyes left the road only long enough to glance at my dash.

"Hey, Cass, I've got to go. That's the furniture company calling me," I shared.

"Okay," she returned. "Call me later and make sure you send me some pictures. I want before and after."

"You've got it."

I disconnected the call with my sister and answered my incoming call. As it turned out, the furniture company was ahead of schedule and was already at my house waiting for me with my brand-new furniture.

Much like the home I shared with my ex-husband, I elected not to take any of the furniture we shared either. I didn't want any reminders of the place he'd allowed another woman, his wife's best friend or not, to come between us. So, when I bought a new house, I bought all new furniture.

This was going to be a fresh start for me, in every regard.

I let the furniture company know that I was on my way and that I'd be there within the next fifteen minutes. Thankfully, they were happy to wait for me.

Upon my arrival, I greeted them, unlocked my doors, and snapped a bunch of photos before they had a chance to bring anything in, so that I could send the pictures to my sister. For the next several hours, I spent my time doling out orders, letting the men know where I needed everything put. I even managed to convince them to bring in the boxes I had in the back of my SUV.

I couldn't fit everything I owned in my car, but figured I'd do a little each day. The rest of my belongings were still in one of my rental units, which was where I stayed from the night I caught Chris and Alicia until last night. In fact, I'd only gone back to the home I shared with Chris a handful of times to get my clothes and other personal belongings.

Hours after I'd walked through the front door of my new place, I had stepped out of the shower and prepared myself for my first night. I'd had a long day of unpacking, mostly in my bedroom and washing bedsheets for my new bed, and I still had a lot ahead of me. The only time I left the house was after the furniture company was finished, so that I could run out to the grocery store and stock up the fridge and the pantry.

After I finished my nighttime routine, I climbed into bed and pulled out a notebook. Occasionally, I'd sketch out some ideas or jot down a few notes for new pieces of jewelry I wanted to make, but tonight wasn't one of those nights. Tonight, I was making a list of things I needed to accomplish over the next few weeks to get myself fully settled in my house.

Once I'd written down more items than I thought there would be, I set the notebook on my nightstand and turned out the light. It didn't take long for me to fall asleep.

My body tensed as I sucked in a breath at the ear-piercing sound surrounding me. As my eyes shot open in the dark room, it took me a minute to figure out what was happening. And when I did, I began to panic.

My alarm was going off.

I wasn't sure what to do because I hadn't even set the alarm before I went to sleep. My reason for that was mostly because I hadn't called and hooked up the service. So, the fact that it had been tripped at all was strange. As odd as it was, I had to admit that I was terrified that someone was in my house.

Immediately, I sprang up in the bed and reached for my phone. After dialing 911, I held the phone to my ear as my heart pounded in my chest. The shrill sound of the alarm was reverberating not only through the house, but my entire body.

"What is the location of your emergency?"

I raised my voice and rattled off my address as I listened to the operator while she, I assumed, typed my information into her computer.

"What is happening?" the operator asked.

"I think someone broke into my house. My alarm is going off," I explained, my insides shaking.

"Okay, I already have units on the way," she assured me. "They should be there within a few minutes. Where are you?"

I swallowed as I stood and answered, "In my bedroom."

The operator continued to type. I knew she had to be on one of those really old keyboards with the raised keys that made a ton of noise when you typed because there was no other way I would have been able to hear her typing like that.

"I just moved here," I started. "This is my first night in my new house."

"Is anyone else there with you?" she asked.

"I'm alone," I admitted.

And the minute the words were out of my mouth I realized I'd found the downside to my divorce.

I was alone.

I didn't mind being alone when it meant that I was no longer living with a man who didn't regard what we had between us as sacred. I didn't mind being alone when it meant that I didn't allow a woman into my home that would betray me the minute I turned my back.

But when being alone meant that when someone broke into my house in the middle of the night and I had nobody there but myself to face the bad guys, that's when I didn't like being alone.

"What's your name ma'am?" the operator asked.

"Quinn. Quinn Jacobs." My ears were beginning to hurt because the sound was so loud. I moved out of the bedroom into my master closet. It was in that moment that I wished my bedroom was the room that had the secret, hidden room in it instead of the room I was going to turn into my office. I made it to the back of the closet where the sound of the alarm was only slightly muted. "I'm in my master closet now," I told her.

"Okay, Quinn. The officers are nearly there. Just hang tight," she urged. "Do you hear anything or anyone?"

It was a wonder I could hear her. "The alarm is so loud," I started. "I can't hear anything else over it."

At this point, even without the alarm, I wasn't sure I would have heard anyone unless they were actually in my bedroom. Since I'd gone into my master closet and hidden myself in the back of it, it wasn't likely I would have known if anyone was in there.

While it felt like an eternity had passed as I waited for the police to arrive, I knew it hadn't been more than those few minutes the 911 operator had told me it would be.

"Alright, Quinn. I've just gotten confirmation that the officers are at your front door and that they've scanned the outside of your house. The door hasn't been broken open and they don't see any other signs of forced entry. Do you feel comfortable enough to go and meet them at the door?"

I shook my head, even though she couldn't see me. "No. Please. I don't care if they break the door down. I'm too terrified to go down there."

"Are you suggesting that you'd rather have them force their way in?" she asked.

"Yes," I responded, my body trembling violently. "Whatever they need to do."

It couldn't have been much more than a minute when I heard a man shout, "This is Officer Kelley with the WPD."

I heard him in the bedroom, but I couldn't move beyond the uncontrollable shaking my body was doing on its own. Seconds passed before my eyes landed on the officer. He took one look at me, came toward me, and took the phone from my trembling hands. He identified himself to the operator and ended the call.

That's when I threw myself into his arms. "Oh my God," I cried, my voice husky and breaking as I tried to pull myself together.

"You're alright, ma'am," he assured me as he brought his arms around me and held me. I didn't care that I didn't know him or that I was only wearing a satin nightie. The only thought running through my mind was that he was a police officer and I was safe.

I'd been holding onto the officer for quite some time when suddenly the alarm stopped. My body froze, and I pulled out of his arms.

That's when another officer walked in and shared, "Hey, Kelley, Chavez just disconnected the power to the battery on the alarm system. We've checked the premises. There's nobody here and no sign that anyone ever was. It looks like the alarm is malfunctioning."

Their eyes came to mine. "Are you sure?" I worried.

"Yes," the second officer replied.

My alarm.

The stupid alarm that wasn't even hooked up to any service was malfunctioning.

Of course it was.

"I'm sorry," I murmured. "I had no idea. I just moved in, and this is my first night here."

"Ma'am," the first officer started before I cut him off.

"Quinn," I corrected him. "You can call me Quinn."

He gave me a nod and insisted, "You do not need to apologize, Quinn. This is our job. I'd rather be called out to a scene a million times for a false alarm than not show up one time because someone thought they were being a nuisance only to find out they really needed our help. I'm not the least bit concerned that we had to come out here tonight and find nothing. In fact, I'm thrilled that it's just the alarm that's the problem."

I dipped my chin and responded, "Okay. Then, thank you for coming out."

"Are you sure you're okay?" he asked.

"I will be," I confirmed. "What time is it anyway?"

"Just after five," he answered.

It was much earlier than I'd normally wake up, but at least I wasn't going to have to try to find a way to get myself back to sleep.

"Time for coffee," I stated. "Can I at least make you a cup for your trouble?"

I'm not sure if he really wanted a cup of coffee or if he realized I wasn't quite ready to be left alone so soon after I thought someone was coming into my house to kill me, but he agreed.

And before he left my house two hours later when the sun was out and shining, he held out a card and said, "Give these guys a call. One of the other officers checked out your current system. It looks pretty dated; so, since you said you haven't yet hooked up your service, we highly recommend them."

I took the card from him and looked at the name.

Cunningham Security.

I'd heard the name before.

"Oh, these guys have done some work on my rental properties," I announced.

"So, then you already know them and how good they are?" he asked.

I shook my head. "No. Well, I assume they're good because I've never had any problems with the systems at my places, but I've never met them. My ex-husband used to handle all of that."

He lifted his chin in acknowledgement. "Ah, I see. Well, I'd recommend you have them come out and check this out for you."

"Absolutely," I agreed. "I'll do that in a few hours. Thank you again for staying here for a little while. I really appreciate it."

"No problem," he returned. "Have a nice day, Quinn."

"Thanks, Officer Kelley."

With that, he walked out my front door, which somehow did not need to be busted in. I didn't ask how they managed to do that because it really didn't matter to me. They were in, I was safe, and I didn't need to replace the door in the process.

After I locked up again, I decided it was best to get back to unpacking until it was time to call the security company and beg them to come and check out my system before the day was over.

CHAPTER 2

Tyson

"Are you sure you don't need me to do anything?"

"You know I love you, little brother," my sister, Kendra, started. "But let's be honest. This isn't really your thing."

"It's my niece's fifth birthday," I noted. "That alone makes it my thing."

Kendra laughed at me. "Being the cool uncle that the kids can climb all over is your thing. Not planning a party or helping with decorations."

She wasn't exactly wrong. My older sister was the third eldest in a family of five kids. Before Kendra was my older brother, Beau. Before him was our sister, Vera. I came after Kendra, and after me came Kyle.

We all had our strengths, and no matter how much I loved my nieces and nephews, of which there were many, party planning and décor really wasn't my thing.

But I loved the kids. Vera was married with three of them, two boys and a girl. Beau and his wife already had two girls and a boy on the way. Kendra had a set of seven-year-old twin boys and one girl. Kyle and I were the only two without children; however, he was fresh off a break-up. I had no doubt that it wouldn't be long before he'd be down for the count.

When it came to my family, I considered myself blessed. Just looking at my parents, my brothers and sisters, and all of their spouses and children, we were a large bunch. It didn't end there, though. Both of my parents came from large families. My dad was one of six; my mom was one of four. With all their siblings having large families of their own, we had more cousins than anyone else I knew.

Despite the amount of parties I'd had to go to over the years for everyone, I never managed to pick up any party-planning skills.

But if you got me outside with Vera's older boys when the weather was nice, I had no problem throwing a football around with them. And when the girls wanted me to push them higher on the swings or watch them perform whatever song was the latest craze in princess movies, I'd do it.

So, I had my place in their lives, and I was okay with that.

Even still, I always offered to lend a helping hand whenever one of the kids was having a birthday party or a celebration for some special occasion or achievement in their lives.

"I don't have to do the planning, Kendra. But if you need me to pick up any drinks or food so you don't need to worry about it, I'm more than happy to do that for you," I assured her.

"I know you are. And you know I'll be certain to have you flex those muscles the day of. For now, I'm good," she promised. "Vera is helping me with the brunt of the work. Mom's lending a hand, and Beau offered up Josie."

"Josie's pregnant," I said.

"Being pregnant doesn't make her an invalid," Kendra shot back. "If I told her you said that, she'd shoot you herself!"

I couldn't stop myself from laughing. I hadn't intended for that to come out the way it did. "That's not what I meant, and you know it. I just meant she shouldn't be overdoing it or stressing herself with your shenanigans."

"I'm going to pretend you didn't just say that," Kendra warned me.

"Whatever it takes," I returned.

"Yeah, well, I'm letting it go because we have more important matters to discuss."

"We do?" I asked.

Kendra hesitated a moment before she shared, "We need to discuss your date."

I had no clue what she was talking about. "What date?"

"Exactly my point!" she shouted. "You need to have a date for the party."

This woman. This woman and her crazy ideas. I wasn't sure I wanted to participate in this conversation with her because I knew that if she'd reached the point where she was talking to me about it, then she'd already discussed it with the masses. And that meant they'd all be getting on my case, too, if Kendra was unsuccessful.

"Let me get this straight," I started. "You expect me to meet a woman and ask her on a date to my niece's fifth birthday party?"

"Why not?" she asked incredulously.

"Um, considering you're a woman, I'd think you know that that's really not romantic," I explained.

"So, take her on a date before the party," she shot back. "You've got two weeks until then. Make them count."

I shook my head. If I didn't know better, I would have thought she was kidding. But I knew Kendra. She was as serious as ever.

"Why is this such a big deal to you?" I asked.

"Because you're you," she started. "Do you know how

happy you're going to make a woman some day? Why are you waiting to make that happen?"

"You're crazy."

"No, I'm not. There's a woman out there waiting for you to come along and show her what it's like to be loved by a real family man."

I wasn't going to get anywhere with this. Since I was at work and needed to get back to it, I decided it was best to get myself out of the conversation without making any commitments.

"Alright, I'll see what I can do," I acquiesced.

I figured that would be enough to pacify her.

"You better actually try!" she ordered.

"I will. But I've got to go now because I just got to work."

She let out a frustrated sigh. "Okay."

"Kiss the kids for me."

"I will," she promised.

With that, I disconnected the call with Kendra and walked through the parking lot to the front door of the Cunningham Security office where I worked.

No sooner did I make it into the building, greet our receptionist, Deb, and make it to my private office when I turned around and saw Levi had entered behind me. Levi was my boss and the owner of the business.

"Hey, boss," I greeted him as I walked around my desk.

He grinned. "Morning."

That look told me there was more than just a friendly greeting being offered. Levi had something else going on.

"Everything okay?" I asked when he didn't explain the reason for his visit or his mood. He and his wife, Elle, had recently found out they were expecting their first child. I wondered if that was occupying his mind.

"Yeah. I'm actually great. Mostly, anyway," he started as he sat down in the chair on the opposite side of my desk. "But I got two phone calls this morning."

Dipping my chin in acknowledgement, I sat down and responded, "Okay. New cases?"

"Just one," he confirmed. "But both calls were about it."

My brows pulled together as I waited for him to explain.

"The first call came in from a woman who said that she recently moved into a new house and needs a security system installed. Apparently, last night was her first night in the house, but the alarm went off in the early morning hours today."

"An intruder on the first night she's in her new house?"

Levi shook his head. "Nope. The system is malfunctioning. When I asked her who provided the service, she mentioned that she hadn't had it hooked up yet. The police showed up at her place last night and disconnected the battery for her just to get it to stop blaring. She didn't know a whole lot about the specifics of the system, but I had her give me some information off the panel. It's not just an old system; it's ancient. The company who installed it was listed on the panel, but they're no longer even in business."

"Alright, so do you want me to go on a service call and check out what she needs?" I offered.

Levi simply nodded his head.

Then it dawned on me that he said he had received two calls.

"What was the second call you received?" I asked.

"It was from Mitch Kelley over at the WPD," he answered. "He was the one who referred us to this woman when they responded to the 911 call this morning. Mitch was mostly calling to give me a heads up that we'd probably be hearing from her, but also because he wanted to be sure that we gave it priority."

Confusion washed over me. We had a mutually beneficial working relationship with the Windsor Police Department, but they didn't usually make requests like that.

"Family member?" I guessed wondering if that was the reason Mitch had asked that we make this woman a priority.

Levi shook his head, "No."

"Then what is it?" I wondered.

I watched as my boss' jaw clenched before he replied, "Officer Kelley said no sooner did he find this woman curled up and trembling in the back corner of her master closet and disconnect the call with the 911 operator when she threw herself into his arms. She was terrified that someone had broken into her home. Once they confirmed the issue was just related to the alarm and that nobody actually attempted to break in, he could tell she was still terrified to be left alone. He ended up hanging around for a couple hours until the sun came up and she settled a bit."

I shrugged and nonchalantly threw out, "Okay, well if you want me to cover it, I'll head over this morning and get it taken care of right away."

"That's exactly what I want you to do," Levi instructed, but his grin was back in place.

Not understanding the shift in his mood, I finally asked, "What's your deal? Why are you looking at me like that?"

"I forgot to tell you that Officer Kelley told me when he found her she was in nothing but a sweet, satin nightie. He's a happily married man, but he thought it was worth mentioning."

"And you're telling me this because?" I pressed, even though I already knew why.

Levi hesitated a moment, but ultimately declared, "I'll probably regret mentioning this because I don't really need you having this image, but I think it's important. Elle's in satin nighties every night. When I got the call about this case from the woman, I looked at who had light caseloads right now. Once I got the call from Mitch and he shared this bit of information with me, my list was narrowed down to you and Gunner."

At that, Levi stood and threw a file folder on my desk. After, he moved to the door of my office, but before he walked out, he turned back and looked at me.

"I figure you might like waking up to sweet, satin nighties."

Then he walked out.

I simply sat there staring at the empty space that now occupied the doorway. I had no idea what it was with everyone around me thinking I needed a love-life intervention. Sure, I wasn't in a serious relationship right now, and it had been a while since I'd been in one. But I wasn't desperate to be in one either.

If I left it up to everyone around me, I'd already be married with five kids. That didn't mean I didn't want to get married one day and have a big family. I just didn't feel the need to rush or force something. I had no doubt that when the time was right, it would happen.

Just as I was about to reach out and grab the folder from the spot on my desk where Levi threw it, my phone rang. I looked at the display and saw it was Beau calling.

"Yeah?" I answered.

"Tyson, it's Josie," my sister-in-law returned.

I immediately grew concerned and repeated, "Josie? Are you and the baby okay?" Before she had the chance to respond, I realized that since she was calling from Beau's phone, it was likely that he was the one who wasn't okay. "Is Beau alright?"

"Relax, Tyson. Your family doesn't just call you because someone is in trouble, you know," she scoffed.

I had to admit that it was just in my nature to worry about them. "Sorry," I lamented. "It's just that I wasn't expecting you to be on the other end of the line considering Beau's name came up on my phone."

"That was on purpose," she claimed. "I used Beau's phone because I knew you wouldn't suspect anything. But if you saw me calling, you never would have answered."

"Yes I would have," I insisted.

"Tyson," she stated.

"Josie."

She sighed. "You're a smart man. You just got off the phone with Kendra. If you saw my name pop up, you would have taken a minute to consider why I might be calling you, and then you would have made every effort to avoid taking the call."

It had been mere minutes since I'd gotten off the phone with my sister, and she'd already talked to Josie. If I didn't love her so much, I'd have to kill her. Because I knew that it was only going to be a matter of time before my phone rang again and Vera was on the other end.

Evidently, I'd taken too long to confirm or deny her assessment because Josie went on, "Anyway, I'm just calling on behalf of myself *and* your brother. He'd never do it, but I know he agrees with me and your sisters and fully supports our efforts to find you a woman. We're all ready for you to start putting some effort into growing this family."

"You're not seriously calling me about this right now, are you?"

"What?" she exclaimed. "It's obvious you need some encouragement. We're just doing our part to make sure we give it to you."

I made a mental note to have a chat with my brother. Mostly, I planned to tell him that he needed to keep his phone with him for no reason other than to ensure his wife wouldn't be able to call me up in the middle of a workday just so she could join my sisters in getting on my case about finding a woman.

"Just because I'm not dating anyone seriously right now does not mean that I need my sisters and my sister-in-law meddling," I asserted.

Josie gasped. "Meddling? That's such a negative word. I think you just mean that we're such passionate women who care about you and want to see you happy."

I wondered who sent them a memo that stated I wasn't happy. "Who says I'm not?" I countered.

"Oh, we know you're happy generally speaking. But we're talking about romance. Do you realize how happy you could be with the right woman?"

I started to consider whether or not a woman I might be interested in would want to stick around after she met my family. With their boisterous personalities, it wouldn't be a far stretch to think that a lot of people might not be able to handle them.

That said, I was happy, and I knew it was likely I'd be even happier in a romantic relationship with the right woman. But I had every confidence in myself to find that woman on my own. Even still, I loved that my family cared about me the way they did, so I'd take them intruding over not caring at all.

"I know, Josie," I finally admitted. I'd learned a long time ago that if I was ever going to get anything done, I needed to appease them for the time being and deal with their prying the next time they decided it was on their agenda. "It'll happen."

"Okay. Well, I just wanted to make sure you know that we're all excited to meet whoever the lucky lady is that you're bringing to Jordyn's birthday party."

I rolled my eyes. It was Kendra's daughter's birthday party, but she was more concerned with me bringing someone for the whole family to fawn over. I wouldn't be doing myself any favors if I subjected a poor woman to something like that.

"I've got to go," I started. "I need to head out and get a security system installed. Keep yourself busy growing that baby, Josie. And if I don't see you before then, I'll see you at the party."

"Sounds good," she returned. "And Tyson?"

"Yeah?" I answered.

"When I knock you upside the head the next time I see you, just know that it's because I'm only trying to make sure you understand that being pregnant does not mean that I can't do things," she warned me.

"Fucking Kendra," I bit out.

Josie laughed and ended, "Later!"

I disconnected the call, grabbed the folder, and looked up the address to where I needed to go. I had to get out of the office and start working so I'd have a legitimate excuse for not answering when Vera's call came in. I'd had enough meddling for one day.

Noting the address, I realized exactly to which house I'd be heading. It was a huge, old farmhouse that had been built at least a hundred years ago. I knew it had been on the market for a while, and I hadn't realized it sold. Part of the reason I believed it took so long to sell was that it wasn't a home the average person could afford. It was a beautiful home, one I hated seeing sit empty for so long. Whoever this woman was that owned it now definitely had money and good taste. Because even if the home needed some minor updates, like the security system, there was no doubt it was a gem.

I saw the name and number in the file, lifted the office phone out of the cradle, and dialed. Two rings later, I heard, "Hello?"

"Hi, is this Quinn Jacobs?" I asked.

"Yes, who's this?"

"Hi, I'm Tyson Reed. I'm with Cunningham Security. I'm responding to your request to have your security system inspected for repair or possible replacement. Are you available for me to come take a look at it?"

"Oh yes, that's great. Um, I ran out for a few minutes, but I'm on my way back to the house now. If you get there in the next ten minutes, you'll have to wait for me. Otherwise, I'll see you soon."

I smiled and said, "I'll be there in fifteen."

"That's perfect."

I hung up the phone and gathered a few supplies I'd need for my appointment, including some of the standard security equipment we'd use for any brand-new installation. Then I got in my truck and took off.

Fifteen minutes after I'd gotten off the phone with Quinn, I arrived at her house. And she wasn't there.

I got back in my truck and decided to give her a few extra minutes before calling her. When another ten minutes passed and she still hadn't arrived, I grew concerned. Just as I pulled out the paper with her number on it, something caught my eye in the rearview mirror. Assuming it was her, I put the paper away and got out of the truck again.

At the same time, Quinn opened her door and stepped out. When she closed the door, I could barely see her face.

She was bundled from head to toe in a hat, scarf, gloves, and a jacket.

I almost had to laugh. Looking at this woman, I recalled Levi telling me that she was found last night wearing just a nightie. It was a bit hard to imagine that now.

I moved toward her and asked, "Are you Quinn? I'm Tyson. We spoke on the phone about your alarm."

I knew she was going to respond when she used one hand to pull the scarf away from her mouth. She hadn't spoken a single word, and I was already mesmerized.

Her lips.

Fuck me, I had never seen a more perfect pair of pink lips.

And that's when I knew that I needed to know what this woman looked like wearing a sweet, satin nightie.

CHAPTER 3

Quinn

WAS THIS SERIOUSLY MY LIFE NOW?

I honestly thought that after getting divorced things were going to start turning around. It had certainly seemed that way initially. After all, I happened to stumble upon a smoking deal when I purchased my home. I believed that was just the beginning of all the good things to come.

Considering my first night in my house resulted in me cowering in the darkest corner of my master closet while I called the police, I was beginning to doubt just how great this new start was going to actually be. And not even twelve hours later, I was late to meet the guy who was coming to deal with my security system all because I got pulled over for rushing home to meet said guy.

As if all of that wasn't already enough, when I finally pulled into my driveway and saw him get out of his truck, I no longer had any doubts. My luck had gone from bad to worse. Because for some reason it was not once mentioned to me that the guy who was going to be coming out to check out my security system was the world's hottest man.

This was not an exaggeration in the slightest.

Tyson was the very definition of tall, dark, and handsome.

While I was sure anybody else would think this was a great thing, I didn't feel so lucky. Because it had been a really long time since I'd looked at a man who wasn't Chris that way. That didn't mean that I never gave another man an appreciative glance over the years. It's just that I was happily married and very satisfied with who I had. Until, of course, I no longer did.

So, seeing this man now, even all bundled up like he was, I knew he was something special. And that terrified me because I didn't know how to do this anymore. I didn't know how to be attracted to a man that wasn't Chris and not act like a total fool in the process.

As I walked up to him, he spoke. "Are you Quinn? I'm Tyson. We spoke on the phone about your alarm."

I pulled my scarf away from my face so he'd be able to hear me. Then, my nerves took over, and instead of answering him, I began to fret, "I'm so sorry I'm late. I was making great time, but then I got pulled over because I was speeding. Luckily, I managed to get away with just a warning. The officer was ready to give me a ticket, but once he asked why I was in such a hurry and I explained that you were going to be meeting me here, he tore it up. Nevertheless, I'm still late."

I was slightly out of breath having rattled all that off, so I took a moment to try and regain my composure. Unfortunately, I was unsuccessful because I tipped my chin up and stared at Tyson. He was easily a good six or seven inches taller than me. Up close he was even more breathtaking than he was from a distance. He had a great mouth, and I was struggling not to drool over it or throw caution to the wind and leap into his arms so I could plant one on him.

Thankfully, Tyson put me out of my misery and offered,

"We have a mutually beneficial working relationship with the WPD, so I'm not surprised you got off with just a warning."

"That's good to know. I hope you won't mind if I use that excuse from here on out," I teased.

"Do you get pulled over frequently?" he asked.

I shook my head. "No, but considering how my luck has turned lately, that doesn't seem like it's out of the realm of possibility at this point."

Suddenly, Tyson's face and voice turned serious. "I heard you had a rough night last night," he shared.

I closed my eyes and looked away. "I feel like an idiot," I admitted. "I was hiding in my closet from nobody."

"Better that than the alternative, though, don't you think?"

I shrugged.

When I made no move to do anything else, he prompted, "Do you want to stand out here all day, or can you show me where the panel is so I can get to work on figuring out what we're dealing with here?"

That snapped me out of it. "Oh, gosh. I'm so sorry," I lamented. "Follow me."

A minute later, I was walking him through the front door and toward the alarm panel.

"Here it is," I declared.

He took one look at it and decided, "This had to have been put in when the house was built a hundred years ago."

As he fiddled with the panel, I asked, "Did you just toss that number out there or did you know it's a hundred years old?"

Tyson didn't look at me when he responded because he continued to inspect the panel. "I didn't know the exact number was a hundred, but I did know that it was old."

"Oh," I mumbled.

He said it in a way that made me think he thought the house was terrible. I didn't know why I thought his opinion on my home mattered, but for some reason, the idea that he didn't like it bothered me.

As if reading my thoughts, he declared, "It's a beautiful home. I've known about this house being for sale for months. I always knew whoever bought it would be one lucky person."

That certainly lifted my spirits. "Thank you."

"But I get the feeling this alarm system is a nightmare," he warned me. "Are you hoping to keep this one and make it work, or are you open to getting something more modern and reliable?"

"I want whatever you have that won't randomly go off in the middle of the night unless someone is trying to break in," I answered.

Tyson glanced back at me, smiled, and decided, "Then I'm more than ninety-nine percent sure we'll be needing to get a whole new system put in here."

"That works for me," I returned. "Do you need me to do anything?"

He shook his head. "Nope. I think I'll be at this for a little while as I try to figure out what the last place did here."

"Okay, then if it's alright with you, I'll leave you to that while I bring my boxes in and finish unpacking," I explained. Even though I'd done okay pulling myself together a bit, I knew I'd benefit from a little bit of space from Tyson.

"Do you need help?" he wondered.

My eyes widened. "Unpacking?"

Tyson laughed. "Carrying boxes," he clarified.

"Oh, right. Um, I should be okay. There are only a few out there because I couldn't bring them all. I grabbed as many as I could before I just got too tired," I explained, belatedly realizing I was rambling again.

He gave me a once over, looked toward the front door, and back at me before he asked, "Are they in your car?"

I nodded.

He jerked his head in that direction and decided, "I'll help you carry your boxes in. Then I'll get started on this."

"You don't have to do that," I insisted.

"If my father ever found out that I sat back and did nothing while I watched a woman lug a bunch of heavy boxes from her car to her house, I have no doubt he'd disown me."

I gave him an inquisitive look and reasoned, "Well, you won't exactly be doing nothing, so he shouldn't disown you."

"If I did that, I'd give him the papers myself," Tyson added. "I'm sorry, but that just wouldn't be right. So, we can either stand here and argue about this, or you can just give in and let me help you."

Realizing Tyson wasn't going to back down, I figured it was best to just give in and let him help me. Besides, the longer I stayed and argued, the longer it would be until I was free to freak out alone in my bedroom.

I gave him a nod and moved toward the door. Then Tyson helped me carry in my boxes. This meant he also carried them to my bedroom. The first time he stepped into the room, I watched as his gaze lingered a bit on my king-size bed.

"Anywhere specific?" he asked, his voice husky.

I pointed in the direction of the closet and said, "Right on the floor over there would be great."

Tyson dipped his chin and did as I requested. He helped me carry in the remainder of the boxes from my car before he announced, "Okay, I'm going to get back to work on the alarm. I suspect it'll be a full day just to remove the old system. I don't want to leave you here without something functional tonight, so I'm going to push harder to get the old one out and get something basic in here for you just for tonight. As long as it works for you, I can come back tomorrow to get the good stuff installed for you with all the bells and whistles."

"I hadn't realized there was a difference in security systems," I admitted as I began removing my hat, scarf, gloves, and jacket. "I had no plans for this week other than unpacking, so if you can make it so I'm safe while I'm here, I'll do what I've got to do to make sure you can get in and get it done for me."

Tyson did not hide the fact that he appreciated what he saw once I'd taken all my layers off. He was quiet for a moment while he took one last look around my room, allowing his eyes to land on my bed again before they moved to my feet. After his eyes traveled up my body and settled on my face, he turned and walked out.

I stood there motionless for a long time trying to process what had just happened. It was the first time in more than a year that I noticed a guy checking me out, and it felt really good to be appreciated in that way.

When I finally managed to snap myself out of it, I looked back at the stack of boxes I had waiting for me and took a deep breath. For the next couple of hours, I did my best to stay focused on my task of unpacking.

But it was really difficult.

Because all I kept thinking about was the fact that I had a gorgeous man in my house installing a security system that would keep me safe.

Somehow, I managed to get through half the boxes despite my thoughts about Tyson.

It was around that point when my stomach started growling. That's when I realized it was already lunchtime. I went downstairs and found Tyson elbows deep in wiring.

"Everything going okay?" I asked.

"I don't even know how this alarm ever functioned properly," he replied. "I've never seen such a mess in all my life."

"Yikes. I'm sorry," I lamented.

He glanced back at me and pointed out, "You've got nothing to apologize for unless you were the one who did the installation."

I shook my head. "Nope, that definitely wasn't me."

As I watched Tyson continue to remove the wires, I offered, "I took a break from unpacking to come down and have some lunch. Can I make you something, too?"

Tyson's body froze. He turned his head to the side and looked back at me again, but he didn't say anything for a few seconds. I started to wonder if it had been the wrong thing to do when he finally said, "Sure."

"Is there anything you don't like?" I asked.

"If it's edible, I'll eat it. I'm really not picky," he answered.

"Okay."

With that, I moved to the kitchen and made lunch. Pulling out a French baguette, deli turkey, cheese, mayo, mustard, and all the trimmings, I put together some sandwiches. I brought out a few bags of chips and drinks so Tyson would have a variety to choose from and set everything out on the counter bar top that also served as a kitchen island with barstools.

Just as I was about to go in search of Tyson, he walked into the kitchen.

"You've got perfect timing," I noted.

He smiled and held up his hands. "Are you cool with me washing my hands at this sink?"

Dipping my chin, I replied, "Sure."

After Tyson washed and dried his hands, he sat down

next to me at the island. "Thanks for making lunch," he started. "It's normally not one of the perks of the job."

"What do you normally do then?" I asked.

"Most days I'll run out and grab something," he returned.

"You don't pack yourself a lunch?"

A small smile tugged at his lips as he replied, "You'd need to know how to cook to be able to do that. I don't cook."

"I didn't exactly cook this," I shared. "All I had to do is go to the grocery store and pick up a few things. Surely, if you can deal with that mess out there, you can handle making a sandwich."

Tyson shrugged. "Paying to have someone do it for me is a lot less hassle, though," he reasoned.

I couldn't argue with that, especially when I knew that I'd had those days I just didn't want to cook dinner. While it didn't happen very often, it was nice to be able to just go out and have someone else do all the hard work when I wasn't feeling up to it.

"You've got no argument from me on that one," I said.

After we'd both taken a few bites of our sandwiches, and Tyson had settled on classic potato chips, he asked, "So, where are you moving from?"

"One of my rental properties," I answered.

He lifted his chin in acknowledgment. "Ah, finally got to a point where you wanted to buy then?"

I shook my head. "No, I was only in the rental for roughly a year," I started. "I moved there the day I walked into my previous home and found my husband in our bed with my best friend."

Tyson jerked his head back in surprise and gave me a look that told me he felt for me. "You're kidding?"

"Nope. After packing up a few things to get me through

the night, I left. I only went back to get the rest of my personal belongings. I never slept there again."

"Wow," he marveled, his shock evident. "I'm sorry to hear that, Quinn."

"Thanks, but I'm over it now. Prior to the divorce being finalized, I'd been searching for a new place to make my home. I found this, knew I wanted it, so the day my divorce was finalized, I had my realtor make an offer. I paid the down payment with the money I got when he bought me out of our house."

Tyson smiled at me. "No offense, but it sounds to me like your ex-husband is an idiot."

"None taken. And yep, he is," I agreed.

"You still have things left at your rental property that you need to move then, right?" he asked.

Nodding, I explained, "Yeah, I have a few more hauls to make."

"Not enough room to fit it all in your car?" he wondered.

"No, it's just that it's a lot to carry all in one shot. That, combined with having to carry it all out in the super cold temperatures, I just do what I can and tell myself that I can only unpack so much in a day anyway."

Tyson finished chewing and swallowed before he offered, "Well, if you want, I'd be happy to help you. After lunch, I need to run back to the office to grab a few things so that I can get you set up with something tonight. If you want to come along, we can make a stop and get whatever is left."

"Really?" I asked. "You wouldn't mind?"

He nodded. "Not at all."

I was shocked at Tyson's generosity. My parents might have told me that I needed to be cautious around new people, but Tyson didn't give me any weird, creepy vibes. Add to that the fact that he also worked for one of the most highly-regarded security companies *and* that I got out of a ticket because I told a police officer I was rushing home to meet Tyson, I figured he was a standup guy.

"Okay," I agreed. "I'd really appreciate that."

He grinned at me and ordered, "Eat up, gorgeous. We've got work to do."

I swallowed hard and felt a wave of excitement run through me at Tyson's endearment. Chris never called me anything like that. In fact, unless I'd gotten dressed up for a special occasion, Chris never really communicated that I was pretty. Prior to us getting engaged, he'd shelled out compliments on a more regular basis, but they were still few and far between.

It was nice to hear someone say something like that to me again.

And because I was feeling so good, I beamed at Tyson before taking another bite of my food.

CHAPTER 4

Quinn

"These are the last two boxes," I declared as I moved to pick one up.

Tyson lifted the other box into his arms and instructed, "Load that one on top."

"What?"

"Put the box you have on top of this one so you can free your hands and lock up before we go," he explained.

I hesitated briefly. "Can you carry this one, too?" I asked.

Tyson cocked an eyebrow. "Yes, Quinn, I think I can manage a box of clothes."

Still holding the box in my arms, I lifted my shoulders and assured him, "I didn't mean to insinuate that you were weak or anything. I just didn't want to make any assumptions. Maybe you have chronic back pain or something."

He let out a laugh. "Are you always this goofy?" he questioned me.

I scrunched up my face at him. "I'm not being goofy. I'm being serious."

"I know," he began. "That's the point."

When I made no move to do anything, Tyson call my name and prompted, "Just put the box up here so we can get going."

I did as he asked and followed behind him to the door. Then, I locked up and we made our way to Tyson's vehicle.

It wasn't more than a fifteen-minute drive from my rental property to the Cunningham Security office. When we walked through the front door, we were met by a woman with short auburn hair.

"Hey, Tyson," she greeted him but in a way that had all sorts of questions lingering behind it.

"Hi, Deb," he replied. "This is Quinn Jacobs. She owns the home I'm doing a system install in right now."

Deb lifted her chin in understanding before directing her attention to me. "It's nice to meet you, Quinn."

I smiled and returned, "You too."

"Is Levi still around?" Tyson asked.

I perked up at the mention of somebody I knew. Well, I didn't exactly know Levi, but I'd spoken to him earlier this morning. I thought it'd be nice to put a face to the name.

"Yep," she confirmed. "I've been here all day, and he hasn't left."

With that, Tyson put a hand to the small of my back to guide me away from the reception desk and to what I could only assume was going to be wherever he planned to find Levi.

Unfortunately, I hadn't had a man touch me like that in more than a year, and it caught me off guard. I ended up stumbling, but Tyson was quick to catch me before I went down.

"Whoa. You alright?" he asked with both arms wrapped firmly around me.

"Yeah," I rasped. "Sorry."

"It's okay," he assured me as he made sure I was steady before pulling his hands away.

I couldn't quite decide if I was relieved he was no longer touching me, or if I was upset about not having that connection anymore. Sadly, I didn't come up with the answer.

Tyson stopped in the doorway of an office and knocked on the open door. The man sitting behind the desk looked up, took both of us in, and grinned. Something about the way he did it was strange and made me feel like I was missing out on an inside joke.

"Levi, this is Quinn Jacobs. You spoke to her earlier this morning," Tyson introduced us.

Levi quickly recovered and stood to come around his desk. "Yes, that's right. Hello, Quinn. It's nice to meet you."

I extended my hand to Levi. As he took it in his, I said, "You too. And thank you so much for getting someone to come and help me out so quickly. I really appreciate it."

He dropped my hand and insisted, "It's not a problem at all. Tyson's current caseload was light without any urgent, pressing matters he needed to tend to, so it wasn't as much of the sacrifice that you might think."

"Oh, I'm relieved to hear that," I admitted. After a brief pause, I realized what I'd said and added, "To be clear, I'm relieved I didn't cause any inconvenience. I didn't mean to imply that I was happy you weren't busy with a lot of work. Obviously, that's never good."

Levi laughed and looked at Tyson. He barely had the chance to take him in when Tyson warned, "Don't."

My brows pulled together, confused at his single-word demand.

Appearing unaffected by Tyson's warning, Levi asked, "What's going on?"

"I've spent the last several hours trying to fix this mess of an installation that was done at her place," Tyson stated.

Before he could continue, someone called, "Hey, what's going on?"

Everyone turned their attention outside Levi's office, where another handsome man was standing. His eyes quickly moved from Levi to Tyson, but eventually settled on me. He extended a hand to me. "Hi, I'm Gunner. You are?"

"Quinn," I replied as I shook his hand. Gunner didn't let go, though.

"Hayes," Tyson called.

I looked around trying to figure out what that meant, but saw Tyson was pinning his gaze on Gunner. When my eyes went back to Gunner, he looked down at our joined hands and back to Tyson before he let my hand go.

"So, did you finish Quinn's system?" Levi asked from behind us.

Tyson turned and answered, "No, not yet. Honestly, I don't even know how it worked at all. I'll tell you what, though. It's clear to me why that company is no longer in business. They did an awful job."

"Are you looking for an extra set of hands?" Levi wondered.

"I can help," Gunner offered. "What's going on?"

"Quinn's got a dated security system at her place," Tyson explained. "It malfunctioned last night and the WPD ended up at her place. She thought someone was trying to break in."

"Ah, I see. Do you want some help?" Gunner asked again.

Tyson shrugged. "I think I'll be alright," he decided.

Gunner and Levi both chuckled, but it was Levi who spoke. "I have no doubt about that," he said, but it was evident he was teasing.

Tyson ignored that and jerked his head in the opposite direction. "I'm going to go grab a few extra things I need to finish this up for her today. Then, I'll need to go back tomorrow to add all the extras she's going to want."

"The extras she wants?" Levi asked.

Tyson narrowed his eyes. "The ones I'd want any woman who's living alone to have," he asserted.

"Right. Well, you better get to it," he ordered before directing his attention to me. "It was nice meeting you, Quinn. I hope everything works out well for you."

"I'm sure it will. You guys have always done excellent work for me before," I praised.

His confusion was evident in his features. "We've worked with you before?" he asked.

Nodding, I explained, "Yes, my ex-husband and I had a bunch of rental properties together. He always handled all of the maintenance stuff and meeting people at the locations, so I was never really involved in that part of it. I always just paid the bills."

"Oh, okay. Well, then I appreciate you giving us the opportunity to take care of you this time around, too."

I offered a friendly smile in return just before Tyson put a hand to my elbow and declared, "We've got to go."

"Whatever you need for time on this, Tyson, take it," Levi instructed. "Quinn's a long-standing client who is obviously loyal to us. Make sure her needs are met."

Tyson's fingers tightened on my arm just briefly. Then, he shifted out of the way and urged me from Levi's office ahead of him.

The two of us walked toward the back of the building and behind a set of closed doors that led to what could be best described as a storage room. There were rows of shelving with boxes of equipment on them. Tyson moved through the rows, found the few things he needed, and said, "Okay, we're good to go."

"That was fast," I noted.

With a look of nonchalance, he revealed, "I've been doing this for twelve years. I figure if it took me any longer than that to get what I needed, Levi might need to reconsider my employment status."

"Point made."

At that, Tyson opened the door and let me walk out ahead of him. As I did, I was greeted by two men, both just a bit larger than Tyson, and a French bulldog. That meant, compared to me, they were huge. Because I felt small next to Tyson.

Both of the men looked at me then Tyson then me again before they looked at the now-closed door behind us and finally settled on Tyson. Once they did, they both grinned. And they did it huge.

Tyson sighed and announced, "Quinn, these are two of my coworkers, Dom and Lorenzo. Guys, this is Quinn."

If it was even possible, their grins got bigger.

"Hi," I greeted them with a wave. I couldn't be bothered with much more than that because all my focus was on the little guy sniffing at my ankles. I crouched down and started to fuss over him. "Hey, you. What's your name? You're so cute," I proclaimed.

"That's the official Cunningham Security mascot, Ollie," Dom declared. "Lorenzo got him for my sister, Jolie, but whenever she's at work, Ollie's here."

As I scratched Ollie's head, I looked at Lorenzo and wondered, "Wait, so you're with his sister?"

"Yep," Lorenzo confirmed.

"And that doesn't bother you?" I asked Dom.

"Nope."

"Wow," I marveled. "I always thought that was like a big no-no."

Dom shook his head. "It's only that if the guy trying to date one of my sisters is an asshole. Lorenzo's not, so I'm cool."

"*One* of your sisters," I repeated.

"I have two," Dom clarified. "I also have two brothers."

My eyes widened. "Your parents had five children?"

Dom laughed and said, "Ekko said those same exact words to me once."

I had no idea what he was talking about, so I replied, "What?"

"Ekko is my wife," he clarified. "But five isn't a lot. Just ask Tyson."

My head snapped in Tyson's direction. The minute our eyes locked, he declared, "Three boys and two girls in my family, too."

I gave Ollie one last pat on the head before I stood and asked, "Really? Isn't that... crowded?"

"I live on my own now, so I manage alright," he assured me.

I nodded my understanding. "Right. That makes sense."

"What are you doing?" Lorenzo asked, tipping his head to the load of goodies in Tyson's arms.

"Quinn bought the old farmhouse out on Cottonwood Road," Tyson started. "The security system in there is nearly as old as the house. I stopped by here to pick up a couple of things, and it's taken more time to get them than it should have. That's mostly because everybody seems eager to meet Quinn."

The guys got the hint and reasoned, "We're just being nice."

"Yeah, I know what you're doing," Tyson muttered. "Anyway, we're going to get going."

"Okay. Nice meeting you, Quinn," Dom said to my departing back since Tyson was already on the move.

"You too," I called back as I picked up my pace to match Tyson's.

Before I knew it, Tyson and I had pulled back into the driveway at my place. When he shut off the truck, he advised, "I'll get your boxes brought inside before I get back to work."

"That works."

When we got out, I met Tyson at the back of the truck, and he instructed, "Why don't you go ahead of me and open the door?"

"Okay, just let me grab a box," I suggested.

"I've got them," he insisted.

"Tyson, you can't carry all of these in on your own," I protested.

"Not in one trip, but I can do it," he maintained.

I moved my legs back and forth as I tried to fight off the biting cold and remarked, "Let me rephrase that then. It wouldn't be nice of me to expect you to carry these all in for me."

"Do you?"

"Do I what?"

"Do you expect me to carry them in?"

I shook my head. "Of course not."

"Alright, so go open the door, get out of the cold, and let me bring them in for you," he demanded.

Realizing this was not a battle worth fighting, but not completely wanting to give in, I moved toward the truck, grabbed a box, and huffed, "Fine. But I'm taking in at least one."

"Goofy and difficult," Tyson stated.

I mustered up my most scathing look and shot it his way. He just laughed at me.

It was quite a few hours later when I finally called it quits.

I'd managed to unpack another bunch of boxes. I'd had my fill for the day and decided to check in on Tyson's progress. I didn't want him to think I was micro-managing him, but I also wanted to be sure he knew that I was around if he needed anything from me.

I walked up to him and tapped him on the shoulder as I called, "Tyson?"

He turned and smiled at me. "Hey," he said softly.

I jerked my chin toward the shiny, new alarm panel on my wall and asked, "How's it going?"

"Perfect timing. I just finished," he answered.

"Wow."

Tyson declared, "So, I'll explain what you need to do for tonight so you'll be covered. And then I'll be back first thing tomorrow morning to finish it up for you."

"That sounds good to me."

With that, Tyson walked me through the basics of the system he installed and the code he programmed for the time being. When he finished, he asked, "Got all that?"

I nodded. "Yeah, I think so."

"Do you have your phone?"

"Why?"

"I'll give you my number. If you have any problems with it, you can give me a call," he stated.

"That makes sense," I returned. "Let me go grab it."

When I came back with my phone, I held it out to him. Tyson punched in the numbers, called himself, and handed the phone back to me.

"Thank you so much for coming out today and doing this for me," I said after he put his jacket on and pulled out his keys.

Tyson smiled and claimed, "It was my pleasure."

I felt the nerves in my belly take over and could do nothing but nod and smile in return. It was crazy. Unless I was focused on something specific when I was around Tyson, I couldn't seem to control my reaction to him. Part of me thought that perhaps it was because for the first time in a year I was around a guy that I thought was handsome and who seemed to like me, too. The other part of me wondered if I was getting it all wrong, and Tyson was just a friendly guy.

Either way, it scared me.

Because on one hand I wasn't sure if I was in a place to trust my heart to someone, Tyson or otherwise.

And on the other hand, if he was just being friendly, I wondered if I'd ever be able to find happiness with someone again.

I must have taken too much time to contemplate everything because Tyson spoke again. "I'll see you tomorrow morning, Quinn. Does nine o'clock work?"

"That'll be perfect," I confirmed.

With that, he opened the door and walked out.

I waited until he got in his truck and drove away before I closed the door. And after I did, I couldn't seem to wipe the smile off my face for the next few hours.

In fact, it was shortly after I'd crawled into bed that night when I thought I'd successfully stopped thinking about Tyson. It lasted only a few moments, though, because my cell phone chimed on the nightstand. When I looked at the display, I saw it was a text from him.

Tyson: Alarm all set?

Me: Yes! Thank you again.

Tyson: No thanks needed. And full disclosure?

Reading those words bothered me, and it took a moment to figure out why. The implicated deception. And after being betrayed by people I trusted, I didn't want to think I'd so easily trusted a man I'd just met only to have him prove that I'd misjudged yet another person.

Me: Sure.

Tyson: It's not protocol to hand my personal number out to random clients after I install their systems.

While I was relieved he wasn't going to share some horrible news that would have me questioning my sanity, I wasn't quite sure how to take what he did share.

Me: Okay?

Tyson: I gave it to you because I was hoping you'd want to call me sometime.

Me: Oh.

Tyson didn't respond, and I wasn't sure if I'd screwed up with my single word reply. The truth was I had no idea how to react to what he said.

CHAPTER 5

Quinn

As tired as I was considering the blaring alarm and 911 call the night prior, I tossed and turned all night last night. After the day I'd had with him, followed by the texts, I really struggled to come to terms with it all.

He was not only the first man since Chris that I'd been interested in, but he showed an interest in me. While I hadn't been certain about it earlier in the day, wondering if he was perhaps just this nice normally, the minute I received his last text message, it was clear there was more than just a nice guy behind all of it.

And that terrified me because I did not want to find myself getting caught up in something that was going to destroy me all over again.

So, I thought it might be wise to come up with a game plan. I'd been thinking all night long, and I came up with what I thought was my only option.

Play it cool.

Play it cool until Tyson pushed for something more than just friendly conversation and banter.

Then, I was going to hope that I'd know what to do next.

It was a terrible plan. Which was likely the reason why I

couldn't sleep all night. At least, that's what I kept telling myself was the reason I couldn't sleep. While I didn't doubt that was part of it, I knew the much bigger reason had to do with the fact that I hadn't been with a man in a really long time.

And after such a long hiatus from sex, Tyson seemed like a guy who could make my return to the activity a whole lot of fun. I'd spent hours with him yesterday, and I got to see the way he filled out a shirt and his jeans. There was no denying the man had a body that was to die for. Between that and the way he smelled, a girl could be very happy.

But that wasn't all Tyson had to offer.

He also had a really beautiful smile, great manners, good conversation, and a voice that could get so soft and gentle it made my heart melt.

Now that it was morning and Tyson was going to be here any minute, I was panicking. Because I was certain I'd screwed up last night. I didn't know if he was disappointed with me for not reaching out to him last night, and that bothered me. The last thing I wanted was for Tyson to be disappointed with me.

I was completely out of sorts, feeling flustered, when I heard the knock at the door. Panic gripped me as I moved to the alarm panel, disabled it, and opened the door.

Tyson grinned at me, held out a box of donuts, and greeted me, "Good morning, Quinn. Since you did lunch yesterday, I'm doing breakfast today."

Taking the donuts from him, I smiled and replied, "Morning, Tyson. Donuts are, quite possibly, my favorite breakfast splurge."

"I got a variety, so hopefully there's one in there you'll like," he shared.

I lifted the lid, peeked at what was inside, and felt my

mouth instantly water. "And here I was worried you were upset with me," I mumbled to the box.

The minute the words were out of my mouth, I regretted saying them. Because Tyson got close and asked, "What? Why would you think that I was upset with you?"

Shooting him a look of disbelief, I scoffed, "Oh, please. Don't pretend you don't know."

"I don't," he assured me.

I stared at him a beat and realized he was being truthful. He had no idea why I thought he was upset with me.

"Well, it's just… I didn't…" I stammered.

"What is it?" he wondered, growing impatient.

I sighed. "I didn't call you yesterday. The alarm didn't give me a problem, and I remembered how to do everything you showed me, so I didn't call."

"Quinn, gorgeous, relax," Tyson said, his voice the perfect tone of gentleness that I adored. "Yesterday you told me that you recently got divorced and that you were married for seven years. All things considered, I figured it's been a long while since you've dated. I had a feeling you didn't catch on to what I was doing when I took your phone and called mine yesterday. So, when a few hours passed and I hadn't heard from you, I knew I needed to reach out to you."

"Do you have any idea how much trouble you could have saved me if you'd somehow communicated that to me earlier?" I scolded him.

"Why? What kind of trouble are you in?" he asked.

I turned around with the box of donuts in my hand and walked toward the kitchen. Once there, I set them on the counter, found one that looked enticing, and took a huge bite. After I'd swallowed that bite, I took another. As soon as I'd gotten that one down, I declared, "I barely slept last night.

Normally, this girl can go a night getting crappy sleep. But between the alarm and the cops two nights ago and then being worried about this last night, I've yet to have a decent night's sleep since moving in here."

Tyson walked up to the counter, grabbed a donut, and took a bite. "I'm sorry to hear that. What can I do to help make sure you sleep better tonight?"

I stared up at him and swallowed hard. There were a million ideas I had in my head of things he could do that would likely help me sleep a whole lot better. I just wasn't sure they were things I should be mentioning to him.

So, I did the only thing I could do. I shrugged my shoulders and took another bite of the donut before turning away from him and moving to the coffeepot. After I turned it on, I looked back at Tyson and found him eyeing me in a way that wasn't just curiosity. It was much more than that. And everything about it told me that he might have been thinking about things he could do to me to help me sleep better.

No way.

There was no way I could continue this.

I needed to find a safe way out of this conversation and into another one that resulted in far less discussion of things that would be detrimental to my sleep for the third night in a row.

"What's on the agenda for today?" I finally asked.

Tyson shook his head at me and chuckled. Evidently, he found my tactics for topic avoidance amusing.

"I'm going to spend my time today finishing up your system," he started. "But you knew that already."

Crap.

Was he seriously going to call me out on this?

I needed to think fast.

After taking another bite of my donut, chewing it slowly while keeping my eyes on Tyson, and swallowing, I finally asked, "Want to know what I'm going to do today?"

He leaned his hips against the counter, held his donut to his mouth, and demanded, "Tell me."

"I'm going to take a break from unpacking because I think I'm going to lose my mind if I have to hang up one more thing," I started. "Instead, I think I'm going to do some actual work."

Tyson tipped his head to the side. "Work? Are you leaving me here alone today?"

I shook my head. "No, why would I do that?"

"I thought you had rental properties you managed," he replied.

I confirmed, "I do, and that's how I pay my bills. But I also have another business I officially opened seven or eight months ago and it's been steadily growing ever since."

"What do you do?" he asked.

"I make jewelry."

"Jewelry?" he repeated.

"Yes."

"And this is something you enjoy doing?"

"I love it," I assured him. "I've been taking classes for over a year now to learn new skills. I always had a plan to make it into a business, but I never imagined it would grow this quickly."

Tyson looked genuinely intrigued. Maybe he was just being nice, but I didn't mind either way. I'd been wanting to talk to someone about my jewelry for a long time. Of course, my sister always made time to listen to me, but it wasn't like I could spend time showing her all of my new ideas since she lived in another state.

"When I finish up with your alarm today, will you show me some of your work?" he asked.

"Really?"

"Yeah."

Tyson wanted to *see* my jewelry. Shock didn't begin to describe what I was feeling.

I didn't respond to him. At least, not immediately. With the exception of my parents and Cassie, I hadn't really had the chance to talk to anyone over the last year. Maybe calling it a chance wasn't accurate. The truth is, after Chris and Alicia's betrayal, I spent most of my time focused on healing myself and getting through the divorce. I wasn't in the right frame of mind to be able to go out and find new friends. I'm not sure I would have trusted myself then to make any rational choices anyway.

So, while it had been lonely for quite a few months, it seemed things might be turning around. Perhaps the purchase of my home was the start of something new and wonderful for me. Maybe the malfunctioning alarm wasn't the bad thing I initially thought it was. And if that was the case, Levi sending the hottest guy I'd ever met to come and fix it for me was simply a hint of the good things to come.

"Okay," I agreed. "When you're done with my alarm, I'll show you some of the pieces I've made."

Tyson finished his donut and smiled at me. Then, he plucked another donut out of the box and walked away.

Right then and there, looking at his incredible backside, I decided to start taking baby steps. I'd start doing little things to give myself just a tiny little shred of happiness. Maybe it wouldn't amount to anything in the end, but at least I'd be trying. And I couldn't feel bad about that, especially not after everything I'd been through.

Tyson

When Levi walked into my office yesterday morning telling me about a client needing her security system checked out and possibly replaced, I never expected this.

I never expected her.

I never expected her quirky personality.

Her gorgeous face.

Her beautiful lips.

I never dreamed I'd walk into the home of a woman I'd want to invite to my niece's fifth birthday party.

But there she was.

All spitfire and sweetness.

And ever since that moment she got out of her car, pulled down her scarf, and started ranting about being pulled over, I didn't want to leave her side.

As much as I felt that way, I was glad when she decided to go upstairs and unpack her things because I had no doubt that if she hung around me while I worked, I wouldn't have gotten as much accomplished yesterday as I did. Quinn was the kind of distraction I wanted to have while I was working. Even still, it wouldn't have been good to have her hanging around either.

Once I got over the shock of her when I first met her, I never expected to be thrown again when she openly shared not only that she was divorced, but also the reason why. And as the day went on, all I could think was that her ex-husband was a fool.

While I knew it was possible I felt that way because I'd just met her and everything always seems to be rainbows and sunshine in the beginning, I had a feeling I wasn't going to find out she was just some crazy woman. Even if this just turned out to be a good first impression, I never agreed with someone stepping outside their current relationship if they were unhappy.

Things happen. People move on. Bringing someone else into the equation is never a good idea. Bringing your significant other's best friend into the equation is unforgivable.

So, it was no surprise that I spent the day yesterday trying to figure out how I was going to keep myself connected to Quinn. Giving her my number so she could call in the event she had an issue with the alarm seemed like the perfect opportunity.

Part of me didn't want to, but I couldn't help getting my hopes up last night that she'd reach out to me. But I also knew she probably didn't pick up on what I was doing, and it became all too clear how oblivious she was to that when I received her responses to my texts.

Moving forward, I knew I'd have to make my advances obvious; however, I knew I had to be careful. I didn't want to push too hard too quick and risk scaring her off either. Given how her marriage ended, I had no doubt Quinn was going to be cautious moving forward.

For the time being, I'd stick to friendly conversation. No matter how much I couldn't stop thinking about kissing her lips, I decided I would wait until either she made a move or gave me the slightest inkling that it was okay with her for me to proceed and take the lead.

If it was up to my family, they'd have me jumping the gun and going in for the attack right off the bat. As much as I might have wanted to explore something deeper with Quinn, even after only one day of being around her, I wouldn't do that to her. I'd already waited thirty-five years to find someone special. Now wasn't the time to rush it.

So, today was all about bringing her donuts for breakfast and trying to find subtle ways in so I could learn more about her.

And, lucky for me, it didn't take long.

The minute she mentioned her jewelry, I knew that was how I'd do it. And it wasn't about some tactic I had to get her to trust me long enough for me to take advantage of that. I was honestly surprised when I learned she made jewelry. Having worked in my father's construction business from the time I was a kid until I got hired at Cunningham Security, I knew what it felt like to build something by hand and to want people to see it.

After snatching up a second donut from the box and walking away from Quinn, I got to work. For the next several hours I pushed hard to get everything set up on her system. I didn't want to drag my feet and take away from the time I had to possibly spend with her.

By one o'clock that afternoon, she found me and declared with a big smile on her face, "Lunch time!"

Since I was approaching the end of what I needed to accomplish anyway, I stopped what I was doing and followed her out to the kitchen. This was another thing I liked about working at her place right now. She was not only making lunch but also offering good company.

"How's it going out there?" she asked when we sat down.

"Almost finished," I said.

"Wow," she marveled. "You don't waste time, do you?"

Not that I didn't always put forth effort to be diligent about my work, but today I was especially efficient.

I shrugged. "I'm on the second day, though," I reasoned.

She pursed her lips and thought for a moment. "This is true. Maybe Levi should reconsider your employment status."

I laughed. "Levi's not going to fire me because this job took me a second day to complete. Based on the actual number of hours I've put in and the amount of work that actually needed to be done, I'm probably ahead of schedule."

Quinn nodded and stated, "I figured as much."

"So, how was your morning?" I asked.

She swallowed a bite of her food before her eyes widened and she replied, "Really good. In fact, today was the first time I checked my email since the day before I moved. I've just been so distracted with the move and unpacking that I kind of let it go by the wayside for a few days. But when I checked it this morning to get caught up, I had a few orders for some of my pieces."

"That's awesome."

"It is, but that's not even the best news," she began. "I actually had an email from a potential new client who is looking to have me make a few custom pieces for him. It's the type of project that could make me a lot of money. But it won't be an easy one since he wants high-quality precious stones. I got back to him with some questions about specifics of what he's looking for, but ultimately, told him I'd sketch something out first to make sure it's what he wants."

"What is he looking to have you make?" I asked.

I noticed Quinn's expression grow a bit solemn. She hesitated briefly, but ultimately shared, "He's got the sweetest thing planned," she started. "He's looking to have me make a set of earrings, a necklace, a bracelet, and a ring. In a few months, he's planning to take his girlfriend on a trip, and each night they're away, he wants to give her a new piece. The ring will be the last thing, and he's hoping she'll accept it along with his proposal."

As soon as she said the words I realized why her mood had changed. If doing this was what made her happy, it might prove to be difficult for her when someone wanted an engagement ring or a wedding band made. I believed she'd eventually get past that, especially once she was in a healthy, committed relationship again, but there was no doubt it would take time.

"Sounds like he has a great idea," I agreed. "Unless he wants it to be a surprise, and she figures out before the last day that he's working up to a proposal."

Quinn hadn't thought of that. "Oh no, you're right. That would be terrible. When I speak to him again, I'll have to mention it to him and see what he thinks. It's possible he either never considered that, or he might think that she isn't the type who'd figure it out. Thanks for pointing that out. Maybe I can add proposal planning to my list of services?"

I let out a laugh. If that meant she was interested in keeping me around to help her out, I'd take it. Deciding it was best not to put her in an awkward position if she just said it off the cuff, I asked, "So, is that how you normally do things? Sketch them out before you make them?"

She nodded. "Yeah. I mean, I've had a few occasions where I've just picked up my tools and supplies and simply started on something without a clear plan in mind. But the results are hit or miss when I do that. So, I've decided it's much better to sketch them out ahead of time."

"That makes sense. And it's great that you enjoy what you're doing."

"I really do," she began. "I mean, it doesn't really bring in enough for me to live the life I do in a house like this quite yet, but that's not really what's important to me. I've always loved accessories and I have a bit of an artsy side, so this is the perfect combination of the two for me."

"I can understand that. I've always needed to do something where I worked with my hands," I offered. "From the time I was old enough, I worked with my father in his construction business."

"Really? What made you leave and go into the security business then?"

"As much as I loved the work and being with my family, I always knew I wanted to go into this field. When I was younger, I got hooked on crime shows about unsolved cases. And it always bothered me that bad things happened to good people, and sometimes they never received any justice. I wanted to be the person who tried to make sure there was one less unsolved case in the world."

Quinn stared at me in silence for a long time before she said, "That's very honorable of you."

I shook my head. "I appreciate you saying that, but it just feels like the thing I was meant to do."

"Did your family support your decision, or were they upset that you didn't stay in the construction business?" she asked.

Smiling, I shared, "I'm not sure my family could support me any more than they already do. Sometimes, they want to be too involved in my life. But I don't let it get to me because their support is boundless. No matter what I do, they'll always be there for me. And I'd do the same for them."

"That's great you have that," she stated.

"And you? Are you close with your family?" I asked.

Nodding, she replied, "Yes, but not in physical distance. I'm actually originally from Montana. About five hours from here. So, while I talk to them on a regular basis, I don't see them nearly as much as I'd like."

"Five hours isn't too bad. It's close enough that you can

drive it and not kill your entire day," I reasoned. "When was the last time you saw them?"

"I saw them all at Christmas. But my sister is coming out to visit me this weekend."

"Do you have any other siblings or just one?"

"Just Cassidy. But what we lack in numbers is made up by my sister's sheer joy for life. She doesn't let a moment go to waste," Quinn remarked.

"Sounds like she's been hanging around my family," I teased.

"Are they wild?" Quinn asked.

It took everything in me not to give her the full truth because that might send her running. Instead, I simply answered, "Maybe a little."

When we finished eating lunch, I asked, "So, I need about another thirty minutes to finish up your system. Do you want to show me what you've been working on today now or after I'm done?"

"We can do it after," she decided.

With that, I got back to work. When I finished up, I sat with Quinn while she showed me some of the jewelry she'd already made. Then, she brought out some that were still in progress. And through it all, I had no doubt about her talent for it.

"This is amazing," I said. "You're really talented."

Quinn beamed at me. "Thank you."

I held her gaze for a long time. There was something in it urging me to do what I'd been thinking of doing since she pulled the scarf from her face. I leaned toward her, noticing the rapid rise and fall of her chest as I did, when suddenly her phone rang, killing the moment.

"Sorry," she lamented. "Excuse me."

When she returned a few minutes later, she apologized, "I'm sorry. That was my sister."

"No problem," I assured her. "I should probably show you the alarm and head out."

She swallowed hard. "Okay."

Then, Quinn and I moved to the alarm panel where I showed her all the bells and whistles. And when I left for the day, I hoped she would use my number and call me.

CHAPTER 6

Quinn

I WAS STANDING IN MY FOYER PACING.

It had been the longest week ever.

And I knew that made no literal sense given the fact that unless daylight savings was beginning, every week had the same amount of time as the one before.

But it felt like it had been longer than usual.

Because I'd spent every day that week since Tyson left my house on Wednesday wanting to call him. I wanted to call him and talk to him and tell him to come back to see me.

I wanted him to finish what he started on the couch.

Or, at least, what I was pretty sure he was going to start on the couch after I'd showed him my jewelry.

That day. That day was the best day I'd had in a *really* long time. And just when it was about to get even better, my sister called and ruined it.

I still hadn't told her, but I planned on it. The minute she walked through my front door I was going to let her know just what she'd done. I couldn't wait to give her a piece of my mind.

Sure, I could have done it that day. I could have yelled at her over the phone, but I wanted to see her face when I did it.

I knew what she wanted for me, and I knew it was going to absolutely kill her to know she'd ruined my shot at a good time. I mean, at the time, I hadn't actually suspected that Tyson and I were going to take things to that level, but given how I'd been feeling since that day, I wasn't so sure I'd turn him down now.

I wanted sex.

I wanted good sex.

And I wanted it with Tyson.

I knew it wasn't rational. And I knew I promised myself baby steps. Something I truly believed I'd be able to do. In fact, it was something I thought was crucial for me moving forward.

But we were talking about more than a year. That was a long time to go without sex. There was only so much waiting a girl could do.

And just when I worked myself up into a full frenzy, there were several brash taps on the door.

I stomped over, flung open the door, looked in my sister's eyes, and blurted, "You cock blocked me!"

"What?!" she shrieked.

I let out a breath, which did nothing to calm me down, as she stepped inside. After I closed the door behind her, I rattled on, "He was right there. Right *there*! I was so close after so long, and then you called me."

"What are you talking about?" she asked.

"Cass, I met a man," I breathed.

She stopped moving and stared straight into my eyes. Then she dropped her bags and threw her arms around me. "Oh, that's great news! I'm so happy for you. When did you meet him?"

"Tuesday morning," I stated.

Her head jerked back. "This past Tuesday? Like only four days ago Tuesday?" she wondered.

"Yes, Cassie. You should remember the day clearly. Because it was the one after that when you decided to call me and tell me about all the things you wanted us to do when you came out to visit me," I reminded her.

"Why are you just now telling me?" she asked. "And what exactly do you mean when you say that I cock blocked you?"

"I'm telling you now because I wanted to yell at you in person," I began. "And cock blocking means just that." I held my thumb and forefinger up, pinched them together until they were just barely touching, and continued, "I was this close to having a man kiss for the first time in more than a year, and you decided to call me!"

"You were seriously going to let him kiss you after only knowing him a day?"

"It's been so long, Cass," I reasoned, not ashamed to admit that I was also whining a bit. "And he's so freaking handsome, it would be a shame not to get at least a kiss from him."

I knew she wasn't judging me when she asked me about letting him kiss me that quickly. If Cassidy got one look at Tyson, she would have asked why I waited so long.

"Alright, I feel like we need to open a bottle of wine right now so you can fill me in on what I missed since the last time I saw you. And by that, I mean I want to know all about this man. I do not care to hear about anything but him right now," she ordered.

Nodding, I agreed, "Okay."

She held my gaze a moment, and with the wind out of my sails, I sighed, "I'm so glad you're here, Cass."

She grinned, threw an arm around my back to the opposite shoulder, and insisted, "I know. I missed you, too."

With that, we moved out of the foyer.

I grabbed a couple of wine glasses, a bottle of wine, and some finger foods before getting comfortable on the living room sofa.

After she'd taken a sip of her wine, Cassie ordered, "Tell me everything."

So, I did.

I gave her every last detail. And she didn't interrupt once, which was saying something since that wasn't exactly her thing.

When I finished telling her everything, I asked, "So what do you think?"

"I'm trying to figure out why you have his number and haven't called him yet," she wondered. "Especially if you're so upset about me calling and interrupting!"

"He has my number, too," I reasoned. "And he hasn't reached out to me either. What if he realized that almost kissing me was a mistake? I mean, wouldn't he have called me if he was interested in me?"

"Maybe. Or maybe he's waiting for you to let him know that you're interested, Quinn," she guessed. "There's no law that says that the guy always has to be the one to call."

"I'm out of the loop, Cass," I admitted. "And am I playing with fire? I've never been one to just hook up with someone. I'm not sure it's something I can do without having any feelings for the guy."

"You do, though," she reasoned. "Based on everything you told me, you two covered a lot of stuff in two short days. He's no longer just some random stranger. You've met how many of his co-workers for crying out loud. And feelings or not, if a couple of nights of fun are something you both want, there's no reason for you to feel shame about it."

"But I feel like it's so quick to just jump into something. There are so many things I don't know about him. Maybe I should reach out to him, but take the time to get to know him a little better before I do anything too crazy," I suggested.

My sister, who was mid-sip, pulled the wine glass from her lips and deadpanned, "I love you, Quinn, but you honestly make me crazy. Why would you deny yourself something you want simply because you have this idea of it being too quick? Let's face it... you and Chris were together how long and there were obviously things you didn't learn about him until the end. I'm not saying that to upset you or make you feel bad. I'm saying it because you need to realize that the time doesn't matter. What you feel and what you want is all that matters."

I hadn't thought about it like that. And I didn't take any offense to what she said about Chris. If I took the time to think about it and let my mind wander there, sometimes I'd find myself questioning where I went wrong with him. Deep down I knew that him cheating was all about him, but I still found ways to question myself and the role I played in the eventual demise of our relationship.

"I guess you're right," I began. "I never really looked at it like that."

She grinned and asked, "So, what exactly is it that you want, big sister?"

"Sex," I groaned. "Really fantastic sex with Tyson Reed."

"Then you should call that boy," she urged.

I nodded and assured her, "I think I will. But not today. Today is just you and me. You've got to fill me in on everything happening back at home while you help me unpack the rest of my boxes. Then, I want to show you the jewelry I've been working on. Tonight, we can go out for dinner. We'll keep it low-key for your first night."

She pulled her brows together and wondered, "Are we keeping it low-key for me or for you?"

I just shook my head and laughed. "Come on," I urged as I stood from the couch. "I need you to help me finish unpacking."

With that, my sister got up and followed me upstairs to my bedroom where we spent the next several hours laughing, catching up, and getting through a good chunk of the boxes I still had remaining. When we finally called it quits so we could get ready to go out for dinner, there were only three boxes left.

Two hours after that, we hopped in my car and went out for dinner. We were fortunate enough to not have to wait too long once we arrived at the restaurant.

"Follow me," the hostess ordered after she'd called my name for our table.

We fell into step behind her, and I was so excited about having the time to spend with my sister that I didn't pay much attention to what was going on around me.

Cassie and I were still following the hostess when I heard, "Quinn?"

I knew that voice, and the instant I heard it my heart began racing. I stopped, turned, and saw him.

Tyson.

It seemed he had the idea to come out for dinner as well. Only, Tyson was not alone. No. He had an entire brood of people with him.

Oddly enough, as my eyes scanned the faces of the people he was seated with, I realized all the conversation had stopped, and they were all staring at me.

I snapped myself out of it, looked back at him, and said, "Tyson."

"Tyson?" my sister repeated from beside me.

Oh God.

Oh no.

She had zero filter.

And that became evident to the people sitting at the table because she asked, "The same Tyson you just spent the entire day telling me all about? The Tyson that I cock blocked?"

I pressed my lips together and shot daggers from my eyes at my sister.

She ignored them, turned her attention to Tyson, and held out her hand. "Hi, I'm Cassidy. I'm Quinn's sister."

I watched as he took her hand and said, "It's nice to meet you."

But he wasn't looking at her. His eyes were still focused on me. And they communicated something for which I wasn't sure I was prepared.

"Likewise," Cassie returned.

My eyes didn't leave Tyson's until I heard a woman at the table start speaking. "Quinn? Since when has there been a woman named Quinn in your life, you had the opportunity to get cock blocked, little bro?"

Okay, so this was apparently one of Tyson's sisters.

"Ladies?" the hostess called from beside us. "Are you coming?"

I didn't even have a chance to respond when Tyson's sister declared, "No, they're joining us. Can you bring us two additional chairs and place settings?"

"Oh no," I refused. "We appreciate the offer, but my sister's here visiting from Montana. I promised lots of sisterly bonding with her."

Cassie didn't even seem to be listening to what I said. At least, not in a way that prevented her from doing exactly what I hoped she wouldn't. She looked around the table and assured them, "I'm here to have a good time. My sister and I have been talking all day. I'm just ready to have some fun."

I noticed as she spoke, she did it with her eyes on the man sitting by Tyson.

The hostess had managed to pull a chair up to the table. "Well then, you've come to the right table, girl. Have a seat over there next to Kyle. If you're looking to have a good time on your trip, he'll have no problem helping you do just that."

I watched as my sister took in Tyson's brother with a devious look on her face. And I envied her for her ability to do that. Just like that, she walked away from me and toward Kyle.

The hostess then pulled another chair up and placed it next to Tyson. I was left with either walking away to have dinner by myself, looking like a fool, or I could join my sister, the man I hadn't stopped thinking about for days, and his family. I didn't know which was worse.

No sooner did I sit down when Tyson leaned toward me and whispered in my ear, "How long is your sister staying?"

My brows pulled together as I replied quietly, "She's staying through next weekend. She'll be heading home first thing Monday morning."

"Fuck," he muttered, looking away.

"What?"

He turned his attention back to me and advised, "I'll be at your place shortly after she's gone. And then I'll finish what she interrupted earlier this week."

I swallowed hard and stared at him.

"What?" I rasped.

"Did you really talk about me all day?" he asked in a soft voice meant only for me to hear, with a smile on his face.

I pressed my lips together and stayed silent. The one who didn't was my sister.

"This is so great meeting all of you," she started. "It's always so hard going back home after coming to visit her. She's here by herself while our whole family is five hours away. It's not that far, but it's not easy enough to just get here at the drop of a hat either."

The same woman who'd been speaking from the start assured Cassie, "Well you don't need to worry about her now. She's got all of us. I'm Kendra. This is my husband, Tony."

Kendra then went around each of the people sitting at the table and introduced everyone. In addition to herself, her husband, Tyson, and their brother, Kyle, we were also introduced to Vera and her husband, Dave, as well as Beau and his wife, Josie.

"So, how did the two of you meet?" Vera cut to the chase.

Tyson answered, "Quinn recently moved into a new home and needed her security system updated."

"Where'd you move from?" Kendra asked.

"Well, I'm originally from Montana, but I've lived here in Wyoming for ten years," I explained.

"What made you leave your family?" Vera wondered.

Answering that question was going to be tough. Because I did it for Chris, and the life I thought we were building together. How did I tell the people who obviously thought there was something serious happening between their brother and me that I was recently divorced?

"She fell in love," Cassie answered for me. "And she got married."

When the looks of confusion came over nearly everyone at the table, my sister continued, "But her ex-husband is a cheating asshole. He slept with her best friend."

I watched as the men at the table winced and the women gasped.

Cassie went on, "Thankfully, Quinn's a smart girl. The day she found out, she left and never went back."

I didn't know if it was because they were doing it for me or for their brother, but Beau stated, "The guy was obviously a fool."

"And you're clearly better off without him," Kendra added.

"Good for you for not sticking around to allow him to do that to you again," Vera approved.

They were all being so nice about it, I felt I had to say something. "Thanks," I murmured. "I'm happy now, so it's all good."

"I love that necklace, Quinn," Josie piped up. "Where did you get it?"

Thankful for the change in topic, I brought my hand up to touch my fingers to the necklace. "I made it," I replied.

The smile left her face as a look of astonishment took its place. "Are you serious?"

I nodded and Tyson added, "This isn't just a one-time thing she did. Quinn makes jewelry."

"And she's really, really good at it," my sister chimed in.

I came out to this restaurant tonight expecting to have a small, low-key dinner with my sister. Now, I'd somehow become the topic of conversation at Tyson's family's Saturday night get together.

"I'd love to see your stuff sometime," Josie declared.

"She's got a website," Cassie announced. "You can check out most of her pieces there. Considering you now have the personal connection, you can just reach out to her and set up a time to come and see everything she's got in person."

With her eyes on my sister, Kendra approved, "I like her."

"You like everyone," her husband teased.

Her brows shot up as her head snapped in his direction. "No, I do not," she shot back. "May I remind you about your old boss? I did *not* like that guy. Or what about that lady that works at —"

Tony cut her off. "Alright, woman, you made your point. Relax. It was mostly meant to be a compliment."

As if nothing happened, Kendra looked back at Cassie and asserted, "I like you because you don't play around. You might not know us, but you know your sister and how you feel about her. You're sitting here singing her praises in hopes she's going to find something good that she deserves after what she's been through. That's what family does. That's what any one of us would do for the other. As a sister myself, I'm telling you not to worry about her, Cassidy. If my brother and Quinn are a thing, we've already got her back."

The tension left Cassie's body, and she sat back in her chair.

"How long are you here for?" Josie asked Cassie.

"Through next weekend," she replied. "I leave early the following Monday morning."

Josie's eyes went to Kendra's and Vera's. They both grinned and Kendra insisted, "Then the both of you need to join us next Sunday. It's my daughter's fifth birthday party. If you're up for good food, good company, and lots of laughs, Jordyn's party will be the place to be."

I was about to respond, but Cassie beat me to it. "We'd love to come," she declared. "Of course, we'll be there."

"Perfect. It's settled then."

And just like that, I went from feeling anxious all week about what I should do regarding Tyson to having my sister set it up so that I'd be attending his niece's fifth birthday party.

While it wasn't how I'd planned to have things go, I

couldn't exactly be angry about it. I was more concerned about what I'd do once Cassie went back home to Montana, and I was left in Wyoming with Tyson wanting to finish what he'd almost started.

CHAPTER 7

Quinn

The sound of my phone ringing is what woke me up the next morning.

My eyes stayed closed as I reached out for it. Once it was firmly in my hand, I opened one eye to see who was calling.

Tyson's name was on the display.

"Hello?" I answered.

There was no response.

Alarmed, I rolled to my back and called, "Tyson?"

"Is that what you sound like first thing in the morning?" he asked.

I pulled my phone from my ear, noted the time was only eight-thirty, and held it back up to the side of my head.

"It's eight-thirty, and I'm still in bed, so that would be a yes," I answered. Then, because I had no idea what he was getting at, I asked, "Is that a bad thing?"

"Gorgeous, it's only bad in the sense that I'm not there with you," he returned.

My eyes closed, and his words made me smile. Keeping my eyes closed, I rolled to my side, tucked the phone between my ear and the bed, and asked, "Why are you up so early?"

"I've been up for a while now," he informed me. "I'm usually up early for work, so I'm used to it."

I groaned.

Tyson laughed in my ear. "I take it you're not a morning person," he surmised.

"That would be correct. In fact, I'm not normally a morning person or a night owl. Last night was an exception."

Cassie and I had dinner with Tyson and his family. We all spent several hours eating, talking, and having a great time. Before I knew it, it was approaching eleven o'clock. By the time we finally said goodbye to everyone, left, and got home to bed, it was just before midnight. That was two hours past the time I was already usually sleeping.

"Well, I'm just happy to hear you survived," he began. "It seems like your sister is just like mine."

"In what way?" I asked.

"She does whatever she's got to do to feel like she's in control of your life," he stated.

I let out a small laugh. "You have no idea."

"Three nosy women say I do," he challenged.

He had a point. I had Cassie to deal with and thought she was more than enough. Tyson had Vera, Kendra, and even Josie.

Smiling in my fake sleep, I acquiesced, "Okay, you win."

"Yeah, but it's not always a bad thing," he concluded. "They all mean well and want the best for me. I'll take that any day over having them not care at all."

I knew exactly what he meant. Cassie was a bit more animated than I was. She had an air of confidence about her, but she didn't abuse it or use it in a negative way. Sure, she sometimes shared things I'd have preferred her not to share, but she never did it with any malice. And deep down, I knew she, like Tyson's family, always wanted whatever was best for us.

"I agree," I sighed into the phone. "So, I have a question."

"Okay? What's up?"

"This little niece of yours named Jordyn," I began. "What is she into?"

"Pardon?"

"For her birthday, Tyson," I explained. "Cassie and I are planning to get manicures and pedicures before lunch. After, we're going shopping. What can we get Jordyn for her birthday?"

There was a moment of hesitation before Tyson insisted, "Oh, Quinn, that's not necessary. You haven't even met Jordyn. And there will be so much there for her already that she won't notice. I don't want you to think you've got to get her something because my sister insisted on inviting you there as my date."

"She's a little girl," I started. "I wouldn't feel right just showing up empty-handed. I can get her something small if you're worried about her feeling spoiled."

After a moment of hesitation, Tyson said, "Anything that screams princess will be right up her alley."

I smiled. She was a girly-girl. I immediately had an idea on what to give her for her birthday. As excited as I was about that, though, I couldn't wait to see how Tyson was around her. He seemed so big and tough, but for some reason I had this feeling that deep down he was a big softie.

"Oh, I can't wait," I bubbled. "This sounds like so much fun."

"Yeah, you might want to wait until after the party to make that statement," he warned. "You heard all about the size of my family last night, but it's different seeing everyone all together."

"I'm sure it'll be fine."

"It will be," he assured me. When the silence stretched between us, he asked, "So, you've got a full day planned today?"

"Yeah," I confirmed. He didn't respond, so I asked, "Why?"

"Can't stop thinking about what your sister said yesterday when you first arrived," he answered honestly.

"Sorry," I apologized. "She has no filter."

"Quinn?"

"Yeah?"

"Do you really think I need you to apologize for her making it known that you wanted that with me?" he questioned me. "If I hadn't thought it might be too much too soon for you a few days ago, I wouldn't have ever left."

For the second time that morning, I groaned.

I didn't know if I could handle having this conversation with him right now. "Maybe we shouldn't talk about this right now," I suggested.

"Okay," he immediately agreed.

Just like that, without any hesitation, he gave me what I needed. Even if it was something he really wanted to talk about, he was putting that aside for me. It wasn't that I didn't want to have the discussion. It was just something I thought we shouldn't necessarily do over the phone where we were both bound to become more sexually frustrated.

"Thank you. I should probably get going now so I can get up and get ready for my day with Cass."

"Alright, gorgeous. I hope the two of you have a great day," he said.

"We always do," I assured him. "And Tyson?"

"Yeah?"

"I want to talk about it, but I'd rather do it when you're here with me," I said softly.

His voice had dropped an octave when he replied, "Looking forward to that."

"Me too."

With that, Tyson and I said goodbye and disconnected. Then I spent the next few minutes staring up at the ceiling. I would have continued to do that, but my door flew open and Cassie came barreling in.

"Guess what?" she burst as she flung herself onto my bed.

"I honestly can't imagine what news you could possibly have since it's only been about eight hours since I've seen you last, and you spent it all in bed," I noted.

Cassie was on her belly, propped up on her elbows and forearms, grinning at me. "I was in bed, but I wasn't sleeping the whole time," she shared, her voice devious.

"Let me guess. You were on the phone with Tyson's brother, Kyle," I guessed.

"Now you're learning," she replied in a tone that indicated she was proud of me.

"I don't even want to know any more," I sighed.

Cassie rolled to her back so her shoulder was touching mine when she teased, "Oh, but I think you do."

My eyes left the ceiling and came to my sister. "The way you're saying that makes me want to know even less."

She grinned and shared anyway. "You and I are going out on Thursday night with Tyson and Kyle."

"What?"

Cassie nodded. "Yep. Kyle and I talked for a while last night, and he wants to show me a good time while I'm here. Of course, I told him that I was here to spend time with my sister and didn't want to just ditch you, so he said that he'd convince Tyson to join him and the four of us could go out together."

"What if Tyson doesn't want to go?" I asked, directing my gaze back up to the ceiling. "I just talked to him, and he didn't mention anything to me about this."

"Kyle and I were on the phone late," she reasoned. "He probably just hasn't had a chance to call his brother and tell him."

"Ask him," I corrected her.

"What?"

"Kyle's not going to tell his brother to go. He has to ask him," I explained.

"Not according to Kyle. Apparently, he believes that Tyson will need very little convincing once he tells him that you'll be there."

While Tyson made it clear that he was interested in me, he didn't make mention of wanting to see me before Jordyn's party. If it was really as easy as Kyle was telling Cassie it would be, I wondered why Tyson hadn't asked to get together with me sooner.

Instead of trying to analyze it all, I asked, "What's the deal with you and Kyle?"

"Nothing."

"Being on the phone all night does not tell me that it's nothing," I noted. "And furthermore, how the heck are you this awake and alert if you were up all hours of the night?"

"I'm trying to enjoy this trip to the fullest," she remarked. "Talking to Kyle last night was worth losing some sleep over. Besides, I can close my eyes for a few minutes when my toes are being freshened up later this morning."

I didn't reply. And Cassie didn't say anything else. The two of us laid there for a long time, allowing the silence to stretch between us. It was quite a while later when I said, "I hope he's everything he seems."

Cassie reached out and grabbed my hand. She gave me a squeeze and assured me, "He will be."

I didn't know how she could make a statement like that

with such confidence, but I didn't question it. Partly because I wasn't sure she'd have an answer, but mostly because I wanted it to be true.

A few minutes later, we got up for breakfast.

"So, Kyle, what do you do?" I asked.

My sister and I were out with Tyson and his brother. They took us out of Windsor and drove us to the neighboring town of Rising Sun. There, they brought us to Big Lou's Restaurant and Saloon.

I'd been here only once before and loved it. Unfortunately, my ex-husband didn't like the scene, so we never came back.

Big Lou's was a two-story establishment, and like the name suggested, it was a restaurant and saloon in one. The first floor held the restaurant, which had been designed to give it a true western feel. The saloon was on the second floor, where a variety of events took place beyond just drinking and dancing. There were also live performances and karaoke nights.

There weren't any live performances or karaoke scheduled for tonight, but the Jacobs sisters wouldn't need that to have a good time.

Currently, we were still down in the restaurant and had just finished our dinner when I questioned Kyle.

"Construction," he replied.

I looked to Tyson who confirmed, "Kyle and Beau took over running our father's business. I'm the odd man out."

Suddenly, it hit me. I didn't know why I didn't think of it before when Tyson told me about his family's construction business.

"Can I hire you to do routine maintenance on my rentals?" I asked.

"Sure," Kyle answered. "You don't have a company that handles that already?"

"One of the few things her ex-husband did that was good," Cassie chimed in. "He was handy and maintained their properties."

"How many do you have?"

"Three single-family homes and one apartment complex," I shared.

"Did you get all the properties in the divorce?" Tyson wondered.

I shook my head. "We split them. We had four homes and four apartment complexes together."

Tyson's eyes narrowed. "Seems like he has far more earning potential depending on the size of the complexes."

I nodded. "He does. But I'm completely okay with it. I'd been handling our finances from day one, so I knew that while those properties brought in more money, they also had a lot more expenses and maintenance. After splitting the properties, he definitely grosses more every month. But I profit much more after costs are factored in. He never considered that and thought he won."

"My sister's no fool," Cassie announced. "She's smart and talented."

I smiled at her and added, "I'm determined to be successful with my jewelry business, and don't want to spend my time dealing with the headaches that come with owning the apartments. It's a lot of work. I'm already offsetting the difference with my side business. And the only expenses I have now that I've acquired most of the tools is the cost of the actual materials for each piece I make. Since that's always factored into the selling price, I've got nothing to worry about."

"Good for you," Kyle began. "One day that guy is going to regret his decision."

"Yeah, and it's not just going to be about the properties either," Tyson added.

I had to admit it was nice to hear those words. For a while I struggled with the fact that I'd been betrayed by Chris. He took vows. He broke them. And I was the one who was left feeling like my world had ended. Obviously, I'd gotten past that point, but it was nice to think that Chris would get to a place where he'd regret what he'd done to us. I hoped somehow that Alicia would get a similar lesson.

"Anytime you need something done at any of the properties, just give me a call. We'll get it taken care of for you," Kyle offered.

"Thank you. And thanks for saying such nice things. All I want is to accomplish what I set out to do. I know if I can do that, I'll have the best revenge." I returned before lifting a finger and pointing it at my sister. "Of course, I know I'd reach my goal faster if I could convince this girl to move here and become my partner."

"Oh, here we go again," she sighed, being overly dramatic about it.

The guys laughed as I pressed, "I don't understand why you don't even consider it. It's not like you're working at a job that you love. Just look at it from that perspective. Instead of sitting there in a medical office handling their billing, you could be seeing my face every single day."

"Gorgeous, you really know how to sell something, don't you?"

I rolled my eyes and leaned my shoulder into his side, hoping to knock him off balance. He didn't even budge.

"What's stopping you from even considering it?" Kyle

asked. He looked genuinely curious, and I liked thinking that perhaps he was interested in Cassidy in a way that he'd be on my side and help try to convince her.

Cassie shrugged. "Montana's home. It's not that easy to just pick up and walk away from everything I love about it. I have friends and family there."

"You can have that there and have it here too," he noted.

"I like him," I announced, pointing at Kyle using nearly the same words Kendra said about my sister. "He's clearly on my side and sees how you can have the best of both worlds. It's only a five-hour drive away, Cass. You can come here, build a new life, start a new career, and make new friends. And when you need it, you can always go home for a visit."

Cassie looked around the table at all of us, but it was Tyson who spoke next. "Quinn's right. If you've got nothing there that's tying you down, like a significant other, kids, or a job you love, why not give it a shot?"

My sister threw her hand out and scoffed, "Oh, you're just on her side because you think she's pretty and you want to kiss her."

Tyson didn't argue. "No use denying it."

Cassie and Kyle laughed. I squirmed in my seat next to him because I wanted him to kiss me. If he did, I had no doubt it would lead into other things I wanted him to do to me.

"Alright, so what do you ladies think? Are you ready to head upstairs?" Tyson asked, changing the subject.

Cassie and I looked at each other and grinned before turning our attention back to Tyson and nodding.

When we made it to the second floor, we found a booth against the wall in the room off the main bar area. We'd barely sat down and started our first round of drinks when Cassie declared, "Time to dance. I've only got a few more days left here.

I'm not going back to Montana without shaking my booty at least once."

I tipped my head back to look at Tyson. "It's my sisterly duty," I explained. "I've got to go dance."

Tyson stood up and moved out of the way so I could slide out of the booth. No sooner did I land on my feet when Cassie wrapped her fingers around my wrist and dragged me to the dance floor. The two of us spent a long time out there just enjoying doing something we'd always loved to do. And it was during that time on the dance floor when I realized just how much I wished I could convince my sister to make the move to Wyoming.

I missed having her around all the time.

CHAPTER 8

Quinn

I HAD TEN MINUTES LEFT TO SPARE BEFORE I NEEDED TO MAKE A call to Patrick Dane, the man who was interested in having me design the pieces for his girlfriend to whom he was hoping to propose.

It was Friday afternoon.

I'd just finished lunch after spending my morning working on another project for which I'd come up with an idea. I was surprised at how well I managed to focus on my work today considering the evening I'd had last night.

After Cassie and I spent entirely too long dancing, we joined the guys at the table again. And it wasn't even minutes later when my sister and Kyle got up to get another round of drinks for themselves. Since Tyson was driving, he'd cut himself off.

When it was just Tyson and I left in the booth, I asked, "Do you think he can convince her to move out here?"

"My brother and your sister?" he wondered.

"Yeah."

Tyson shrugged. "I don't know your sister that well," he started. "Kyle has always been the kind of guy that goes after what he wants and won't stop until he gets it. But being ambitious in most facets of your life and trying to convince someone else of what they should do in theirs are two different things. If this was about Kyle going over something he had his heart set on and he was his only obstacle, I'd have no doubt. Persuading your sister to pack up her life and move away from the place she's grown up is not that. So, I'm sorry, but I just can't say."

"He'll try though, right?" I pressed.

"From what I've seen so far and the very little he's told me, I have no doubt that he likes her. But I don't know if what they might feel for one another translates into a long-term, serious relationship. Cassie knows she's going home in a few days and seems to be completely content to just have a good time."

I looked away in the direction the pair had walked off. "Yeah," I sighed. "She's always been like that. I've always envied her confidence when it comes to that."

"You think you aren't confident?"

"I mean, there are things that I'm confident about, but not like that. She isn't afraid to put herself out there, even when she doesn't know what the next day will bring. I'm too scared to do anything like that," I admitted.

Tyson burst out laughing. I watched with avid fascination as he threw his head back, and his body shook with amusement. As much as I enjoyed seeing him like that, I didn't understand what he found so funny.

"You're kidding me, right? Quinn, your sister is scared shitless and you're one of the bravest women I've ever met."

I blinked in surprise. "What?"

"Your sister doesn't even want to consider moving out here when she knows you're here," he started. "You moved here because you thought you found someone you were going to spend the rest of your life with. When that didn't work out like you planned, there isn't a soul on Earth that would have blamed you if you went back to Montana. But you didn't. You stayed here. On your own. And you took a chance on yourself by opening your own business when you'd originally planned on having your best friend by your side through it. All of that is not something that someone who is scared does. That, my gorgeous girl, is the mark of a confident woman."

My lips parted. I'd never really looked at the decisions I'd made after the divorce as brave. Mostly, I'd thought of it as being stubborn. I didn't want what Chris and Alicia did to make me leave a place I'd grown to love. Hearing him say that he thought it was courageous of me to stick around and not let them beat me made me feel really good.

"Quinn?" he called.

"Yeah?" I rasped.

He leaned closer, and his voice dipped lower when he shared, "I'm really glad you decided to stay here."

"Me too," I whispered.

Tyson moved closer, his lips mere inches from mine, when Cassie's voice surrounded us. "We're back!"

Tyson's eyes closed, the disappointment written all over his face. I took that in for a brief moment, but ultimately turned my attention to my sister.

Her eyes moved back and forth between Tyson and me when realization dawned in her features. "Did I cock block you again?" she asked.

Tyson didn't look at her. He simply cocked an eyebrow at me and asked, "You're sure you want her to move here?"

I bit my lip to stifle a grin as I nodded.

Tyson groaned.

And sadly, for the remainder of the night, we didn't get another moment like that again.

Now, as I sat preparing to call a client that, if he decided he liked my designs and the price, had the potential to be huge for my business, all I could think about was how much truth there was behind Tyson's assessment.

I had been brave to stay in a place where I had no family or close friends left. It took guts to dig my heels in and stick around after I'd been betrayed by those who were supposed to have loved and cared about me.

I was starting to realize that no matter what happened with Tyson or whether my sister decided to move out here, I'd be fine. Because even though Chris and Alicia's betrayal left me broken for a bit, I found a way to pick myself back up. And in the end, I knew I'd be much stronger for it.

Feeling a sense of pride and determination, I picked up my phone and called my potential client.

After three rings, he answered, "Hello?"

"Hi, Mr. Dane. This is Quinn Jacobs. How are you?"

"I'm great, Quinn. Thank you so much for taking the time to call me this afternoon to discuss the jewelry. And please, call me Patrick."

"Sure. And it's no problem at all," I assured him. "Did you get a chance to take a look at the sketches of the designs I sent over?"

"I did," he replied.

He hesitated to say anything else, and the nerves instantly built in my belly. Not wanting to miss the opportunity to create the pieces he was looking for, and unable to stand the wait, I assured him, "Please understand that the sketches are just a rough idea of what is possible. They are, by no means, set in stone. I did my best to try to match the style with the details you gave about your girlfriend's style. If what I sent is really off the mark, we can definitely work to make some changes that'll make it all perfect for her."

"Quinn, forgive me," Patrick lamented. "It's just that every time I think about what you sent over, I can't help but feel overwhelmed. I can't believe I'm preparing to ask her to marry me. The thought of spending the rest of my life with this woman just leaves me speechless. Sometimes I wonder how I got so lucky. Anyway, I think what you designed was exquisite. Every little intricate detail matches her style and personality perfectly. She's feminine grace personified, and that's precisely what you delivered."

To say I felt relieved was an understatement. While I'd hoped Patrick would like the designs, I thought they were just going to be a jumping off point. I had no idea he was going to have such a positive response.

"I'm so happy to hear that," I said.

"I do have one tiny addition I want to make to the earrings. While I want all of the stones in each piece to be diamonds, I do want one slightly larger focal point in the center of the earrings using a different gem. If you think that's doable, I will send over some specifics on what I'm looking for."

"Absolutely," I confirmed. "Like I said before, these were just meant to be preliminary sketches. I had suspected we'd need to do some tweaking. The fact that there's only something minor is great news."

"Perfect. Now the big question is regarding time," he started. "How soon are you able to get started on this, and do you have any idea on when they'll be completed?"

I took in a deep breath and blew it out before I explained, "Well, that really all depends on what you want. Currently, I don't have any other major custom projects I'm working on, so that's the first hurdle out of the way. The second thing we need to consider is the specifics on the diamonds and the other gem you want to add. While you gave me an idea on what you want for shapes of the diamonds, we have yet to really discuss the specifics of carat size, clarity, cut, color, and price. Depending on what you want, it could delay getting the project completed in a reasonable amount of time. But I can assure you that once I have all the diamonds here and ready to go, it won't take long."

"Alright, so could you email me a list of my options on those things with a rough idea on time. I'm not necessarily concerned about the costs, but you can throw them in there if you'd like. After you show me what my options are, I'd very much appreciate your recommendation. Ultimately, I want her to have the best there is, but I don't want her to have to wait forever for me to give it to her. So I think whatever we can do to balance those two will be perfect."

"Sure, I can do that. As soon as we're off the phone, I'll put that together and get it sent over to you."

"Great. I'll look forward to receiving that then. Thank you again, Quinn."

He was thanking me, yet I thought I was the one who should have been grateful. While my business had been steadily growing, this project had the potential to really launch my career to another level. Knowing that, I replied, "You're welcome. And thank you for giving me the opportunity to be part of such a special time in your life. I can't wait to see it all come together."

With that, Patrick and I disconnected. I spent the next two hours doing a little research on what readily available options were out there for diamonds in the size and shapes he'd requested. I generated a list for him that included specifics on the clarity, color, and price of those diamonds. Then, I did a bit more work and put together a list of other options that might delay getting the engagement ring completed. Once I had everything together, I sent an email over to him with my recommendations based on what he said was most important to him. I also included two back up choices, just in case.

Once I'd finished, I went to check on my sister. She'd decided after lunch that her lack of sleep had caught up with her, and she needed a nap. Since she knew I had some work to get done, it was the perfect opportunity for her. But given that she was heading home on Monday, we didn't want to waste the little time we had left together.

Tonight, we were planning to have dinner and a movie at home. With our time dwindling, we both just wanted a quiet night hanging out on the couch being lazy and eating. And since Cassie specifically requested it, I had every intention of giving it to her. Right now, I'd do anything to convince her to change her mind.

The weekend was flying by. It was already late Sunday morning, and Cassie and I were just about ready to head out to Jordyn's birthday party.

I called Tyson yesterday afternoon to get the address, but he didn't want to give it to me. He had been planning to pick us up and take us himself, but with Cassie leaving early Monday morning to head back home, I didn't know how late we'd stay at the party. As a result, I told Tyson I didn't want him to pick us up because I didn't want him to have to leave his niece's party.

"Cass!" I yelled from the bottom of the stairs up to her. "Let's go! We're going to be late for the party!"

"I'm coming!" she shouted back.

I could tell by the way she sounded that she wasn't actually coming. If we were going to have any hope of making it to the party at a decent time, I knew she was going to need some encouragement. So, I climbed the stairs and hustled down the hall to the guest bedroom where she was staying.

"We've got to go, Cass," I coaxed her as I opened the door and walked in.

I froze on the spot and took in my sister. While she looked dressed and ready to go, she still managed to look completely out of sorts.

"What's wrong?" I asked her.

"I wish I could be like you, Quinn," she mumbled.

"What?"

She flopped down on the bed and sighed, "I love being here. I love seeing you all the time. I love not having to go to work at a job I don't like. And I love that I feel more like myself here than I do anywhere else."

I walked over and sat down next to her. Placing my palm on her forehead, I stroked backward into her hair. "So, come here," I urged. "I can come back to Montana as soon as you're ready and I'll help you pack up to move. You can stay with me as long as you need, and if you don't want to work anywhere else, I could really use your help with the new business."

She shifted her gaze to mine. "Why does it scare me so much?" she asked.

"Because it's scary," I confirmed. "Don't you remember what it was like for me when I moved here originally with Chris? I was terrified of leaving everything I'd ever known. But I still did it because I knew I had to take a chance. If I hadn't, I would have regretted it for the rest of my life. Go home, think about it, and if you really aren't happy, come back. I'm here for you. And I always will be. So, if you're scared of being lonely, you don't have to worry about that. Worst case, you try it out for a while and realize it's not what you want. You can always go back home."

She closed her eyes and smiled.

"Besides, I know this great guy who'd be thrilled to hear that you're thinking of moving here. While I wouldn't recommend making a move like that for a guy considering I've been there and done that, it should help you decide a little easier."

I was doing my best to keep the tone of my voice neutral and calm. On the inside, I was totally freaking out. If my sister made the move to Windsor, I'd be the happiest woman in the world.

"I really like him," she admitted.

I smiled at her and said, "And I'm pretty sure he really likes you, too, Cass."

"What if... what if I take a chance on him and he does to me what Chris did to you?" she worried.

"Then I'll be there to help you through it," I assured her. "But in all honesty, Cassidy, I don't think Kyle has that in him."

"You don't?"

I shook my head. "No. He's too much of a family man, in my opinion. There's something about him and Tyson and the rest of them that's not like other people. It's... it reminds me of you and me. It's loyalty."

"How did you do it?" she asked. "How did you not go crazy being fearful about you and Chris? I know you were in love at the time, and you probably never imagined you'd end up where you did. But still. Like right now, how is it that you're even considering another relationship?"

I held her worried gaze for a long time wondering how to tell her what I felt. The last thing I wanted to do, especially if there was a chance she'd consider moving here, was tell her the truth and scare her more.

Because I pondered it so long, my sister got the wrong idea and began to fret. "Oh God, Quinn. I'm not trying to make you question Tyson or anything like that. I think he's a great guy, and I hope he's the one for you. I want to see you happy in a relationship again with a man who treats you the way you deserve to be treated. I'm just struggling to understand how you got through it and to the point where you can even think about another relationship."

"Because I've got you," I stated. "You saw me at my worst, right after it happened. If it weren't for you dropping everything an hour after I called you and hauling your butt down here, I'm not sure I'd be sitting here right now. My sister saw me through the worst time in my life. That's why I'm so strong now. Because when my life was spiraling out of control, you were my constant."

"I love you," she whispered through her tears.

"I know. I love you, too."

I gave Cassie another minute in the bed before I admitted, "As much as I love you, I will not hesitate to leave you here right now. This is Tyson's niece's birthday party. And I know we've met most of his family, but we haven't met his parents. I don't want to show up late and make a bad impression."

The minute the words were out of my mouth, Cassie shot up in the bed. "You're right," she exclaimed. "Kyle's parents will be meeting me for the first time, too. We have to go."

She didn't even wait for me to get up. Instead, she bolted out of the room and down the stairs.

I followed behind her with a smile on my face because I had a feeling I was going to get my sister back.

CHAPTER 9

Quinn

"I KNOW THERE ARE FIVE SIBLINGS, BUT THIS SEEMS LIKE MORE cars than necessary for that amount of people."

"I think you're right, Quinn," Cassie agreed. "But at least we know we're in the right place."

"Yeah. And I know the houses are on the larger side here, but there can't possibly be this many people in the house," I reasoned.

"Maybe there's another party happening in a different house today," Cassie suggested.

I shot her a look of disbelief and asked, "What are the chances of that?"

She shrugged in response.

We'd arrived at the address Tyson had given me for Jordyn's birthday party. Minutes after we pulled into the neighborhood, I'd taken a few turns and gotten us to the street where Kendra's house was located. And no sooner did we make that turn onto her street when Cassie and I saw the line of cars parked all along the road from one end to the other.

I managed to find a spot to park my car at the end of the road. We got out, grabbed Jordyn's presents from the back seat, and started walking down the sidewalk that still had remnants of the last big snowstorm piled up on the curb.

Being from Montana, Cassie and I were accustomed to the cold. It didn't bother us in the least. I think that was one thing that made the move to Wyoming easier. Even though I didn't have the same people around me any longer, the temperatures remained mostly the same.

A few minutes after Cassie and I started walking down the street, we finally made it to Kendra's driveway. We weaved ourselves through the cars parked there and up to the front door. Cassie rang the doorbell, and a moment later, a woman neither of us recognized opened the door. She eyed us, saw the presents we were carrying, and must have assumed we belonged there because she stepped back and allowed us to come inside.

Immediately, I shifted my body closer to Cassie's. While we were the only people standing in the foyer, the noise that surrounded us was like nothing I'd ever heard before in my life. I had no doubt we were about to walk into a massive crowd of people. In fact, both of the rooms off to either side of us were filled with people. But with everyone so caught up in their own conversations, they didn't notice us standing there.

Just then, one little boy ran by us followed shortly thereafter by three more children.

"Who are you?" the woman who opened the door asked.

"I'm Quinn and this is my sister, Cassidy," I answered.

"Are you from the twins' school?" she wondered.

"Twins?" I repeated.

The woman grew confused, but thankfully Cassie chimed in. "We're actually friends of Tyson and Kyle," she started. "Sorry, we don't really know too many people here. Kendra invited us to the party when we met her last weekend."

Realization dawned in her features. "Oh, that's right. I remember Vera telling me about Tyson's new girl and her sister. What's your name again?"

"I'm Quinn," I replied, not sure how people were calling me Tyson's girl when I hadn't even managed to kiss the guy yet.

"And she's the one that's Tyson's girl," Cassie added. "I'm Cassie, and I'm here visiting her from Montana, so I'm here now by default."

"Right," the woman returned. "I'm Louise. And I'm Tyson and Kyle's aunt. Can I take your coats for you?"

Cassie and I removed our coats and handed them to her. Then she ordered, "Go ahead in. The boys are out there in the mix somewhere."

At her instruction, we walked from the foyer straight ahead and entered the kitchen.

"Oh my goodness," I whispered to my sister as I curled the fingers of my free hand around hers.

"Tell me about it," she returned, leaning her body into mine.

While I knew it hadn't been more than a few seconds, it felt like we stood there for hours when we finally heard someone shout, "Quinn! Cassie! You made it!"

I looked in the direction the voice was coming from and saw Kendra walking toward us. It was a bit of a relief to see a familiar face, but not much. When Kendra made it to where we were standing at the mouth of the kitchen, she threw her arms around the both of us. Then, she took a step back and asked, "Did you find the place okay?"

Feeling like I'd lost my voice, all I could do was nod my head.

She smiled and replied, "Great. Come on in, grab a drink and something to eat. I'll introduce you to everyone."

Everyone? I thought.

I was so consumed with panic at the sheer number of people she had in her house that she didn't seem to be giving a second thought to, I was going to do anything to avoid meeting *everyone*. So, I held up the presents we'd brought for Jordyn and finally said, "These are for Jordyn. Is there somewhere special you want us to put them?"

I asked the question, but I wasn't sure there was actually any space left for presents.

"You really didn't have to do anything," she insisted. "We truly just wanted you here. But you'll definitely score big points with my girl for it. Here, let me take them for you."

Just as we handed over the gifts, she declared, "Oh, look. Here are the boys."

That's when I saw that Tyson and Kyle had materialized seemingly out of nowhere. I felt mildly relieved as my eyes connected with his.

"Hi, Quinn," Tyson greeted me as he got close. Kyle was talking to Cassie, but I couldn't pay attention. I needed Tyson to explain.

"You said this was a party at Kendra's house," I reminded him.

Tyson grew confused by my words and looked around. "This is her house," he assured me.

"Right. But you said it was a small gathering," I said.

"It is," he insisted. "She only invited the immediate family members."

My eyes left Tyson's for the first time since they'd landed on him and moved through the kitchen. In the back of my mind, I recalled the number of people I'd seen mingling in the two rooms off either side of the foyer. It was then I realized that perhaps Tyson didn't know about the extra people.

"Immediate family?" I repeated.

He nodded.

I shifted closer to him. He instantly noticed my anxiety and put an arm around my shoulders.

Tipping my head back, I looked up at him and shared, "I don't even know this many people. This is your immediate family? I expected a small gathering of your brothers, sisters, their kids, and your parents. This is... I don't even know what this is. I don't know what to do."

Tyson gave my shoulder a gentle squeeze and promised, "Everyone is nice. You have nothing to worry about. Most will be loud. Some will be nosy. But they're all the most genuine, loving people you'll ever meet. Just stick close to me, and you'll be fine."

"Will Kyle make sure that Cassie's not left alone?" I worried.

Tyson looked over my head. When he returned his gaze to mine, he assured me, "He's got her covered."

Satisfied with his response and confident about my sister's well-being, I shifted even closer to him. Tyson felt it, squeezed me tighter, and brought his mouth to my ear. There, he whispered, "I don't like that you're uncomfortable right now, but I love that you keep pressing your body tighter to mine."

His breath at my ear, so close to my neck, caused a shiver to run down my spine. Tyson didn't miss it and added, "I love that, too."

"Tyson," I whispered.

"Is this her?" an unfamiliar voice asked.

Tyson lifted his head and turned to face the individual. "Yes," Tyson confirmed. "Dad, this is Quinn. Quinn, this is my father, James."

I knew I was going to meet him, but I hadn't expected it

would be like this. First thing. I had to pull myself together. And fast.

I snapped out of it and extended my hand. "It's so nice to meet you," I said.

"Likewise, dear," he returned, taking my hand and kissing the back of it. Mr. Reed looked at his son and asked, "Has your mother met her?"

Tyson shook his head. "Not yet."

"You better get on that now," he ordered. "She hasn't stopped talking about this all week long."

Yikes.

All week.

It seemed that me coming to this party was a bigger deal than the actual reason for it, which made me wonder which of the kids was the birthday girl. I felt like I'd already had a hundred children scurry by me, but didn't know if any of them were Jordyn.

Tyson nodded, put a hand to the small of my back, and ushered me along. On the way to meet his mom, we were stopped several times. I saw Vera and Beau at different intervals. Tyson didn't allow us to stop too long, and every time we moved I noticed the glances we both got from members of his family. I was still a little unsettled by the fact all these people were his close family members.

Eventually, we stopped in a room where there were more kids than adults. In fact, there were only two adults. Josie and another woman. That's when I realized two things. The first was that we were in a playroom. It was littered with toys, and kids were squealing with delight. But the second, more important, thing I noticed was that the other woman in the room was Tyson's mom. She hadn't even looked up from what she was doing, playing with a little girl in a princess dress, but I knew it was her. I also knew the little girl had to be Jordyn.

Suddenly, she looked up and bubbled, "Uncle Ty!"

"Hi, princess," he returned, melting my heart, as he squatted down to catch the girl who was running full force toward him.

Her body collided with his in a way that would have knocked me to the ground. Tyson was unaffected, wrapping his arms around her and lifting her. He stood next to me as his mother moved toward us.

I looked at her and noticed she hadn't taken her eyes off me. Thankfully, I was able to pull my gaze away from her scrutiny when I heard, "You're pretty."

I found the little girl in Tyson's arms staring at me in awe. "Thank you," I said. "But I'm not nearly as beautiful as you. I love your dress."

"Aunt Vera got it for me," she shared.

Tyson cut in and offered introductions. "Jordyn, this is Quinn. Quinn this is the birthday girl and my little princess, Jordyn."

"Uncle Kyle said I was *his* princess," she informed her uncle.

Tyson laughed. "We'll let him think that, but you and I know the truth, right?"

Jordyn stared at her uncle a moment before she beamed at him and nodded. Then, he turned his attention to his mother and said, "Mom, this is Quinn. Quinn, this is my mother, Sandra."

I held my breath wondering what she was thinking. Just as I was about to extend my hand to her, she moved closer, put an arm around me, and gave me a hug. Then, she kissed my cheek and remarked, "It's so nice to finally meet you."

Wow.

Wow.

I hadn't been expecting her to be so welcoming. I knew I must have looked like an idiot to her, Tyson, and probably even Jordyn because I stood there completely, utterly shell shocked and silent.

"Quinn?" Tyson's voice penetrated my brain.

But I didn't move. I started feeling a bit hot and really dizzy. I came to the quick conclusion that skipping breakfast was probably not the best idea. I'd been so nervous about meeting Tyson's family that I was worried I'd get sick.

Now, I knew I was going to regret that decision.

I vaguely heard Tyson order, "Take her."

The next thing I knew, both of his arms were around me.

"Quinn, honey, are you with me?" he asked.

I was, but I knew I wasn't going to be much longer.

The last thing I remembered hearing was Josie's voice asking, "Is she okay?"

Then, my body went slack against Tyson's as everything went black.

"Quinn?" Tyson called.

"She needs food," the voice I recognized as belonging to his mother declared.

"Can someone find her sister?" Tyson asked.

"I will," an unfamiliar voice said.

"Quinn?" Tyson called again.

"Here's another cool cloth," Josie announced.

Just as I felt the cloth hit my forehead, my eyes fluttered open.

Initially, I opened them and saw Tyson looking back at me. He was worried. "There you are," he rasped, his relief undeniable.

I managed to take in his relief for a few fleeting moments before I shifted my head in his lap and saw entirely too many sets of worried eyes staring back at me, most of which I didn't know to whom they belonged.

The embarrassment must have been written all over my face because Tyson barked, "Give her some space."

Immediately, everyone dispersed.

I felt bad that he'd yelled at his family like that, but loved that he knew what I needed right then and didn't hesitate to give it to me.

When it was just the two of us, Tyson asked, "Are you okay?"

"I think so," I whispered. "What happened?"

"I'm guessing you passed out."

I closed my eyes. "I'm mortified," I stated when I opened them again.

He shook his head and insisted, "Don't be. Have you eaten anything today?"

I shook my head. "I was too nervous."

Tyson's jaw clenched. "It was too much for you," he surmised. "All these people all at once."

"I'm sorry," I apologized.

"You don't have to be sorry. I didn't think."

"She hugged me," I deadpanned.

"What?"

"Your mom hugged me."

I felt his body stiffen underneath mine. "Do you have a thing about people touching you?" he worried.

A lazy smile spread across my face. "No. It's just that your dad kissed my hand and your mom hugged me. I've gotten all this affection and kind words from them and your siblings. It was unexpected, especially considering you haven't even managed to kiss me yet."

"Is that what you're waiting for?" he asked, seeming amused.

I shrugged my shoulders. "It'd be nice, I think."

His thumb came up and stroked my cheek. "Yeah," he whispered in return.

Tyson stared at me a bit longer, his finger gliding softly over my skin. It felt nice, but it was interrupted by my sister shouting, "Quinn! Oh my God! Are you okay?"

I had no choice but to smile at Tyson as I slowly sat up. "I'm okay, Cass. Relax. And stop shouting. I've already been embarrassed enough."

"What happened?" she asked.

"She needs food," Tyson's mom entered the room again carrying a plate of food.

Placing it in my hands, she ordered, "Eat, dear."

Then she stood and waited. I had no choice but to look down at the plate, carrying more food than I could ever dream of eating, and pick up the easiest thing. I lifted the fork, speared the pasta, and put it in my mouth. Only after I'd taken a few bites did she ease up on her inspection.

That was when I said my first words to her. "Thank you, Mrs. Reed. And it's nice to meet you, too. Sorry about all that."

"Don't you worry about that," she ordered. "And call me Sandy."

"Okay."

Sandy's eyes moved to my sister. "Have you eaten anything?" she wondered.

Cassie shook her head.

"My sons," she muttered her displeasure. Then she demanded, "Come with me. We'll get you fed, too."

Cassie hesitated, but ultimately stood and went with Tyson's mom out to the kitchen. And from that point forward, Tyson stuck by my side. He constantly had a hand on me. Apparently, me passing out had scared him a bit.

After we rejoined the party, I was thankful to see that his family welcomed me, but also gave me a bit of space. Part of that might have had something to do with the fact that Tyson seemed to be putting a wide berth between me and anyone who got too close.

Eventually, I had to reassure him that I was okay and that he didn't need to give every member of his family a death glare. I wanted them to like me, and I didn't think his behavior was helping the cause.

Once everybody had had the chance to eat and mingle, the birthday girl begged to open her presents. So, somehow, everyone managed to fit themselves into the room surrounding her as she began tearing the paper off of each one. One by one she went through them, her excitement permeating the room. She finally made it to the two presents Cassie and I had brought.

Just like she'd done with all the presents before, Kendra took the card, read it, and said, "This is from Quinn and Cassidy."

Jordyn was entirely too excited to pay any attention to what Kendra was saying and opened the first box. When she did, she cried, "Another princess dress!"

I couldn't help but laugh. With all the gifts she received, Jordyn had gotten a plethora of princess dresses. And somehow, she hadn't yet received any duplicates.

After examining her new dress, Jordyn moved to the

smaller square box and ripped the paper from it. When she opened the box and saw what was inside, her eyes widened in shock. Tyson's hand squeezed on my thigh as he asked, "What is it?"

Jordyn's eyes came to mine. "I get to be a real princess," she marveled.

I nodded and confirmed, "You sure do."

Kendra looked in the box, saw what was inside, and held it up to Jordyn. "How about you go ask Ms. Quinn to help you put it on?"

Jordyn did as her mother asked. She placed the box in my lap and asked, "Can you put it on for me?"

"Please," Tyson warned her.

"Please," Jordyn repeated.

"Of course."

I pulled the handmade crown out of the box and placed it perfectly on her head. By chance, she happened to have a few barrettes in her hair. While bobby pins would have been a better choice in securing Jordyn's crown, the barrettes would easily get the job done.

Once the crown was secure, I looked at her and stated, "You look magnificent, Princess Jordyn."

She sent the biggest grin my way and announced, "I'm going to go look in the mirror."

"Did you make that?" Kendra asked.

I nodded.

I felt Tyson's body go solid beside mine as Kendra declared, "It's gorgeous. I get the feeling she's going to want to sleep with it on."

Kendra went on to tell everyone that I was a jewelry maker. I fielded a bunch of questions from the women in the room about my work for the next half hour. When the conversation turned to another topic, I leaned toward Tyson and asked, "Can you show me where the bathroom is?"

He nodded and stood.

Just as we made it to the bathroom on the first floor, we saw one of the kids run in and close the door. Tyson took me by the hand and led me upstairs. "I can wait," I assured him.

"It's okay. We can get away from the noise for a minute," he returned.

Tyson stopped outside the bathroom and held his hand out to the side for me to enter. "Thanks."

I quickly did my business, washed my hands, and gave myself a once-over in the mirror. When I opened the door, I found Tyson waiting outside.

"Hey," I said, not expecting him to be there.

"Hey," he replied, putting a hand to my hip and turning me so my back was against the wall.

That's when I understood why he didn't go back downstairs. Tyson was going to take advantage of being away from the crowd and the noise.

His hand squeezed my hip as he warned, "That crown you made for my niece better not have a single real diamond in it."

I grinned at him. "It doesn't," I promised.

"You're going to be her favorite person in the whole world now," he noted.

"That works for me."

"If you let me kiss you now, I might be able to decide if you're my favorite person, too," he teased.

I swallowed and rasped, "Okay."

Leaning forward with one hand planted on the wall beside my head, he brought his lips to within inches of mine. He just barely brushed them against mine when we heard, "Are you helping her in the bathroom like Uncle Kyle?"

"Fuck," Tyson whispered.

He pushed away from the wall and looked down at his niece. "What?"

"Uncle Kyle had to go in that bathroom earlier to help the other lady who got me the princess dress," Jordyn shared.

I pressed my lips together to stop myself from bursting out laughing. Kyle and Cassie had snuck away at some point to do what Tyson was trying to do with me right now. But, just like us, they were also caught in the act.

Not missing a beat, Tyson bent down and picked up Jordyn. "Yeah, I needed to help Quinn in the bathroom."

"Sometimes, Daddy has to help Mommy when she's in the shower," Jordyn shared.

Tyson's horrified eyes came to mine. "Make it stop," he begged.

Now it was my turn to burst out laughing as we started walking toward the steps. As we descended the stairs, I decided, "I should probably find Cass and get going. She's got to get up and get on the road early. And I want to make sure I get some time with her tonight before she leaves again."

"What time is she leaving?" Tyson asked.

"She wants to be on the road by six."

He thought a moment and agreed, "Yeah, it's probably a good idea to get her back to your place then."

With that, I went and located my sister. We made rounds and said goodbye to everyone. I thanked Kendra again for inviting us.

Cassie and I both said goodbye to Tyson and Kyle after they insisted on walking us to my car. But it wasn't until we were on our way back to my place that I remembered something.

The day I first met Tyson's family at the restaurant, he

leaned over and whispered in my ear that he'd be at my place shortly after she left to finish what he'd started on my couch days before that.

That's when I decided to get home as quickly as possible. Because I needed to find out what was happening between my sister and Kyle. And then I needed her advice and encouragement before I fully committed to this thing with Tyson.

CHAPTER 10

Quinn

It was seven o'clock Monday morning, and Cassidy had just left about forty-five minutes ago. While we thought we got them all out last night, we shed a few tears this morning, which was the reason why she was delayed an extra fifteen minutes.

As always, I hated having to say goodbye to her, but at least this time there was an upside. She promised me that she was going to go home and seriously consider what moving here would mean for her. Given that she had a five-hour drive back home to Montana, I had no doubt that she'd be thinking about it long before she arrived there.

I believed this was the case because I knew I wasn't the only one hoping she'd make the move. When Cassie and I got home last night from Jordyn's birthday party, we made the most of our time. After helping her pack up her suitcase, we sat down in front of the fireplace where I tried to convince her to share what was going on between her and Kyle.

"Okay, Cass, it's your turn to spill," I ordered. "I thought while we were packing up your things, you'd share. But obviously, it seems you aren't going to do that on your own."

"Because you'll probably hate me," she reasoned.

"What?" I asked, completely confused. "What does that even mean?"

My sister pressed her lips together and remained silent. But I could tell by the look on her face that this wasn't simply a matter of not wanting to share the juicy details. This was something else.

Worried, I begged, "Cass, tell me what's going on."

"I'm such a horrible sister," she cried. "If I tell you what I did, you'll never want to speak to me again."

My eyes widened, and I cut right to the chase. "Did you sleep with my ex-husband?"

Cassie jerked her head back and gasped, "What? No!"

"Okay, then there's nothing else you can tell me that's going to make me never speak to you again," I promised.

"I was in the bathroom," she murmured.

"Sorry?"

I watched as my sister took in a deep breath and blew it out. Then, her eyes came to mine and she admitted, "When you passed out, I was in the bathroom."

I shrugged. "Okay. What's the big deal?"

"I wasn't using it for its intended purpose," she huffed.

Understanding dawned, and I replied, "Oh."

"Yeah. Oh. While you were freaking out, panicking, and passing out, I was too busy having an orgasm."

I held my hand up in front of my face and demanded, "Wait. Stop. You're telling me it's true?"

"What? Am I telling you what's true?"

"A few minutes before I found you so we could leave and come home, Jordyn found Tyson and me upstairs and told us about how her uncle Kyle had to help the lady who bought her the princess dress in the bathroom downstairs, too. Are you telling me that you and Kyle had sex in a bathroom at his sister's house on his niece's fifth birthday?"

She shook her head. "No! We didn't actually have sex," she denied my accusation. "We just... fooled around a bit."

"You fooled around to the extent you had an orgasm in the bathroom at a kid's birthday party," I pointed out.

She shamefully dropped her gaze. "That doesn't bother me, though. What bothers me is that my sister obviously needed me, and I wasn't there for her."

"It's okay, Cass. I'm fine now," I assured her. "It really was probably just my own fault for not eating anything this morning. Besides, Tyson managed to take care of me alright anyway. I'm glad you can drive home from this trip with an orgasm to add to your vibe vault."

"Yeah," she agreed. "Thanks for looking on the bright side."

I assessed her mindset, felt she could handle it, and asked, "What are the chances you'll want to come back and get them regularly? And is that even an option for Kyle?"

"It's a lot to think about, Quinn," she began. "Moving here is a big deal. You know I'm usually down to do just about anything without any guarantees, but I'm just not sure if I can handle that big of a step with so much uncertainty."

Since I'd already talked with my sister about how we could manage the move for her as far as work and a place to stay, I knew the doubts she had were related to something else.

"Is that uncertainty about Kyle?" I wondered.

"Based on what he's told me? No. But that doesn't mean I don't have things lingering in the back of my mind that tell me that sometimes people aren't always true to their word. I just met him, and I had no plans for a long-term thing with anyone right now. But Kyle wants us to keep in touch when I go back home."

I thought this was great news, so I assured her, "That's

a good thing, Cassidy. He's obviously very interested in you then."

"Yeah," she returned, but I could tell her mind was elsewhere. After a few moments of silence, I saw her brows pull together as she snapped her head in my direction.

"What?" I asked, wondering what was going on with her.

"What are you hiding from me?" she retorted.

"Nothing," I answered honestly.

She narrowed her eyes and shook her head at me. "Yes, you are. You just told me that Jordyn said her uncle Kyle had to help a lady in the bathroom *too*. Why did she say it like that? And why did she find you and Tyson upstairs, huh?"

I bit my lip recalling Tyson almost kissing me *again*. If it didn't happen soon, I was certain I would combust.

"Unlike you, my dear sister, I actually had to use the bathroom," I began. "But when Tyson showed me to the one downstairs, one of the kids had just run inside. So, he took me upstairs to use the one up there."

She tapped her fingers across her lips, pretending to think. "And yet the little girl believes Tyson was in there helping you. Hmm. Something just doesn't add up."

I rolled my eyes at her. "He didn't go in with me. But he did wait outside for me. And he might have come really close to kissing me, *but* we were interrupted by the little girl."

Cassie burst out laughing.

I sighed and waited for her to settle down before I asked, "What do you find so funny?"

"You and Tyson have had how many opportunities to kiss and they've all been unsuccessful so far. That's just wrong."

"Exactly. It's wrong. Not funny," I scolded her.

She smiled and assured me, "Oh, don't worry. It'll happen eventually."

"Yeah, yeah. I'll believe that when I see it."

"Or feel it," she teased.

"Speaking of feeling it," I started. "I assume you had a good time in the bathroom then?"

"Oh yeah," she returned.

And then she launched in to a candid confession of all the details. It was the perfect way to end her trip here.

Now that my sister was on her way back to our hometown and we'd managed to get all of my things unpacked when she was here, I was free to get back to my work. I hadn't really put a lot of time in on the jewelry since she arrived other than doing the designs for Patrick and making Jordyn's crown.

So, my plan for today was to check my emails to confirm if Patrick had gotten back to me. Once I sorted his situation out, I'd finish up a few of the projects I'd started before my move that I hadn't yet completed.

But before I got to work on any of that, I needed to get upstairs and get myself dressed. After Cassie left, I'd made myself a cup of tea and curled up on the couch for a little while under a soft, fuzzy blanket.

I flung the blanket off my bare legs and moved to the kitchen to set my mug in the sink. Just as I walked back toward the stairs, there was a knock at my front door. Given that I wasn't expecting anyone this early, I assumed that Cassie got so far, realized she forgot something, and turned around.

I opened the door expecting to see her standing there, but it was Tyson instead.

Staring back at me.

His eyes started at my face and then moved down my body. I was only wearing a satin nightie, so he got an eyeful. When he focused his attention on my face again, he spoke. His voice was deep and husky when he asked, "Did your sister leave?"

"Yeah," I replied.

"Are you okay?"

I nodded.

Tyson didn't say anything else. He stepped inside my house, closed the door behind him, and pulled off his jacket while simultaneously kicking off his shoes. Then, one arm was around my waist as the other drove into my hair. Without hesitating, Tyson lowered his mouth to mine and touched my lips with his.

A whimper escaped from the back of my throat.

And that was all it took for him to lose control. Suddenly, his mouth was no longer gentle. The pressure against my lips was punishing as his tongue spiked into my mouth.

It had been so long. Too long since I'd been kissed. And I wasn't sure I'd ever in my life been kissed like this. Like it was something Tyson had been longing for his whole life. Like it was necessary to his survival.

I thought I was going to cry when he pulled his mouth away from mine, but I didn't. Because he didn't allow it to leave my body. His mouth worked its way down my throat to the exposed skin along my shoulders and collarbone. After kissing every inch of my skin there, Tyson didn't stop.

His hands slid down over the silky material of my nightie while his mouth traveled down my chest. I heard him take a deep inhale between my breasts before he shifted to one side and closed his mouth over my nipple. The satin fabric was keeping him from having direct contact with my breast, and I grew even more turned on because of it.

"Tyson," I breathed as my back hit the wall.

He groaned.

I thought he'd pull the nightie down my arms, but he didn't. One of his hands left my hip and traveled up the side of my body. He made it to my chest and gently squeezed my breast. Tyson kept his hand there, playing, as he dropped to his knees. His mouth was kissing my belly through the satin, and all I wanted was to feel his lips on my skin.

When his hand let go of my breast, I expected him to tear the nightie off, but he didn't. Instead, his fingers curled around my thighs. I loved the feel of his hands on my bare skin and wanted so much more.

"Please," I begged when he looked up at me.

The heat in his eyes couldn't be missed, and he quickly looked away. His gaze went to my left thigh where he finally, *finally* kissed my skin. As he peppered kisses over both of my thighs, his hands slid up the backs of my legs and under my nightie. They stopped right at the top of my legs just below the bottom curve of my ass. Tyson squeezed gently as his mouth moved higher. Then, his fingers slid from the back of my legs to my inner thighs. When he lifted them higher, causing them to brush against my very wet, very sensitive vagina, I couldn't stop myself from moaning.

My legs started to buckle, but Tyson held me upright. He moved his hands away and up over my ass. Thankfully, he wasted no more time. Within seconds, he tore my panties down my legs. The second I stepped out of them, Tyson was no longer interested in teasing me.

His hands went to the hem of my nightie and lifted it, exposing me.

He tipped his head back, looked up at me, and rasped, "You're gorgeous, Quinn. Everywhere."

Once he got the words out, I lost his eyes but gained his mouth. Right between my legs. And he was doing things with his mouth and his tongue that I didn't think anyone could do with their mouth and tongue.

Tyson expertly worked me between my legs. Considering it had been so long and because he'd done all that teasing that led up to this point, it took me almost no time at all to find myself on the verge of an orgasm.

With the fingers of one hand toying with my nipple and my other hand gripping his hair, my breathing grew shallow.

"Babe," I called. "I'm going to come."

Tyson worked me harder and sent me over the edge, never once relenting until he'd seen me through to the end. And once he did, he stood and pressed his solid body into mine. His face was buried in my neck, his lips kissing the skin along my throat.

I slid my hands up his arms and gripped his shoulders. Even with the power of the orgasm that had just seared through me, I still craved more. I still wanted Tyson.

"Tyson?" I called quietly.

His hand continued to glide along the smooth material covering my body. I dragged one hand down his chest and abdomen until it settled on his hardened length.

"Yeah, gorgeous?" he whispered in my ear before pulling back to look at me.

I gave him a gentle squeeze and asserted, "I want to feel you between my legs."

Tyson groaned before he advised, "Take me to your bedroom, Quinn."

I didn't waste any time. I took him by the hand and led him up the stairs to my bedroom. The minute we stepped inside my room, Tyson pulled his long-sleeved shirt over his head. His body was amazing. Seeing his solid chest and strong arms, all I wanted to do was run my tongue all over him.

After pulling a string of condoms out of his pocket and tossing them on the nightstand, Tyson's hands went to the waistband of his jeans. He unbuttoned and unzipped them before he pushed them down over his ass and let them fall to the ground. He kept his eyes focused on me the entire time as he bent down and removed his socks and jeans from around his ankles.

Then he moved toward me.

Even though he'd just recently come in from being out in the cold, I couldn't tell. When he got close, I could feel the heat emanating off his skin. I couldn't wait to have it pressed against mine.

Tyson slid his fingers under the straps of my nightie and slowly shifted them off my shoulders. He took half a step back and watched as it fell from my body and pooled at my feet.

I followed his gaze as it traveled from my feet and up my legs. He hesitated briefly at my vagina before continuing up to my breasts. His eyes lingered there a long time, and then he gripped his cock over his boxer briefs. When he brought his attention back to my face, he finally spoke.

In a low voice, thick with emotion, he said, "Look at you, Quinn. You're so beautiful."

"Can I see you?" I wondered.

Tyson didn't make me wait. He shoved his thumbs into the sides of his boxer briefs and pushed them down his legs. For the first time, I got to see all of him.

And it was absolute flawlessness.

"You're perfect," I rasped, taking a step toward him.

I angled my neck, touched my mouth to his, and wrapped my hand around his cock. The second I stroked his length, he groaned. He had one hand planted firmly on my ass, the other behind my head.

Tyson gave me a few minutes to stroke and play with him, but he eventually had enough. I couldn't say I blamed him because I was just as tired of waiting.

While he grabbed a condom from the nightstand and rolled it on, I climbed into the bed. Tyson took one last look at me before he joined me in the bed and settled his body over mine. Once there, he positioned himself between my legs. With the tip of him nudging me open, he whispered against my lips, "I've wanted to be with you like this in your bed ever since I carried those boxes up here for you."

"So take what you want, Tyson," I urged him. "And give me what I've wanted from the minute I laid my eyes on you."

With that, Tyson pushed inside and filled me.

Oh God.

It had been too long.

Entirely too long.

And Tyson felt perfect right where he was. "You're perfect," I breathed again for a completely different reason.

He drew his hips back before thrusting his cock into me again. I moaned in pleasure and was lost. Lost in the feeling. Lost in the passion. Lost in Tyson.

We moved our bodies together, our hands touching and mouths tasting. Tyson rolled to his back as I straddled his hips. I ground down on him while he licked and sucked on my breasts.

When I was on the verge of another orgasm, he rolled us again. His hands gripped my thighs, pushed them tight against my torso, and drove in deep, hard, and fast.

"Tyson," I whimpered, barely able to catch my breath.

"Quinn, baby, fuck," he growled.

The next thing I knew Tyson was with me. We were both completely, utterly lost as sparks of pleasure shot through our bodies. Tyson worked me through my orgasm, and I held on tight. Something about it was so different, so powerful.

Long after he'd stopped moving and was holding his

weight above me, I still felt my limbs and my insides trembling. Tyson eventually pulled his face back to look down at me. I'm not sure what it was he saw on my face, but he asked, "Are you okay?"

I shook my head. "I've never felt anything like that before. My body just doesn't feel right."

Tyson tensed and worried, "Did I hurt you?"

"No, it's nothing like that. It's just… that was the most intense orgasm of my life," I finally shared.

"Really?" he asked as the tension left his body.

"Yeah," I replied lazily.

Tyson pressed a gentle kiss to my cheek before he slid his mouth back toward my ear. "I'll be right back," he said.

"Okay."

He slid out from between my legs, and I immediately missed the feel of having him there.

Tyson left the bed and walked toward the master bathroom. As sated and satisfied as I felt, I still managed to keep my eyes trained to the magnificence that was his backside. And when he returned, I kept my focus on the brilliance that was his front.

CHAPTER 11

Quinn

"SEE SOMETHING YOU LIKE?" TYSON TEASED ME FROM THE edge of the bed when he returned from the bathroom.

My eyes traveled up his body and met his. "You," I replied with a smile.

"I know the feeling," he began. "Only, I'm thinking that standing here looking at you."

I reached my hand out to him. He took it and climbed into bed with me.

Tyson and I cuddled up together and stayed like that in silence a long time. Eventually, I spoke.

"How was the rest of Jordyn's party last night?" I asked.

With his fingertips running gently up and down my back, Tyson answered, "Chaotic. But Jordyn had a blast. I have no doubt she slept well last night."

"She's adorable," I noted.

"Yeah, she's a cutie for sure. But I don't know what we're going to do when she gets older. It's all cute now, but I have a feeling that's going to change."

"Oh, but you've got a long time before she gets to that point," I started. "I'd just enjoy her now exactly how she is. I mean, you've got a real-deal princess in your family."

Tyson laughed. "Well, if there was any doubt about it before, there certainly isn't now with that crown you made for her."

"I'm so happy she liked it."

Tyson squeezed me in response, but made no verbal reply.

Another few seconds of silence passed before I couldn't stand it any longer. I had to know the truth about what they thought.

"So, did I make a complete fool of myself yesterday?" I asked.

"What?"

"Tyson, I passed out when your mom hugged me and welcomed me," I reminded him. "I wouldn't exactly say I made the best first impression."

"Are you kidding me?"

Tyson and I were lying together, our bodies pressed front to front. I pulled my face from his chest and responded, "Um, yeah."

"They adored you," he said. "Though I'll admit that they were just happy to see that I had someone there with me, so you didn't really have to work too hard."

"That's not making me feel very good," I warned him.

Tyson brought his hand up to cup my jaw. Then, he dragged his thumb slowly across my bottom lip.

"I promise it's not a bad thing," he said softly. "I was partially teasing you."

I cocked an eyebrow. "Partially?"

"My family is crazy. And they really want me to find someone that's going to make me happy. They push for it so much that sometimes I joke that they'd settle for anyone I introduced them to. But when it really boils down, they'd never stand for me being with someone they didn't think would give me what I needed in a relationship. Obviously, they wouldn't have a choice in the matter, but they wouldn't hesitate to let me know their thoughts either."

"You have a lot of them to answer to," I noted.

He chuckled and remarked, "That's an understatement."

Tyson rolled to his back, taking me with him so that my body was running the length of his, my thigh hooked over his, and my cheek and palm were pressed to his chest.

"Were you being honest when you said that they were all your closest family members?" I asked.

"Yeah. Mom and Dad are both from big families. He's one of six siblings, and she's one of four. All of my aunts and uncles have gotten married and had their own children. With the exception of two of my aunts who only had two children each, the rest of them have had at least three. The largest is my uncle who ended up having a total of seven kids. And now that all the kids are grown up, there's a new generation of children starting."

While I knew that whatever was happening between me and Tyson right now was still new, I also had to be smart. I wasn't sure what his plans were for having children one day. But if he planned on a brood of seven, I didn't know if it was wise that we continue what we started.

"Do you want kids?" I asked.

"Of course," he returned.

He didn't add anything additional, which started to worry me. I began to think that perhaps he just assumed there'd be no reason not to have a bunch of babies since everyone else in his family did.

His body tensed beneath mine suddenly, and he called, "Quinn?"

"Yeah?"

"What about you? Do you want children one day?" he asked. I could hear the trepidation in his tone, and that's when I knew that he was worried I might not want any. I quickly spoke to ease his fears.

"I do," I assured him. "But I'll be honest, I don't think I could handle seven."

He let out a laugh and admitted, "Not many people can. How many do you want?"

I lifted my cheek from his chest and looked at him. "Two?" I guessed. "Three tops."

Tyson lifted his hand and ran his fingers through my hair pondering my words for a few moments. Finally, he affirmed, "I could do three."

"Is that what you really want?" I wondered.

He shrugged. "Honestly, I hadn't really considered it much beyond knowing I wanted kids of my own, and knowing I wanted more than one. Three's a good number. More might be nice, but I think I could be very happy with three."

I held his gaze a few moments, assessing him. "Are you sure about that?" I finally asked.

"Yeah. But is there a reason you seem overly concerned about it right now? I'm not sure we're at that point yet."

Now it was my turn for my body to tense. I pressed my palm to his chest and lifted myself up. Tyson watched me curiously as I pulled the sheet up to cover myself, and he suddenly made an assumption about my change in demeanor.

"Quinn, I think you misunderstood what I said. I'm not in any way suggesting that you are just a woman I want to sleep with and not someone that I could get there with. It's just that we've really only known each other a couple weeks. I think you're amazing, but this is still new. I mean, I just kissed you for the first time today. Kids aren't really something I'm thinking about right now."

I didn't know how to bring up what was bothering me. I had a feeling if I did that Tyson was going to realize I was a basket case and immediately stop what we'd just started. And as nervous as I was about starting something new, I wasn't sure that not having it at all was something I wanted either. But for the right reasons, I'd end it.

When too much time had passed without a reply, Tyson urged, "Gorgeous, talk to me."

"I'm not upset for the reason you think," I started, knowing I had to be honest. "But as early as this is between us, it's important to me to make sure that we're on the same page."

"I just told you that I thought three was a good number," he reminded me.

"I know, but you also said you *thought* you could be happy with three and that more might be nice," I pointed out.

"Do I have to have all the answers right now?" he wondered.

I shook my head and looked away. "Of course not."

Inside I could feel my heart breaking a little. I thought I could do this. I thought I could start over. But maybe I wasn't ready. Even though I had no doubts about my divorce and knew beyond a shadow of a doubt that it was the right thing for me, I wondered if perhaps it was too soon to be getting into something with a man with whom I'd want something serious.

Maybe I should have been more like Cassie. Maybe I should have found a way to connect with a man on a physical level only, so that I wouldn't question every little thing he said. Because I knew that not only was it not fair to me to live in this constant state of worry, but it also wasn't fair to make him have to pay for the mistakes that Chris made.

I felt movement in the bed before Tyson's hand curled around the side of my neck opposite him.

"Quinn?" he called.

"Hmm?" I replied, still not looking at him.

"Is there something I'm missing here?" he asked. "Because I feel like there's something you're not telling me." His thumb was stroking gently over the skin at the front of my throat. That soft touch, his gentle tone, and the emotions inside me took over.

I turned my head toward him, and with my eyes filled with unshed tears, I admitted, "You don't have to have all the answers right now, Tyson, but I do."

"Why?" he questioned me.

I closed my eyes slowly causing a tear to fall from each one. When I opened them again, I saw the worry and fear in his face. Seeing it didn't make me hold back. Instead, I rasped, "Because you're the first man I've been with since before I got divorced, which means I don't hop into bed with just anyone. This means something to me, Tyson. But I can't get involved again with a man who makes me believe we're on the same page only to find out years later that we're not, and that the grass is greener elsewhere."

"Quinn…" He trailed off.

The lump lodged in my throat was not only painful, but it also made it difficult to speak. Somehow, I managed to apologize, "I'm sorry, Tyson. I know that's probably not fair to say to you, but it's the sad truth of where my mind and my heart are. As much as I hate it, I can't change it. And I realize it probably was wrong of me not to say something sooner. I'm sorry about that, too."

No matter how hard I tried to fight it, I couldn't stop myself from breaking down into tears. Tyson quickly pulled me into his arms and held me tight. It felt nice to be in the comfort of his embrace, but I worried that I'd just dumped a load of stuff on him that he didn't need to deal with.

Most of all, I worried that while the sting of Chris and Alicia's betrayal didn't make me leave town, it did leave a lasting impression on my heart.

Tyson

This was not how I expected things were going to go this morning. Everything had been going great. In fact, they'd been going better than great from the minute I arrived up until Quinn and I started talking about children.

And now that I was sitting here in her bed with her crying in my arms, I realized there was still a lot of hurt and emotional turmoil Quinn was going through.

While I had easily figured out she was new to the dating scene, I hadn't considered that what I'd get with her was going to run so deep. It bothered me a lot to think that her heart was still so battered.

Obviously, I knew that she'd been betrayed by her husband and best friend in the most unforgivable way, but I guess I never really imagined she was still feeling this level of insecurity. Perhaps I should have, and maybe it made me a naïve fool to assume otherwise, but she always seemed so strong and confident. For that reason alone, it never crossed my mind.

Because in my eyes, Quinn had no reason to worry. Her ex-husband had to be the biggest fool on the face of the planet. She was an incredible woman, and you'd think any man who had a chance at something real with her wouldn't let it slip through his fingers. Any smart man, that is.

I did my best to try and comfort Quinn, allowing her a safe place to get out what she was feeling. And when she finally began to settle, I knew I had to set things straight with her.

"Are you okay?" I asked.

She slowly nodded and answered, "Yeah. Sorry about that."

I put her chin between my thumb and forefinger and insisted, "Do not apologize for needing to release whatever emotions you're feeling inside. It's not good for you to hold it in, and I wouldn't want you to, regardless of what it's about. To add to that, if you feel the need to release it, you're always welcome to do that in my arms for as long as we've got what we've got going between us. Okay?"

"Okay," she agreed.

"Good. Now, I want to talk to you about what just happened here," I began. "And I need to do it being honest with you because that's what you deserve. Are you okay with that?"

She swallowed hard, making her anxiety evident, but ultimately replied, "Yes, I'm okay with that."

I let go of her chin, slid my thumb up to her plump bottom lip, and moved it from one side to the other and all along her jaw. Once my fingers curled around the back of her neck, I shared, "I like you, Quinn. If it's not already evident with everything that happened before today, it should be after what happened the minute I showed up here this morning. That said, I did not realize the level of pain you're still carrying around with you. Short of you passing out yesterday, I've not seen this level of vulnerability from you. You were betrayed by someone who promised to love you and grow old with you. I can't imagine coming to the realization that someone you put your trust and faith in proved to be the opposite of who you believed them to be."

"Tyson—" she got out before I pressed my finger to her lips to silence her.

"Let me finish," I urged her.

She dipped her chin slightly in agreement.

I returned a nod and continued, "Like I said, I didn't realize you were still carrying this level of pain around with you. Now that I know what's on your mind and in your heart, I want you to know a few things about me. I like you. I want to explore this with you. And most importantly, I would never make a long-term commitment, such as marriage, to anyone without being sure about all that making that commitment involved. Talk of kids right now is a lot for the stage we're at in this relationship, which is why I was sort of writing it off and not really giving you a definitive answer. But now I understand why you need a bit more than just blasé answers. Because I want to see where this can go, I'm willing to make the effort to give you those answers."

I paused a moment to give her a chance to take in everything I'd just said. After I'd done that, I added, "One other thing I need you to try really hard to believe when I tell you is that I'm a loyal man. In all facets of my life. Whether it be my family or my job, I'm committed. I'm the same in a relationship, too. If there were any reason it wasn't working for me in a relationship, I would not ever stray. I'd stay and figure out why it wasn't working, and then I'd make the effort to fix it. If it wasn't salvageable, I'd end it. But not first without trying to repair whatever was broken, and never after bringing someone else into the equation. That is one promise I can make you, gorgeous. I would never cheat on you. If there's anything you take away from all that I've just said, please take that. Can you try to do that for me?"

"I'll try," she said softly.

"Okay," I returned. "Now what did you want to say to me?"

"Just that I didn't want you to think that I'm upset or crying because I'm still hung up on my ex-husband. I'm no longer in love with him. It's his betrayal that hurts. I didn't realize it until we started talking, though. But if anything, it makes me hate him a little more for what he did. Because now I know that I'm going to constantly question whether I'll be enough."

There were so many things I'd want to say to this guy if I ever met him. I didn't think I was perfect by any means, but I knew enough to treat people with respect. Especially someone who committed themselves to you.

"You are enough," I stressed. "Obviously, he couldn't see that. But to the right man, you will be. Look, I don't know where things will go between us, but I do know that if we go the distance, I will work my ass off every day to make sure you know that it's only you."

She bit her lip nervously, which told me she had something playing on her mind.

"Quinn?"

"Yeah?"

"Whatever you're thinking, just tell me," I encouraged her.

She hesitated a moment before she said, "Well, it's just that you're making a lot of grand statements. How can you be so sure about everything you're saying? Making promises now when everything is good is easy to do, but you don't know what the future will hold."

"If we're going to explore what we have here between us, are we going to be exclusive?" I asked her.

Fear crept into her features, but she managed to answer, "I wouldn't be able to do this if we weren't exclusive."

"Okay, same here. So that's good. Now, can you answer me this? In the amount of time that we're together, will you ever cheat on me?"

Without any hesitation she immediately replied, "Absolutely not. I'd never do that."

"Can you promise?" I pressed.

Suddenly, she seemed to understand where I was going with my line of questioning.

Before she could say anything else, I reminded her, "I get it, Quinn. I completely understand your fear with this. But when I say that I can promise you I'll never cheat on you, I mean it. I am sympathetic to the fact that you'll probably need extra reassurance of that until you finally realize you can trust me. Assuming this is important to me, and it is, my job will be to do what I've got to do to make sure you know you can trust me."

"Alright. And I'll promise to *try* not to make you pay for what he did. I don't know if I'll be successful, though."

"You will be," I assured her. "Maybe not immediately, but I know you'll eventually get there."

"I hope so."

I gave her a smile and a wink before I agreed, "Me too. Because you shouldn't have to live the rest of your life feeling like you do right now."

She returned the smile and teased, "Well, I mean, I *was* feeling really good until we got sidetracked."

Happy to hear her playfulness return, I offered, "I'm happy to get you back on track."

Instantly, all the bad stuff melted away. Quinn let go of the sheet she'd been clutching to her chest and put her hand on my bicep. "How do you plan to do that?"

I leaned forward, kissed the skin along her neck, and worked my way up to her ear. After gently tugging the lobe between my teeth, I whispered, "I have my ways."

When she didn't respond, I pulled back to look at her. That's when she smiled and challenged, "I'm waiting."

So, I got back to work and got us back on track.

CHAPTER 12

Quinn

"HOW HAS YOUR FIRST WEEK BACK BEEN?"

"Ugh," my sister responded. "I'm sorry. I can't explain the reason for my loyalty to this place. The people are nice enough, but I just don't feel happy doing this."

"Come here," I demanded.

Cassie laughed.

It was Friday afternoon, and I was talking with my sister for the first time since she left. Other than checking in with her later in the day on Monday to make sure she made it home safely, we didn't manage to connect all week.

"Please," I begged. "It'll be so great for you. Plus, I think I'm going to be drowning over here really soon if I don't get some help."

"What? Why?" she asked.

"I don't know for sure what happened, but I have a pretty good idea about it," I began. "Earlier this week, I received an email from someone looking to have me do some custom jewelry for a high-profile client. Initially, I thought it was just dumb luck. But yesterday, I got another email from Liliana Mack's publicist. Apparently, they heard about my work and want me to do Lily's jewelry for her next red carpet event."

"What?!" Cassie shrieked. "Are you serious?"

Cassie was freaking out about what I'd just told her because Lily Mack was Hollywood's newest rising star. This was a huge opportunity for me. I had no idea how I'd gotten so fortunate to have something like that land in my lap, but I certainly wasn't going to complain about it either.

"Yes. I think this is all coming from Patrick. He must have told someone who told someone else. And now, my inbox is filled with emails from people requesting custom work. I want to take it on, Cass. I want to do it all, but I can't possibly keep up with the demands of doing what I love and doing what needs to be done. I can't focus on designing and building the pieces along with sourcing my materials and gems knowing I've got a stack of emails I need to get through."

"This is amazing, Quinn. I'm so, so proud of you."

I harrumphed. "I appreciate that. Really, I do. But the truth is that if I can't convince someone named Cassidy to help me, and soon, this isn't going to work. You know I'm not comfortable enough to hire someone I don't know. And I already know your work ethic. You run that doctor's office back home, Cass. I have no doubts about you being able to manage this for me. I can't even think about a schedule because I'm being torn in so many different directions."

"Alright, alright. Relax," she instructed. "I don't have a ton of time right now since I'm on my lunch break, but I'll call you later tonight or sometime tomorrow. We can go over specifics and details then. Here's what we'll do, though. For the next few weeks, I'll handle all of your emails and scheduling. If it's possible, I'll do what I can to help with sourcing your gems. You'll need to walk me through some of the industry related terms and stuff. Let's try this out for a little while and see how it goes first."

"Really? You'll become my partner?" I asked.

"I'm just helping you out right now, Quinn. I'm not your partner. This is your gig, and I'm just being the supportive sister helping you out."

"You're so much more than that, Cassie. I hope you know how much I love you."

"I do," she replied. "But if you really want to prove it to me, you should tell me what's been happening with that man of yours. Has he managed to kiss you yet?"

It took everything in me not to laugh because not only had Tyson and I finally managed to kiss, but he'd had his mouth *everywhere* on my body. Multiple times. And it was utterly delightful every single time.

"Your silence speaks volumes right now," Cassie declared.

I finally let out the laugh I'd been trying to hold back and informed her, "Cass, we've done so much more than just kissing. And it has been the most amazing few days of my life."

Cassie squealed with delight on the other end of the line. I was surprised considering she was at work, but if she wasn't bothered or embarrassed, I had no reason to be either.

When she finally managed to settle herself down, she asked, "And? How was it?"

"Magnificent," I sighed. "I didn't even know it was possible to feel the way that Tyson makes me feel."

That was the truth. Initially, after we'd done it the first time, I'd assumed it was so powerful and the way my body felt afterward was so extraordinary was because I'd gone more than a year without sex. I was convinced that the next time we did it I'd get that confirmation. I didn't expect I'd be disappointed moving forward, but I wanted to go in having realistic expectations, too.

Tyson proved me wrong. Somehow, he managed to deliver each and every time we were together.

And we'd been together several times since Monday.

"You know," Cassie began. "Telling me about Lily Mack's publicist requesting you to design custom jewelry for Lily's next red carpet event is huge. And if it's the start of you becoming Quinn Jacobs, jeweler to the stars, I so want to be there to be a part of that. But hearing this news about Tyson is doing a much better job at convincing me that a move might be worth considering."

"You're going to have to explain yourself because I don't understand what you mean by that," I coaxed her.

Cassie's voice dipped low and was just a hair above a whisper when she explained, "Think about it. You have proof of Tyson's talents, right? That whole family is huge. It's doubtful that they had all these babies all these years just because they wanted to increase the population. My thought is that it runs in the family. They're good lovers. All of them. And big families end up being the result of that. Plus, I've gotten a preview of Kyle's... generosity in that department. While I can't make any bold statements, I'm guessing I won't be disappointed if I manage to get the full experience one of these days. I could really go for some sexual bliss."

Bliss wasn't even the word for it, but I didn't tell her that. She was already crazy enough coming up with her explanation as it was. Adding fuel to her already blazing fire wasn't going to help anything, so I decided to steer the conversation away from the sex talk into something else.

"Speaking of babies," I started. "I almost screwed things up with Tyson and me before we even really got things started."

"Babies?" she repeated. "You didn't go unprotected, did you? Am I going to be an aunt soon?"

"No!" I yelled. "Considering it's not even been a week,

I wouldn't know something like that anyway. But that's not what this is about. Tyson and I were talking about the size of his family and what we both want in our future. He wants kids, but couldn't really say definitively how many. I freaked out because I don't want to be in another situation where I build something special with someone and they end up leaving because I wasn't able to give them everything they wanted."

"Oh my," she worried.

"Yeah, exactly. And of course, this all resulted in me panicking even more because then I realized Tyson would think I was ready for marriage and babies. This happened right after we had sex for the first time. I mean, nothing like making the guy think you want promises of forever and a lifelong commitment simply because he fulfilled your physical desires once."

"How did he handle it?" she asked.

"Really well, actually. He didn't seem the least bit bothered by the subject matter and understands that what Chris and Alicia did to me is a big part of the reason why I reacted the way I did. At any rate, once I confirmed that he knew I wasn't still romantically hung up on Chris, we managed to talk it out. He seems to be willing to work through it with me, so I think that's a good thing."

Cassie was silent for a long time, and I almost started to wonder if we'd gotten disconnected. Just as I was about to call her name, she murmured, "I hate Chris for what he did to you. I hate that he betrayed you the way he did and made you believe that you'll never be enough for someone. His inability to remain faithful has nothing to do with you. And I know that's so much easier for me to say than for you to understand. I just hope one day you see that that's the truth."

I hoped I would, too. I think I knew on some level deep down that it wasn't me that was broken. I'd been betrayed by him. And her. And the reason for it was all on them.

But I think it was the fact that I didn't understand what led to Chris' infidelity that caused me to constantly question myself. Was it that I was no longer attractive to him? Was it that I wanted to go out occasionally and he always wanted to stay in? Was there some stupid thing I did that just began to irritate him? Was it because I pushed myself to do something more with my life by pursuing another career and he was content to keep things as they were?

I had no answers to any of those questions. What I did know was that not having answers caused me to question everything about myself.

And while some things barely bothered me anymore, others were right there in front of my face, unable to be avoided.

Like a future with another man who might want something different out of life than I did.

"Me too, Cass," I finally replied.

"Well, I better get going so I can clean up from lunch and get back to work. I'll call you later tonight or sometime tomorrow. Just let me know what works for you, and we can figure out how I can best help you out with everything you've got on your plate."

"Do it tomorrow afternoon," I stated. "Tyson's planning on coming by tonight, and you should enjoy one more night of freedom before I start utilizing all your free time."

She laughed and admitted, "That's probably not a bad idea. Love you, Quinn."

"Love you, too."

After we disconnected, I got myself back to work. I still had a mountain of emails to get through, plus I had a few loose ends I wanted to tie up on a couple pieces of jewelry I'd been working on. Since I knew my sister was going to help me out and work through a lot of the emails for me, I decided to only tackle the ones that came in more than two days ago. With those out of the way, I got my tools out and prepared to start on the fun stuff. And that was when a call came in.

Looking at the display, I saw that it was Patrick. Normally, I wouldn't give my personal number out to a client, but I'd made an exception with him. Given the nature of the project I was working on for him and the extremely high cost associated with it, I believed it was in my best interest to make myself as available as possible. Sure, I knew I was reliable and trustworthy, but Patrick didn't know me from the next person. I thought it was wise to make myself accessible and transparent until I'd managed to build up a reputation that spoke for itself.

"Hello?" I answered.

"Hi, Quinn. It's Patrick. How are you?"

"I'm doing well. Thanks. And you?"

"Great," he replied. "I just wanted to reach out and confirm whether or not you sent over the contract. I checked my emails just a few minutes ago and still hadn't seen anything come through."

"Oh, I'm so sorry," I lamented. "This week has been so crazy. My sister was out here visiting me last week, so I got a bit behind on things. After you and I spoke earlier this week, I immediately pulled up the contract and completed all the specifics in it, but I think I ended up getting sidetracked by something else and completely forgot to send it to you."

I moved back to my office, sat at my desk, and pulled up the contract.

Then, I continued, "I'm looking at it right now, and

everything is completed just as we discussed regarding the timeline, the payment structure, and the design. Just remember to initial the sheet with the design, assuming it's as you want it. I did adjust for the change to the earrings, so you'll be able to see that there."

"Perfect. As soon as I have it, I'll review it and get it back to you right away along with the deposit to get things started."

"Great. And I just want to reiterate, even though you'll see it there in the contract, that nearly all of the diamonds we're looking to put into all the pieces are readily available. The stones you want in the earrings are also going to be easily sourced. The only one that may cause a delay is the stone for the engagement ring. You've decided to give her the absolute best we can find with regard to the clarity and color, but the cut and size you want makes it difficult to locate. So, while I've got one on reserve with a close contact in the industry who promises to call if he finds another buyer, I'm going to keep searching. Assuming he doesn't call me sooner than our deadline, I'll continue to search up until that point."

"Thank you, Quinn," Patrick returned. "I appreciate your diligence with this, and I'm looking forward to seeing the final pieces once they're complete."

"You're welcome. And again, I'm so sorry about this mess with getting the contract over to you. Thanks for reaching out to me about it. I've just hit the send button, so you should see it any minute."

"No worries at all. I'll get it done and back to you immediately."

With that, Patrick and I disconnected.

I got back to work. And for the next several hours, I didn't do anything but focus on completing the last few remaining projects I had been wanting to finish since before my move. I got all but one done. I probably would have been able to finish it up if I didn't have any other plans, but Tyson was coming over and I wanted to freshen myself up before he arrived.

Considering I had no real plans other than to work a little this weekend, I promised myself I'd find the time to complete it before Monday rolled around.

Once I cleaned everything up, I went upstairs to shower and change my clothes. All week long, when Tyson came over to visit me, I made dinner for the both of us. When we made plans for tonight, he told me I wasn't allowed to cook. Either he could take me out for dinner or he'd pick something up on his way over. I decided to have him pick something up on his way over.

Truthfully, at the time I'd had enough of going out for a while considering I'd been all over town when Cassie was visiting. I was actually looking forward to a quiet weekend in with nothing to do and nowhere to go.

When the knock came at my front door an hour later, I flung it open and smiled at the sight of Tyson. With his hands full, he stepped inside and gave me a kiss.

"Hey, gorgeous. How was your day?" he asked.

I thought about it for a minute and ultimately responded, "Productive. And yours?"

"Meh, it was quiet," he replied. "There were two routine cases I worked on, but nothing too crazy is happening right now. Sometimes, it's nice to have that break."

I dipped my chin in acknowledgement and suddenly noticed he had more than just dinner in his hands.

Confused, I looked up at him and asked, "What's going on?"

"Have you seen the news?" he wondered.

I shook my head. "No."

"Right. Well, then I guess my next question is… are you still planning to have a weekend of sitting inside and going nowhere?"

"Pretty much," I confirmed.

"They're calling for a snowstorm this weekend," he started. "It's up to you, but I thought maybe we could get snowed in together."

A smile formed on my face. "I'd love to do that."

Tyson returned my grin and shared, "It's a good thing then that I decided to bring some essentials."

He set a few bags down by the door, but held onto the food in his other hand while we walked toward the kitchen. As I pulled out plates and drinks, I asked, "When is the storm supposed to start? And how much snow are they calling for?"

"It's supposed to start overnight tonight and end sometime late tomorrow afternoon or early evening. Six inches is the prediction."

"Wow," I marveled. "Have I been that distracted this week that I didn't know they were calling for half a foot of snow?"

"Yes."

I shot Tyson a questioning look before he explained, "You've been working hard all week. I don't know much about it beyond seeing or hearing you talk about the time you're putting in each day. And then when I come to visit, watching the news or talking about the weather is the last thing on either of our minds."

"True," I agreed.

"So, it's a good thing you have a man who's looking out for those things when he's not around you," he teased.

He was right. And because it made me feel good to know he was thinking about me when he wasn't around me, I moved close to him and slid my arms around his waist.

"Yeah," I sighed. "I've been learning this week that I'm really lucky."

Tyson gave me a kiss and a squeeze before he suggested, "How about we get dinner on some plates and grab a seat so you can tell me all about this realization?"

I tipped my chin up to look at him. After beaming up at him, I agreed, "Okay."

With that, Tyson gave me another kiss. Then, we put our dinner on plates and found seats on the couch so I could tell him why I was feeling so lucky.

CHAPTER 13

Quinn

"Wake up, sleepyhead," Tyson whispered in my ear.

I was on my side in my bed, and he was curled up behind me. It surprised me to learn that Tyson liked to cuddle. I knew that he had no problem showing affection and delivering orgasms, but I didn't know what to expect otherwise.

Over the last week, he'd shown me that he enjoyed having maximum physical contact as frequently as possible. And I loved it. It was one of those things that I didn't know I was missing because it was something I hadn't ever really had before Tyson came along.

Last night, after we ate dinner and I filled Tyson in on my blessings for the week, we decided to put on a movie. Once I had it on, he reached out to me, repositioning us on the couch so that he was on his back and I was lying on top of him. Through the entire movie, he traced his fingertips all along the skin of my back, and I thought it was incredible that the simplest, littlest thing could make me feel such big emotions.

When the movie ended, we spent a long time on the couch making out like high school teenagers. I couldn't remember the last time I'd done that, and I liked how doing that made me feel so desired. Tyson wasn't in any rush to get us in bed just to have sex. It was almost as though he was enjoying the two of us just kissing and touching and turning each other on as much as I was.

But eventually, we'd both gotten to a point where we could no longer stand it. Getting to the bedroom wasn't even an option. So, right there, on my brand-new living room couch, Tyson and I made love.

And just like every time before then, it left me feeling completely sated and unable to function.

Now, it was morning, and Tyson was clearly trying to rouse me. But I was exhausted. Because after our session on the couch, he carried my limp body upstairs and brought me to bed. Only, it wasn't just a matter of lights out for him at that point.

No.

Not at all.

He didn't dive right in for another round.

Instead, he took his time again. He used his hands and his mouth to prime my body for the next round he was craving. Tyson kissed and touched my neck, my breasts, and between my legs. He'd trail his fingers over my thighs or along the small of my back. Sometimes, he would offer gentle squeezes on my behind. Other times, Tyson would grip my hair firmly, but tug gently.

And in each of those moments, all I could think about was how good it felt to have someone who not only wanted to, but also seemed to enjoy, giving me that much attention. Tyson was generous. Very generous. He knew in the end he'd get the prize, but he enjoyed the journey and made the most of it.

Before I fell asleep last night, I came to the conclusion that my sister might have been right in her assessment. She's mentioned that Kyle had been generous with her. Knowing that she hadn't experienced the full scope of that generosity yet made me excited for her.

Best of all, I found myself feeling thankful that I hadn't jumped into anything with someone else before now. While I knew there were parts of me that still needed time to heal, I'd done a good deal of it already and was currently in a place where I could fully appreciate what Tyson was giving to me. Because it was so much more than just phenomenal sex.

"Quinn," Tyson's gentle voice rang in my ears again.

His hands were running over the satin material of my nightie. It felt so good, I almost didn't want to respond to him just so he'd continue. But I didn't think that was fair. So, I leaned my shoulder back into his chest and twisted my neck so I could look at him. When I opened my eyes, he was smiling at me.

"Good morning, gorgeous."

"Good morning," I mumbled. "What time is it?"

"Just after eight," he answered. "Are you planning to sleep all day?"

"No, but there's nowhere important to be this weekend. And you kept me up pretty late last night with all your touching and kissing and stuff."

Tyson let out a laugh before he cocked an eyebrow and repeated, "And stuff?"

"Yeah. That stuff was the most exhausting part of it all," I shared.

His features changed and he looked pensive for a moment. Then, he asked, "Didn't you enjoy it?"

Without any hesitation, I assured him. "Yes, absolutely. I

loved it. I'm just being honest with you about it. The orgasms you give me tear through my body like nothing I've ever experienced before now."

He chuckled and noted, "Never in my life did I think I'd ever hear that as a complaint."

"What?" I asked.

"I'm making you feel too good," he remarked. "I didn't think I'd ever have a woman tell me that her orgasms are too enjoyable."

"I'm not complaining, Tyson. They're magnificent. You're magnificent. But it still takes a lot out of me. I need recovery time."

Tyson fell to his back, looked up at the ceiling, and sighed, "Alright. I'll try to take it easier on you from now on."

Fear gripped me. I didn't want that.

"No!" I snapped as I sat up in the bed and looked down at him.

"No?" he questioned me, moving his eyes from the ceiling to me.

I shook my head. "I want you to do exactly what you've been doing precisely how you've been doing it, now and for as long as you want to continue giving it to me. I love it. I love it so much I can't even begin to tell you. It's just that sometimes I want to be able to give you a hard time about it, too."

He looked at me like I'd lost my mind.

I couldn't say I blamed him, though. Because once I'd admitted it and said those words out loud, I realized how crazy I sounded.

When Tyson continued to stare without saying anything, I got nervous.

So, I blurted, "Maybe I should get up and go downstairs to make us some breakfast. Do you like French toast?"

"Are you crazy?" he finally asked.

I bit my lip. "Maybe. Just a little bit, though. I promise."

Tyson took in a deep breath and blew it out. I grew incredibly concerned. Then, he sat up next to me, kissed my cheek, and asked, "Is your French toast any good?"

Relief swept through me. I turned my head in his direction, and with a smile on my face and tears shimmering in my eyes, I rasped, "I think so."

"Whatever you're feeling right now, shake it off," he advised gently. "I need you to feed me so that I'll have the energy to give you more stuff to complain about."

At that, I couldn't help myself. I burst out laughing as the tears escaped. Tyson wrapped an arm around me and pulled me close. Then, through my laughter, he brought a thumb up to swipe at my tears. With my face being held in his hand, he moved his face closer and touched his lips to mine.

When he pulled back, he said, "Breakfast."

At his command, I got up and went downstairs to make breakfast.

I hung up the phone and walked back out to meet Tyson on the couch. It was after lunch and we'd had a pretty eventful day so far.

After I fed Tyson French toast for breakfast, he kept true to his word and gave me some stuff that I'd be able to complain about later. We ended up taking a quick nap afterward, which I desperately needed.

As the snow fell outside, Tyson and I decided to be lazy for a little while watching movies. We cuddled during the first, and on the second, I worked on the necklace I wanted to finish. Cassie had called in the middle of the second movie, so I quickly answered and asked if I could call her after lunch. She was fine with that, which allowed me to stay focused on what I was doing with Tyson nearby.

Once the movie was over and I was putting the final touches on the necklace, Tyson said, "I'm starting to understand why you have started seeing all of this incredible growth in your business over the last week."

I was sitting on the floor at my coffee table working. Tyson was sitting behind me, his legs on either side of my body. Occasionally, when I'd take a break from my work and rest my back against the couch, he'd put his hands to my shoulders and give me a little massage. It was so nice, and I found myself taking breaks more frequently just so I could get a little extra loving from him.

Twisting my neck, I looked back at him. "What?" I asked.

"Jewelry isn't my thing, but I know when something looks nice. Between what you showed me the day after I met you and this, your talent is unparalleled. I'm not surprised you got the opportunity to handle Lily Mack's red carpet event. I'm really proud of you, Quinn."

"Thank you, Tyson. It means a lot that you support me with this."

Tyson tipped his head to one side and asked, "Didn't he do that for you?"

I frowned and shook my head. "He wasn't really interested one way or the other," I explained. "Things weren't always bad between us. I've actually just been realizing a lot lately that there are quite a few things he didn't do for me."

The hand Tyson had on my shoulder gave me a squeeze. "I'm sorry."

"It's okay. I'm fine," I assured him. "I think a lot of it boils down to that saying about how you can't really miss something you never had. It wasn't that he had a problem with what I was doing, at least not one he shared with me. It was just that he never really expressed any interest in it at all."

The expression on Tyson's face did little to make me believe that he thought my explanation was a good one. I didn't necessarily think Chris' lack of support was a good thing. It just was what it was, which was nothing at all. I guess if I really took the time to think about it, it was sad. Because things weren't always bad between us. And in the beginning, Chris had given our relationship the time and attention it deserved.

Maybe he had gotten comfortable. Maybe it was something else. I didn't know, I probably never would, but it really didn't matter anymore. I'd moved on, and he did, too.

Not liking the look on Tyson's face, I shared, "He might not have expressed any interest in what I'm doing, but you do, Tyson. And I really like that you care that much."

That did the trick, and we were back on track.

Tyson waited patiently while I finished up the necklace, and then we had lunch together.

After lunch, I called Cassie back to discuss the specifics of having her help me out with my business. Since she was doing me a huge favor by offering to help when she had free time, I allowed her to tell me what specific roles she was looking to fulfill. In true Cassie fashion, she was willing to go above and beyond the call of duty. But that's just the kind of sister she was, so I shouldn't have been surprised.

We'd just ended our lengthy phone call, and I went back to the couch where Tyson told me he'd be waiting. When I walked into the room, he looked at me and smiled. "Everything go okay with your sister?" he asked.

Nodding, I explained, "Yeah, she's willing to take on a lot

of responsibility to help me out. Basically, as long as it isn't anything that's actually designing or building the jewelry, she was more than willing to take it on. I gave her all the information she'd need to catch me up on emails. And she ordered me to get her pictures of the stuff I've worked on recently so she can get it up on my website for me. I know she'll have no problems with any of that. The only thing I might need to supervise for the next little while until she gets the hang of it is the selection of gems and stones. I have a few different suppliers that I go through depending on what I'm looking for. Since I always know who I go to based on what I need, I've never really written it down."

Tyson tugged me into his lap when I finished speaking. He gave me a kiss and said, "I'm happy you have her to help you out. Hopefully it'll really lighten your load and allow you to create more."

"That's what I'm hoping for," I admitted. "I don't mind talking to a client when I need to figure out what they're looking to have made, but I really dislike all of the administrative stuff. That's right up Cassie's alley, so it works out perfectly."

"Kyle really likes her," Tyson shared.

I smiled inwardly and rested my head on his shoulder. "I already figured that out," I started. "For what it's worth, I think she really likes him, too. But Cassie's not like me. She's able to keep her emotions locked up tight."

"Do I have to worry about him ending up heartbroken over her?" he wondered.

"I honestly can't say. She'd never intentionally set out to hurt him, but she's seen what happened to me, and it scares her to think that same thing could happen to her. I think if Kyle is really interested in her and shows her that there are good men out there, he stands to gain a lot."

Tyson's face softened, and he decided, "I guess I won't worry then."

"What about me?" I asked.

"What about you?"

"Do I have to worry about my sister with your brother?"

He shook his head. "Not at all. I have no doubt that if she's open to it and gives him the chance, he'll show her exactly what she needs to see that'll allow her to open her heart."

With one of my arms tucked behind him and the other draped across his abdomen, I gave Tyson a squeeze.

We stayed like that a long time, not saying anything and really not needing to. I had an inkling we were both feeling pretty thankful for the confirmation that our siblings were going to be in good hands with one another. In addition, it was hard not to feel a tinge of appreciation for the fact that we'd found one another, too.

After a while, I shifted my thoughts from our relationship to thoughts of how we would spend the rest of our snow day. When we checked around lunchtime, Tyson guessed we'd gotten about seven inches of fresh snow. It had started to slow, and it wasn't likely that we'd see more than another half an inch or so by the time it ended.

Since we'd watched enough movies, and I had a feeling there were more in our future, I really wasn't up for another one immediately. I just needed a little break from them for a bit. And that was when it hit me.

I sat up in Tyson's lap and shot him the biggest grin I could muster.

"What?" he asked.

"When was the last time you played in the snow?"

"Sorry?"

"When was the last time you played in the snow?" I repeated my question.

He narrowed his eyes at me, clearly indicating he was thinking about something. Part of me was worried he thought my crazy was coming out again, but there was the other part of me that hoped he was seriously trying to remember when he last played in the snow.

When he finally spoke, the answer he gave wasn't the one I expected to get. Nevertheless, it was still a good one. In fact, it might have been better than what I expected.

"End of January," he declared. "The big storm we had."

I shook my head in surprise. "Wait. Are you serious?"

Tyson dipped his chin. "Why do you seem so shocked by that?" he asked.

With my mouth hanging open, my eyes shifted back and forth. "Um, I don't know. Maybe the fact that you're a man in his mid-thirties who just admitted to me that he was playing in the snow roughly a month ago."

"Being thirty-five means I have to stop playing?"

"No," I insisted. "I just wasn't expecting that."

Tyson laughed and stated, "I've got eight, soon-to-be nine, nieces and nephews. They range in age from five to twelve. That's prime time for playing in the snow."

When he put it like that, it made much more sense.

"I didn't realize you meant that you'd played in the snow with the kids," I explained the reason for my reaction.

"What? You don't think I'll go out and play in the snow with you?"

I shrugged. "I don't know. I'm kind of hoping you will."

Tyson smirked and ordered, "Then you better go bundle up."

I perked up. "Really?" I asked.

"It'd be a total waste of a snow day not to actually go out and play in it," he started. "And, fair warning, I'm a master at fort building. So, if you're planning to have a snowball fight, you might want to wait until after I've built you a fort."

Oh my God.

I loved him.

Honestly.

Seriously.

Totally.

I loved Tyson.

And even though admitting that to myself scared me to death, I let it sink in. Because there was no reason why I shouldn't have been able to fall in love again. I deserved that. I had a lot to offer to a relationship, crazy or not, and I think Tyson knew that, too.

So, I leaned forward and kissed him. It wasn't just a peck either. It was a long, passionate kiss with lots of tongue and moaning.

Then, I pulled back, smiled at him, and went to get bundled up.

CHAPTER 14

Quinn
Two weeks later

"I'm sorry, but it's just too much, Quinn."

My shoulders fell.

I wasn't mad. I couldn't be.

Cassidy had stepped up to help me out of the goodness of her heart. For me to expect that she'd be able to handle her regular work schedule in addition to managing so much of my business was wrong. There was that much work on my end, work that she couldn't exactly do while she was at her other job, that it was an unreasonable request.

And I should have expected she wouldn't be able to maintain that level of stress for an extended period of time.

For me, it had been wonderful over the last two weeks. I was able to put my full focus into the actual jewelry-making part of my business. It was the ideal solution for me, of course, because while I was doing the part that I loved doing, Cassie was handling the part that I didn't necessarily enjoy all that much.

So, while I was disappointed that my sister would no longer be part of the success of my business and that I'd have to take on the role of manager and administrator again, I couldn't be mad. She tried to help, and that was all I could really ask of her. Ultimately, I knew she had to do what was best for her.

"I understand, Cass," I returned. "Don't feel bad about it. I know how time-consuming it is. With your regular work hours at the doctor's office, I had a feeling this might become a little bit too much to manage. It was difficult for me, and I don't have another nine-to-five job to worry about, so I completely get it. I really do appreciate you trying to help me out, though."

"You're welcome. I feel so bad that I can't do it all, but with the office it's just a lot. It's sad, too, because I wake up every morning excited to get some work done for you. But after a full day of working at my regular job, I'm usually pretty burnt out when I get home. Most nights, I've been powering through to get at least the most important things accomplished, but your business is blowing up right now. It needs someone who can devote their full attention to it, but unfortunately, I'm not that person when I've got my regular job to go to every day."

"I get it. Really, I do," I tried to reassure her.

"I just feel so horrible about it," she sighed. "But for two weekends in a row now, I'm sitting here with absolutely no personal life because I'm still working. I wouldn't mind if it was just going to be temporary for a few weeks; however, I can see the potential here. And there's no chance this is going to end or slow down any time soon."

Cassie was on the phone with me telling me how horrible she felt about not being able to continue to do this for me, but I should have been the one who was feeling bad. The growth of my business was consuming all of my sister's free time. And that just wasn't cool.

As much as I hated that she wouldn't be able to continue, I

wouldn't want her to be living like that. Her happiness was far more important to me.

"So, that's why I walked into the doctor's office this past Monday and told them I was officially resigning from my position, and that I'd be leaving in two weeks," she stated nonchalantly.

"What?!" I shrieked.

"I hope Windsor is ready," she teased. "Because it's about to have two Jacobs girls living there. I've decided to move to Wyoming, Quinn."

My eyes filled with tears. "I'm going to cry. Are you serious?"

Cassie's laughter came across the line. While she laughed in my ear, I paced my kitchen. Once she got herself together, she assured me, "I wouldn't joke about something like this. And truthfully, you aren't completely to blame for me not having a personal life right now."

"What does that mean?" I asked.

"I'm not really interested in going out to party all the time anymore," she started. "I've been doing what I can each night for your business, but every night before I go to bed, I talk to Kyle. It's so different for me to be doing this with him, but I'm beginning to really like it. I like him. And I like what I'm building with him, even though we're this far apart."

"It's kind of hard to make it all about sex when you're over five hours away from each other, isn't it?" I joked. "Have you told him you're planning to move here?"

"Not yet. I wanted to tell you first."

I took in a deep breath and let it out. My sister was finally going to be close. I didn't know whether to cry tears of happiness or jump for joy. Even still, I wanted to make sure she was confident in her decision.

"You need to know I'm overjoyed at this news, Cass. Honestly, you've made my year. But I want you to be sure. Are you certain this is what you want to do?"

"I have absolutely no doubt about it," she insisted. "Like I already said, I wake up excited about what I'm seeing happen in your business. There's so much potential for you right now, and as your sister, I want to be part of your journey. I want to take this ride with you. I honestly had no idea how crazy things had gotten for you until I started doing it myself. I'm so proud of you for what you've accomplished in this last year despite the heartache and challenges you've faced."

If she continued to talk like this, I was going to be a mess. I was already pulling tissues out of the tissue box mercilessly and swiping at my cheeks. If she kept it up, I'd have red-rimmed, puffy eyes in no time at all.

Thankfully, it didn't get to that point because she added, "And I'm serious about the thing with Kyle. I've had my fun, Quinn. I'm a grown woman now, and I've been thinking a lot recently about my future. I don't want to be partying my life away only to wake up one day asking myself why I'm alone. I know there aren't any guarantees with Kyle, but I like the way he makes me feel from a distance. It's got to be that much better in person, don't you think?"

I loved this for my sister.

Loved it.

"It's going to be fantastic in person, Cass," I confirmed.

"I hope so."

"So, what are your plans then?" I asked. "When are you going to head out?"

"Saturday morning," she replied.

"I'll come back there on Friday," I declared. "I can visit with Mom and Dad, and then we'll drive back together. You won't be able to fit all your stuff in your car anyway. Have you told them yet?"

"No. I'm going to call them after I get off the phone with you," she responded. "I think they'll be happy about it."

"Yeah. Me too," I agreed.

A bit of silence stretched between us before Cassie asked, "Do you still have one of your apartments available for rent?"

I was caught off guard by her question, but answered, "Yeah, I still have the one I was living in before I moved here available. But why? Wouldn't you rather stay here?"

"Maybe the first night or two after I get there," she started. "But not permanently, Quinn."

"I wouldn't mind you being here," I assured her.

"I know that. And I love you for it. But I'm going to be starting my life over again. I need my own space. You need yours, too. You've got this new man in your life, and I want you to be able to explore that with him to the fullest. Sometimes, that involves having sex whenever and wherever the mood strikes. Maybe it'll be in the kitchen after breakfast or maybe it'll be on the way up the stairs after a long day. But no matter where or when it is, you've got to have the freedom to do that."

"You're crazy."

Cassie laughed at me. "Maybe, but I'm not wrong."

She wasn't. So I couldn't exactly argue with her. Most of all, I had to admit how lucky I was to have her in my life. When I looked at someone like Tyson, I found myself envious sometimes of the amount of people he had in his life to have his back. He'd mentioned on several occasions just how loyal his family was to him and each other. I loved that he had that. But when I sat back and really thought about it, I didn't need a whole brood of people. Sure, I didn't think I'd be complaining if I had in my life all that he had in his.

But I realized it wasn't the number that was important.

I only needed one.

One person who'd be there for me through thick and thin, no matter what.

And that's precisely what I had with my sister.

In a situation like this, it would have been easy for her to just move here and live with me. Of course, I'd welcome her with open arms. I loved her. But I loved that she was able to take a step back and assess the situation so she could make a decision that was best for the both of us.

"Okay, Cassie. So, I'll come out there on Friday, spend some time visiting with Mom and Dad, and then we'll leave Saturday morning to head back here. They'll probably enjoy a dinner out with both of us since it's been a while."

"That works for me."

"I'll touch base this coming week," I stated. "Don't work too hard this weekend."

"I won't. Love you."

"Love you."

Cassie and I disconnected, and I immediately burst into happy tears. I figured there was no point in trying to hold them back. Despite my best efforts when I was on the phone with my sister, I ended up with puffy, red-rimmed eyes.

And because I was so overwhelmed with the news I'd just received, I forgot to keep my eye on the time.

I realized it when there was a knock at my door.

Tyson and I had made plans to go out for dinner tonight, but now I was a mess.

I opened the door, and the minute he saw my face, he worried, "Are you okay? What happened?"

"Cassie's moving here," I declared.

"Isn't that a good thing?" he wondered.

"Yeah."

"So, why are you crying?"

I planted my face in his chest and wrapped my arms around his waist. "I'm just really happy about it and got a little emotional."

I felt Tyson's tense frame relax and start to shake with his laughter. "You're crazy."

I squeezed him in response.

"When is she coming out?" he asked.

"Next weekend," I started. "I'm going to actually go back there next Friday so I can help her finish any of her packing and bring some of her stuff back in my car."

"I'll go with you if you want company on the road," he volunteered.

Just like that. Without hesitating or thinking on it for a moment, Tyson just casually agreed to a five-hour drive to my hometown like it was no big deal to him.

"Would you want to do that?" I asked, tipping my head back to look up at him.

He lowered his mouth to mine. When his lips were a mere fraction of an inch away from mine, he explained, "I want to spend time with you after a long week at work. So, if that's where you're going to be, that's where I'd like to be."

"Okay, but…" I trailed off.

Tyson pulled back and pressed, "But what?"

"I'm going to be going out to dinner with Cassie and my parents. Are you willing to meet them?"

Suddenly, Tyson looked disappointed. I didn't like thinking that he wasn't thrilled at the prospect of meeting my parents.

"Gorgeous, you've met my whole family already. Not only am I willing to meet your parents, I also really *want* to meet them. It's mostly because I want to meet the people that raised such a crazy woman."

"I'm not crazy," I argued. I wasn't really arguing, though, because I knew it was partially true.

"If you say so," he returned. "Now, are you still going to let me take you out tonight, or are we staying here like this all night?"

"I need to fix my face," I murmured. "Then, we'll go."

"Okay, Quinn. Give me a kiss first, though."

What could I do but give in? I mean, he wanted to meet my parents.

And I loved him.

While my days had been filled with work over the last week, it felt like it took forever to make it to Friday.

I was beyond ecstatic, and I was so excited that we'd finally made it to the big day.

I was driving back to Montana to pack up my sister and bring her to Wyoming. Tyson was coming with me, and he was going to meet my parents. That alone was enough for me to consider this to be a special occasion. But what made this day even more special was the fact that Tyson and I were pulling off one huge surprise.

The day after Cassie told me she was going to be moving out here, Tyson got a call from Kyle. Cassie had reached out to him after she told my parents about her plans to move and gave him the good news.

Kyle was ecstatic about it and wanted to share the good news with his brother. When Kyle called, Tyson mentioned that he and I were going to be driving out to help her move. I happened to be there when Tyson got the call and urged him to ask Kyle if he wanted to go with us and surprise Cassie. Kyle jumped at the chance.

So, not only was Tyson going to meet my parents, but his brother would be, too. And my sister had absolutely no idea that it was going to be happening either. I hadn't even told her that Tyson was coming with me.

Sometime in the middle of the week, Tyson declared that we'd take his truck on the mini road trip to Montana since it had more room to put any extra stuff Cassie needed to bring back. I didn't fight him because I knew it was an argument I wouldn't win; and quite frankly, given that his vehicle was larger than mine, it made sense.

Just over five hours after we left my house this afternoon, Tyson, Kyle, and I arrived in my hometown. We didn't leave too early because Cassie was going to be at work until five. I wanted to make sure we saw her before we met up with my parents.

I picked up my phone and called her.

"Are you still on the road?" she greeted me.

"I actually just made it to town," I answered. "I'm about five minutes from your place. Are you home from work yet?"

"I'm leaving now. I should be there in about fifteen minutes. You still have your key to my place, right?" she asked.

This was actually perfect. "Yeah, I do. I'll go in and see what you've left for me to do before we meet up with Mom and Dad."

"Okay. See you soon."

I looked to the guys and relayed my conversation with Cassie to them. Kyle seemed like he was about ready to burst. He was doing his best at trying to play it cool, but I could tell he was excited to see her.

We made it to Cassie's, and I used my key to get us inside. I didn't do what I told her I would and go through the items that she packed up or that still needed to be packed. I stood and watched out the window for her. The apartment complex she lived in had a large parking lot, so I doubted she would even notice Tyson's car.

Not long after we arrived at her place, I saw my sister pull in.

"She's here," I announced.

It wasn't more than two minutes later, when I heard her fiddling to get her key in the front door. I could have gone over to open it up for her, but I didn't want to ruin the surprise.

The next thing I knew the door opened and a bunch of balloons and flowers entered before my sister did. Her eyes were looking down at the key in the door when she called out, "Quinn, I'm here. Sorry I'm late, but they decided to throw me a par—"

Cassie stopped in her tracks as she stared at Kyle standing a few feet in front of her. She was frozen on the spot for several long moments, and none of us said anything.

Suddenly, she dropped everything just inside the door and flung herself into Kyle's arms. "Oh, my God," she cried. "What are you doing here?"

Seeing that, I no longer had any doubt about it. My sister was falling in love. And judging by Kyle's reaction to seeing her for the first time in weeks, I knew he felt just as much for her. Overwhelmed with happiness at the sight of the two of them, I leaned into Tyson. He wrapped an arm around my shoulders and curled me into his body. When I looked up at him, I saw that he felt what happened between our siblings just as much as I did. And what he saw made him a happy man.

When Kyle finally loosened his hold on Cassie, she turned toward me with tears in her eyes. I knew she found a similar look in mine. And when she got close to me and wrapped her arms around me, she whispered, "Thank you so much."

"Love you, Cass."

She squeezed me in return before letting go and saying hello to Tyson.

"Okay, so have plans changed now or are we still meeting up for dinner with Mom and Dad?" she asked.

No sooner did she get the words out when the reality of it all hit her in the face. She snapped her gaze in Kyle's direction. "Oh my God. Wait. Did you know that we're supposed to be having dinner with my parents? It's okay if you don't want to go."

Kyle was mostly unaffected by her words and teased, "What? You're not going to let me eat?"

"Of course," she returned. "I just didn't know if you knew that was the plan and were comfortable with it."

"I'm looking forward to it," he assured her.

"Cassie, how about you tell Kyle and me what is ready to go in the cars so we can start loading them up for you?" Tyson suggested. "We'll get some of it done tonight, and then tomorrow morning when Quinn and I come back, we'll take care of any of the last few things that you still need here tonight."

"Where are you going tonight?" she asked.

"I booked a room at a hotel for us," he replied.

Cassie's eyes went to Kyle as she squirmed. He had a knowing look on his face.

I interrupted their moment before it got too awkward for all of us there and ordered, "Alright, let's get this show on the road so we can surprise Mom and Dad with boys."

"You didn't tell them either?" my sister gasped.

"Nope."

Then I shot her a smile and walked to where she had her suitcases and boxes piled up. Everyone else followed behind me.

CHAPTER 15

Quinn

"ALL JOKING ASIDE, ARE YOUR PARENTS GOING TO LOSE THEIR minds that you're both showing up with a man by your side without you having given them some kind of warning or heads up?"

Tyson was sitting behind the wheel of his car driving us to dinner as he followed behind Cassie, who was in her car with Kyle ahead of us.

I understood why Tyson was suddenly worried about how my parents might react to having something like this just thrown at them. But I knew my parents, and I knew this would not be an issue for them.

"No, they won't lose their minds," I promised. "My parents have always been the kind of people who just roll with the punches. Life is what it is. There's not much you can do to change what's going to happen in someone else's life. They love Cassie and me, but know that my sister and I need to make our own choices in life. We're both grown women, so we're old enough to decide what's right for us. They have the attitude that as long as we're happy and not hurting anyone, they'll support us, no matter what."

Tyson seemed to relax a bit at the confirmation he wouldn't

show up to a dinner and have my dad ready to put him through the wringer. I guess I understood his nerves. I'd felt the same way when I met his family. But from my perspective, Tyson had it much easier. He only had two people to meet.

"I thought they might be concerned about you being in a serious relationship again after your divorce," he explained. "Not that you aren't old enough to make your own choices, but I can't imagine I'd be thrilled about my daughter dating again after she'd been betrayed and had her heart broken by her husband and her best friend."

Hearing Tyson talk about his future daughter made my heart race just a little bit. As much as I wanted to focus on that, I wanted to make sure he understood that my parents were good people.

"I can understand what you're saying. And I know they worry about me. But just because they have more of a hands-off approach now that Cassie and I are adults doesn't mean they don't want to be involved in our lives. Their door is always open. And if either of us ever needed advice that we can't or don't want to get from one another, they're always there for us."

"As long as you're sure, I'm good," he insisted. "Honestly, I'd be good with it either way. But if there was the possibility of them freaking out a bit about it, I might have tried to convince you to let them know now. Even if we're only a few minutes away."

It was nice that he was considering their feelings in the matter, and it only served to remind me of just how good a man Tyson was. I knew my parents would see that almost immediately after meeting him, and would welcome him with open arms.

We made it to the restaurant, and I spotted my parents'

car right away. Once I saw it, I felt butterflies in my belly. I wasn't worried that they wouldn't like Tyson. I think I was just a mix of nerves and excitement to tell them that I'd finally gotten to a point in my life where I'd moved on from something that hurt my whole family deeply.

After we parked, the four of us walked into the restaurant together, and Cassie gave our name to the hostess.

"We've just seated the other two people in your party," she said. "Follow me."

Tyson took my hand in his and held onto it as we followed the hostess through the restaurant. I spotted my parents at their table before they noticed us and instantly felt myself smile. I hadn't seen them since the Christmas holiday and had missed them terribly.

"And here we are," the hostess said. "Your server will be over shortly."

"Thank you," Cassie returned.

My parents were wide-eyed as they stared at the four of us. Their eyes darted back and forth between me, Cassie, Tyson, and Kyle.

Suddenly, my mom declared, "Looks like Quinn brought a boy home, Bill."

"I can see that, Helen," my father remarked. "I'm just glad she brought one for her sister, too."

I loved my parents.

And it took everything in me not to burst out laughing that they were looking up at Tyson and Kyle calling them boys when they couldn't have been further from the truth.

Belatedly, my parents stood and introduced themselves. Extending his hand, my father said, "Hi, I'm Bill."

Tyson took his hand and returned, "Tyson Reed. And this is my brother, Kyle."

"Oh, a brothers and sisters thing. I love this," my mom swooned.

"This is my wife, Helen," Dad introduced her to the guys.

They both greeted her with a hug and a kiss on the cheek, and I knew she was doing her best not to start fanning herself.

"Sit, sit, sit," my mom ordered after she and my dad had both given me and Cassie a hug each.

We all sat down just in time for the waiter to come over and take our drink orders. While everyone perused the menu, we made small talk. My parents asked about how my drive back was and if we'd run into any major traffic. That was one of the things I found so strange about them. My parents always wanted to discuss the traffic patterns.

After the waiter returned with our drinks and everyone ordered food, my mom asked, "So, how did you all meet?"

She asked the question in a way that made it seem like she was talking to all four of us, but her eyes were directed at me. I decided that meant I was supposed to be the one to provide an answer.

"Tyson actually works for a private investigation and security firm. Do you remember how I called you a few weeks back and told you that the police were at my place because my alarm went off in the middle of the night?"

"I do," my dad muttered. "Your mother didn't stop talking about it for days."

"I was just worried about our girl being out there all alone," she reasoned before she batted her eyes and looked in Tyson's direction. "But it seems that's no longer an issue, is it?"

"No, ma'am," he confirmed. Then he turned his attention to my father and added, "I completely replaced Quinn's entire security system. The one that was in there had been installed by a company that's no longer in business, and they did a terrible job, which explains why it was malfunctioning. She's all set now, though."

My father smiled proudly. "Thank you for doing that for her," he said.

"And now, Kyle," my mom started. "What do you do?"

"I actually took over my father's construction business," he answered.

Just as I had suspected he would, a wave of relief moved through my father. "Oh, that's such good news. My baby girl, I love her to death, but she makes me crazy. If she ever needs anything fixed or hung, she's always trying to do it herself. She never asks for help from the start, and I love her independent, capable attitude. But she's really not good at any of that kind of stuff. And then she always ends up calling me after she's put about a thousand holes in her walls."

"I am not *that* bad," Cassie huffed.

I started laughing and insisted, "Yes, you are. Kyle, it's true. She's awful with a hammer."

"I'll be sure to remember that," he said.

"Oh, stop. This isn't nice. Quinn really has no room to talk. At least I try to fix something before I go crazy. She's the biggest drama queen on the face of the planet," Cassie shot back.

"I am not a drama queen," I maintained.

"No?" she returned before turning her attention to Tyson. "Tell me, Tyson. Have you seen Quinn's crazy dramatic side yet?"

Tyson looked a bit nervous. His eyes went from Cassie's to mine to my parents. Then, he stated, "I feel like this is a trap."

"It is, son," my father confirmed. "Go with your gut on this one."

With that advice, Tyson looked at Cassie and lamented, "I'm sorry, but I'm not sure what you're talking about, Cass."

My sister growled.

"Good man," my father approved.

At that point, my mother jumped in and asked, "So, Tyson, how long have you been in the security business?"

And just like that, my mom took us out of our downward spiral to a much better place. And from that point forward, dinner with Tyson, his brother, my sister, and our parents was a veritable success.

A couple hours later, we were outside in the parking lot saying goodbye. It was going to be quick because it was frigid outside.

My father came up to me, pulled me into his arms, and hugged me. When he took a step back he praised me. "Your mom and I are so proud of you. You picked up the pieces of your broken heart and put it back together again. You've always loved freely, Quinn. And I'm happy to see that one lousy experience hasn't ruined your ability to give yourself a little slice of happiness."

"Thanks, Dad."

He turned to Tyson and stated, "You're a lucky man. Treat her better than the last one did."

"You have my word on that, sir."

With a nod, their conversation ended. My mother gave me one last hug before both my parents moved to say goodbye to Cassie. Tyson and I got in his truck, warmed up a minute, and took off to the hotel.

"Thanks for not passing out when you met my parents," I said as I walked out of the bathroom toward the bed where Tyson was waiting for me.

I climbed in, and he immediately pulled me close to him. Our bodies pressed together, my front to his, he joked, "I'm surprised I didn't pass out from utter shock. I don't know what I was expecting, but it certainly wasn't them being as laidback as they were."

"I told you that's how they are."

"I know, but I think it's one thing to hear it and something else entirely to see it. That was, by far, the easiest meeting of the parents I've ever experienced."

"Have you had a lot of them?" I asked, hating that I did.

Tyson gave me a squeeze. "No. Just a few. I enjoyed yours the most, though."

I inched my way closer to him. When I did, he brought one hand up and ran his fingers through my hair.

"Quinn?" he called after some silence had stretched between us.

"Yeah?"

"I want to tell you something, but I'm worried about how you might react to it," he warned me.

Panic gripped me. While I didn't believe that I knew all of Tyson's deepest, darkest secrets, I hadn't expected that there was something he was intentionally keeping from me. No matter how terrified I was, I had to know what he wanted to say to me.

"Tell me," I rasped.

Tyson hesitated. Just when I thought he was going to tell me, he stopped himself.

"Tyson, you're scaring me."

"I love you, Quinn."

"What?" I breathed.

"I love you," he repeated.

His eyes searched my face, presumably looking for

something that might tell him what was going through my head. I wasn't sure that he found the answer to that because I hadn't yet figured out what to do with his admission.

Obviously, it meant everything to me. I had admitted to myself a week ago that I'd fallen in love with him, but I didn't think that was as big of a deal. Tyson was an easy man to love. He didn't come with a bunch of emotional baggage. His family might have been large, loud, and a little crazy, but it was all in a good way.

So, wanting Tyson to know exactly how much hearing those words meant to me, I took my hand and pressed the palm of it to his shoulder. When he fell to his back, I climbed on top of him, my thighs straddling his hips. His hands started at my thighs and moved up until they ultimately made it to the satin material of my nightie.

Over the last several weeks, Tyson made it abundantly clear how much he enjoyed my nighties. I always wore them to bed, so it wasn't like I had to go out of my way to be cute for him.

I lowered my face and touched my lips to his before we fell into a much deeper kiss. The second my tongue touched Tyson's, the nightie was gone, and we became a mess of tangled limbs, soft moans, and sweat.

Tyson rolled me to my back, settled himself between my parted thighs, and asked, "Are you protected from pregnancy right now?"

"Yes," I whispered.

"I want to make love to you, Quinn. And I'd never put you at risk. I wouldn't ask you for this if I had any doubts. It's okay if the answer is no, but I want to know if I can have you without anything between us?"

I knew he was verbally communicating now that he

wanted to make love to me. I think he believed it would be the first time he would be doing that with me. I knew differently because I'd felt him doing it so many times before. And because I trusted that he was telling me the truth, I replied softly, "Yes, Tyson. You can make love to me."

That was all the encouragement Tyson needed to hear because the next thing I knew, he was filling me. Completely and slowly. Without anything between us.

And it was beautiful.

"Quinn," he groaned the second he was inside me.

"Yes," I moaned. "You feel amazing."

Tyson slowly pulled back before he pushed back in agonizingly slow. He repeated that over and over while his lips kissed me all over. He pressed his lips to mine before he moved them to my cheek, then my jaw, and finally my throat.

And I was, once again, reminded of just how incredible a lover Tyson was. Several times he built me up to the point where I was just about to go over the edge, but then he'd either stop moving or pull out completely.

It was torturous, but in the best way possible.

As was usual with him, Tyson had me lost. Lost in him. In us. In the connection of our bodies. In the movement of our hips. In the touch of our hands. In the taste of our tongues. In the caress of our fingertips.

There was no awareness of time when I was with Tyson like this. It could have been mere minutes and it would have felt like hours. We started with me on my back, but then he was on his back before I was on my belly and eventually on my side.

No matter what position we were in, Tyson never failed to put in the effort and show me just how much he appreciated my body. Sometimes, he was slow and gentle, offering whisper-soft touches and tender kisses. Other times, he was quick and powerful, delivering earth-shattering thrusts and frantic, needy tasting and sucking. Regardless of how he gave it to me, it always, always felt like worshipping.

"Tyson," I whimpered when I felt myself reaching the point of no return.

"You're gorgeous, Quinn," he declared as he picked up his pace. "Every inch of you looks and feels like perfection."

In the next instant, a guttural moan escaped me as my limbs tightened and my back arched off the bed. Tyson moved quicker, working me through my orgasm, but his grunts came louder. And somewhere in the middle of mine, Tyson found his release.

Tyson

I was still buried in the warmth of Quinn. Being here with her like this was like nothing I'd ever experienced before now. Sure, I'd been with other women, and it was always good enough. But never was it like it was with Quinn.

Something about her had me always wanting to prolong our time together in bed. I often found myself struggling to find a way to make sure I'd shown the right amount of attention to every part of her.

And despite all my best efforts, I still wasn't sure it was good enough. Quinn never complained. In fact, she always expressed how great it was for her. I believed her. But it still didn't stop me from wanting to give her more, somehow even better, every single time we were together.

Now that we'd both just come down from the high, I

started to move so I didn't end up crushing her with my body weight. Her body tensed, and I felt her thighs wrapping tighter around me as her fingers gripped my shoulders.

I stopped moving and waited for her to explain.

But after she'd searched my face for a bit without an explanation ever coming, I called, "Quinn?"

"I love you, too," she rasped.

My body stiffened.

And because I didn't say anything, it gave Quinn the perfect opportunity to continue speaking. "I've known for a little while now but was scared to admit it to you."

The tension from the initial shock of her sentiment left me. The thumb on one of my hands that had been framing her face stroked along her cheek as I whispered, "Gorgeous."

She closed her eyes and pressed her cheek into my touch.

"I love so many things about you," she began. "I've honestly never known a man like you. The way you take care of those you love is heartwarming. I see your loyalty and closeness to your family, and it makes me realize how lucky I am to know you. Because you give me all those wonderful things that you give to the people you love most in the world. The way you just offered to drive out here with me because you wanted to spend time with me. Or the way you encourage me with my jewelry by praising the work I've done. I figure these are things that you give to everyone. It's just who you are. But you give me more."

I couldn't imagine what else she'd have to say. I didn't know if I could handle hearing any more than she'd already shared.

Unfortunately, I didn't have a choice in the matter. Quinn's voice was so soft when she spoke again. "It's when you have me like this," she practically purred. "It's in the way you give so much of yourself to me. You touch my body in all the right ways at all the right times. You aren't a lazy lover, Tyson. And that has nothing to do with the pace of your strokes. It's about the feel of your hands on my skin and the way you cover nearly every inch of my body with your kisses. It's about the way our bodies fit together and move in perfect synchronicity. I love it all. And I love that it's a priority to you to make sure I'm so lost in you and everything that you're doing to me. I've felt that way from the very first time we were together, and it's only gotten better every time since then."

"That's a lot of praise, gorgeous," I pointed out. "It seems like I've set the bar pretty high for myself. But I want you to know that it doesn't scare me. Because even though I want you to be satisfied with what I'm giving you every time we're together, it's never felt like work. I love being with you. And I love what I get from you just the same."

"I'm scared, though," she blurted.

As much as I didn't like hearing that, I already had a feeling I knew there was going to be fear lingering there for her.

"I've worked really hard to put my heart back together, Tyson. And now I'm giving it to you," she started. After she paused for a moment, I saw something shift in her features. When she opened her mouth again, tears filled her eyes, she begged, "Please protect it."

Overwhelmed by the emotion coming from her, I couldn't immediately respond. Instead, I swallowed hard past the lump in my throat and moved close to kiss her. When I pulled back, I'd gotten myself together enough to promise, "I will, Quinn. Always."

The moment the words were out of my mouth, I felt her limbs loosen on my body. I took that opportunity to roll to my back and take her with me. For the next little while, the two of us stayed like that, her body draped over mine as my hands traced delicately up and down her back.

"I love this, too," she suddenly shared.

"I'll be sure to keep that in mind then," I assured her. "Do you want to go clean up before we fall asleep like this or do you want me to get you a cloth?"

"I'll do it," she said.

"Kiss first," I ordered.

Quinn kissed me and then moved to the bathroom to clean up. When she came back to the bedroom, she slipped her nightie over her head and climbed in bed beside me. That's when I tucked her tight to me and thanked my lucky stars that Levi thought I'd appreciate being able to wake up to satin nighties.

Because I had no doubt that as long as Quinn was the one wearing them, they'd be my favorite thing to wake up to in the morning… or, if the mood struck one of us, the middle of the night, too.

CHAPTER 16

Quinn

"Just call her."

I bit my lip. "I can't," I hissed.

Tyson stood from the chair in the corner of our hotel room and stated, "Okay, two things. First, why are you getting agitated with me? And second, why can't you?"

I put one hand on my hip and shot back, "I'm getting agitated because I told you two times already I wasn't going to call her."

I was about to answer the second question he'd asked me when he cut in. "Then I'll just call him."

My eyes widened. "Oh no you won't," I warned him.

"Why not?"

I dropped my gaze to the ground and took a deep breath to calm myself. When I looked at Tyson again, I explained, "Because they're probably having sex. We are not going to interrupt them."

He cocked an eyebrow and wondered, "So, you're telling me that I had multiple failed attempts to even just kiss you because of your sister, and you're worried about the fact that she and Kyle are still having sex that we might interrupt?"

"Yes."

"It's nearly ten-thirty, Quinn. Check out is at eleven o'clock," he noted.

I insisted, "She'll call us. And if, by chance, she doesn't call by the time we need to check out, we'll go for a drive until one of them reaches out to us."

"Are you planning on going back to Windsor today?" he asked.

"Of course."

"With or without them?"

I shook my head and rolled my eyes. "They'll call."

As if by some divine intervention, my phone began vibrating on the nightstand. I picked it up, saw my sister's name, and answered, "Morning, Cass."

"Good morning," she chirped.

I smiled and teased, "I'll take that to mean you had a good night."

"Did I ever," she returned.

"Can't wait to hear all about it," I said. "But Tyson is ready for us to break out of this hotel. Are you guys ready for us to get over there, so we can start heading back to Windsor before it gets too late?"

"Um, well…" She trailed off and I knew she was distracted. Likely by Kyle.

"Cassie!" I shouted.

"Okay, okay. We'll be decent by the time you get here," she stated.

"You better be," I warned her.

"We will be. I promise."

With that, I disconnected the call with my sister and looked at Tyson.

"You can't wait to hear all about it?" he asked incredulously.

"What?"

He let out a laugh and shook his head. "You just told your sister that you couldn't wait to hear all about the good night she had," he clarified. "Are you serious with that statement?"

My eyes shifted back and forth as I tried to figure out what I missed that was upsetting him so much. "Uh, yeah?" I finally responded.

Tyson moved toward our suitcases and stated, "That's weird."

"Why?" I asked.

Turning around to look at me again, he said, "You're interested in hearing about your sister's sexual escapades. That seems odd to me."

I cocked an eyebrow and returned, "Well, you're obviously not a woman with a sister."

"You've got that right."

Unable to handle the absurdity of the conversation, I couldn't stop myself from laughing as I walked toward him. "And I love that you're not," I assured him as I slipped my hands around his waist. "But she's my sister, and I love her. I just want to make sure he was good to her."

"Kyle's my brother, and I love him to death. But that is not a conversation I ever want to have with him," he declared.

I frowned at him.

"I'm serious," he went on. "Not only is it not any of my business, but if I'm worried about him, I'm smart enough to figure out that if he appears happy and they continue to see each other, it's all good. I don't need him to share anything with me about it… especially not the details."

Realizing this was one of those topics we were so far apart on, I decided to put an end to it. "Let's just agree to disagree on this one."

Tyson acquiesced with conditions. "I'm good with that.

As long as you promise to make sure I know zero things about what you discuss with your sister regarding any of this."

"Deal."

Tyson was satisfied with that, so he bent to press a kiss to my lips. Then, he grabbed our bags and we managed to check out of the hotel before the deadline.

Fifteen minutes later, Tyson and I arrived at Cassie's. I never mentioned to Tyson that my sister had hinted at the possibility of her and Kyle not being finished when we arrived. I figured it wouldn't bode well for us to worry about something that may or may not be an actual issue. Thankfully, when we knocked on the door because I refused to use my key just in case, Kyle opened the door and was fully clothed.

"Morning," he greeted us.

Tyson narrowed his eyes at his brother. "It's basically afternoon."

I pressed my lips together to stop myself from bursting out laughing. When I got myself under control, I returned, "Good morning, Kyle. Where's Cass?"

"The bedroom."

"Then that's where I'll be," I announced.

"Yeah, she needs help finishing up her packing in there," he started. "Tyson and I will get the rest of this stuff moved to the car."

"Okay!"

I took off toward my sister's bedroom.

When I walked in, I found her standing at the side of her bed trying to pack up a bag with all of her cosmetics and toiletries. As soon as she looked up, I knew she was head over heels.

"Was he generous?"

"Orgasms were plentiful," she confirmed. "But it was so

much more than the number of them, Quinn. I didn't know it was possible to feel that much that many times."

I loved this for her.

"Once you could understand? But when they continued to not only be good but even better, then you started questioning it, right?"

Her eyes widened, realizing I understood and had put into words exactly how she felt. "Yes. And the fact that you're telling me this makes me so happy. It's going to continue, isn't it?"

I nodded slowly.

Cassie's eyes fluttered as she turned and fell to her back on her bed. "Gosh, Quinn, he's totally the best decision I've ever made. I know it's so new and I'm probably crazy for even admitting this, but honestly, it was like I could feel him falling in love with me."

I laid down on the bed beside her and assured her, "It's not crazy, Cass. Because while you felt him falling in love with you, I have no doubt you were falling for him, too."

She turned her head in my direction and rasped, "I'm scared."

"I know. But I think you already know based on how he's treated you that you're completely safe." After a brief pause, I blurted, "I told Tyson I love him."

Shock registered in her features. "Did he admit the same?" she asked.

"He said it first," I shared.

Cassie didn't respond. She didn't need to because her eyes filled with tears telling me everything she was thinking. Seeing it, mine did the same because I knew she was happy for me. She was there right after I found out Chris and Alicia betrayed me. My sister not only came to stay with me for a while immediately after, but she also stayed up many nights talking to me on the phone long after she'd returned home to Montana. She saw me through the worst time in my life, and I knew how much it hurt her to have to see it. I would have felt and done the same if the roles were reversed. Luckily, I didn't think I'd have to worry about that now that Kyle was in her life.

This moment for Cassie was, no doubt, like the end of a really bad dream. She was finally seeing me, her sister, happy again. And I understood her sense of relief over it because I felt it, too. With her help, I managed to put myself back together. And once I was healed, a man who clearly worshipped me walked into my life. There was no better feeling for me than to know that I had the strength to get through something like that and still come out the other side. The best part was that I had a feeling this time would be completely different and far, far better.

Minutes later, Kyle's voice filled the room. "I might be wrong, but I feel like we just walked into something bad."

Cassie and I looked to the door. There was nothing but worry and concern on the faces of the two brothers standing there looking back at us.

Wanting to quell their fears, I sat up and assured them, "No, it's not bad. Everything is actually really, really good."

Kyle shook his head and confessed, "Between our sisters and Josie, you'd think I'd have some kind of clue about how women work. I'm convinced I'll never understand."

"It's best in situations like this to just smile and nod, Kyle," Tyson advised.

I stood up and walked to Tyson while Kyle moved to Cassie. The second I was within arm's reach, Tyson tugged me toward him. His voice dipped low at my ear, and he asked, "Are you sure everything's okay?"

I nodded in his chest. "Yeah," I whispered.

"Okay," he returned. "We got everything moved out to the truck. Is there a lot left?"

I looked around the room, noted that most of it was empty save for her stuff on the bed, and confirmed, "I think it's just the bags on the floor over there and the stuff on her bed."

Tyson gave me a nod, but before he could say anything, Cassie declared, "I think before we leave Montana, we need to stop for lunch at Mo's."

I turned around to see Cassie was standing in Kyle's arms and exclaimed, "Yes! I haven't had Mo's in ages."

She swung her body back toward the bed and began throwing everything there into the open bag. Kyle moved to get her bags that were on the floor.

"What just happened here?" Tyson asked.

I directed my gaze back to his and shot him the saddest pair of puppy dog eyes I could muster up. "We have to go to Mo's before we leave," I pleaded with him. "Please?"

"I don't know what Mo's is, but it sounds like I should," he replied.

"You really should," I insisted. "I know it'll delay us getting back early tonight, but can we please make one more stop before we head home?"

Tyson held my gaze for a long time. For a moment I thought he was going to say that he would rather just get on the road, but he finally agreed by admitting, "I guess this is what love is. Giving the other person everything they want. No matter how silly it may seem."

I threw my arms around him and promised quietly in his ear, "You won't regret it. Even if you don't like Mo's, which is very unlikely, you still won't regret it. Because by loving me enough to give me the silly things that make me happy, you earn yourself things that'll make you happy."

"Like what?" he asked.

I pressed up on my toes again and whispered in his ear, "My mouth around your cock."

Tyson's arm tightened around my waist.

"Go help your sister finish packing up her stuff," he ordered. "We need to get to Mo's so I can get you back home."

I let out a laugh before I did as he asked.

Then, Tyson and Kyle took Cassie and me out to Mo's.

On the way there, I was grinning in my seat.

"What's your deal?" he asked. "Are you that excited over this place?"

I shook my head and said, "Actually yes, I am. But that's not why I'm so happy."

"So, tell me what's going on?"

"Are you sure you want to know?" I asked, but there was a warning in my question.

Tyson either must have missed it or completely ignored it because he said, "Of course I want to know. If it's making you smile like that and it's something I can do to put that smile there again, I'm going to do it."

"Okay, you asked for it," I began. "I'm this happy because as it turns out, it would seem that the Reed brothers are extraordinarily generous lovers. I was ecstatic having found that for myself. Knowing that my sister has it too is just icing on the cake."

"Stop," he demanded. "We had a deal."

I shrugged innocently. "You asked for it."

"Next time, if you know that the answer to the question is going to lead there, you need to explicitly warn me about it. Understood?"

I giggled uncontrollably in my seat, but ultimately agreed.

And ten minutes later, when we arrived at Mo's, all was forgotten.

Suffice it to say that Tyson and Kyle enjoyed it as much as my sister and I did. Even still, I knew that wouldn't get me out of my end of the deal… not that I wanted it to.

We were a mere three minutes away from my house when it happened.

I should have expected after all of the good things that were happening in my life lately that something bad was bound to happen. But it honestly never crossed my mind. Besides, who in their right mind would want to sit around thinking about and waiting for something bad to happen?

I'd dealt with enough strife over the year that followed my discovery of my ex-husband's infidelity. That was more than I cared to ever deal with. Not wanting to experience anything traumatizing again, I tried to always focus on the positive. And while I could admit I wasn't always a ball of sunshine and positivity, I thought I was doing a pretty good job of staying optimistic about all facets of my life.

Everything was going well.

In actuality, other than the fact that it wasn't until nearly three o'clock when we finally left Montana, the trip back home to Windsor had been relatively uneventful. We'd hit one slow spot on our way because of the one-lane traffic on a road that was undergoing construction. Beyond that, it was smooth sailing.

But when we were close to my house and I was rambling on and on to Tyson about something, he suddenly pulled off to the side of the road. He had done it so abruptly that it jerked me a bit in my seat. I looked over to ask him what he was doing when I heard the sirens.

That's when I saw a fleet of police cars speeding by with the lights on and the sirens blaring.

"Well, there goes that," I mumbled.

Tyson glanced over at me. It was pretty dark outside, so I couldn't make out all the details of his expression. "There goes what?" he asked.

"I was thinking I'd be able to give my parents a call to let them know we arrived back here safely, and that the trip was uneventful. Who would have thought it'd be when we were this close to home that there'd be all this excitement? Not that I'm saying the need for the police is exciting. I just mean that other than all my blabbering on about everything, the trip home has been quiet."

Before Tyson could respond to me, the sound of a phone ringing filled the cabin. I recognized the tone as Tyson's and watched as he pulled it out of his pocket.

"It's Levi," he declared. "Hang tight a minute."

I dipped my chin as he answered.

"Yeah?"

A pause while he listened. Then his eyes shot to mine.

"Yeah, she's right here with me. We left later than expected to come back and are less than five minutes from her house. What's going on?"

Silence again.

Tyson didn't respond, but he reacted. He kept his phone pinned between his ear and his shoulder while he maneuvered the truck back out onto the road. Then, he slammed his foot on the gas and took off.

I had no idea what was going on, but I knew it wasn't

good. There was an awful churning in my belly as a million scenarios raced through my mind.

"Alright, thanks for the heads up," Tyson said into the phone before he disconnected.

He tossed his phone down into the center console and sped up. What he didn't do was tell me what was going on.

I called, "Tyson?"

Nothing.

Then I realized why.

Because he'd pulled into my driveway.

And in it, I found that my home was where the police had been racing to.

CHAPTER 17

Quinn

"WHAT'S GOING ON?" I ASKED TYSON AS HE PUT THE truck in park at the top of my driveway.

With his hand already on the door handle, he ordered, "Stay here in the truck. Do not get out until I come to get you."

"Tyson!" I called, but he had already exited the vehicle.

I watched Tyson walk behind his truck to Cassie's car. Kyle was driving and had gotten out to talk to Tyson. After a very brief chat, Kyle nodded and got back in the car. Then, he backed up, turned the car around, and drove away.

As Kyle drove off with my sister, a police officer came over to Tyson. I could tell by their interaction that they knew each other. Beyond that, I didn't know anything else. I simply sat there in Tyson's truck waiting for him to come back to me.

And while I did, I wondered if this was simply another case of a malfunctioning alarm. Of course, I knew that if it was, that would mean that Tyson either hadn't done his job properly or he'd gotten a piece of equipment that was faulty. Deep down, I knew that wasn't the case.

It was at this moment that I wished I'd paid more attention to the news. I never really cared to watch it much mostly because there wasn't much good news being reported. Obviously, I knew it wasn't smart to think that nothing bad happened in the world, but I preferred not to fill my head with it every day. But it was at this moment that I wondered if the price of oblivion was too high. Not that I would have been able to prevent something from happening, but at least I would have known why there was a fleet of police cars in my driveway with their lights on as the officers moved around the perimeter of my house.

I contemplated getting out of Tyson's truck, but the rational part of my brain convinced me to stay right where I was. Even though it was my home and I had a right to know what was going on, I also knew that my area of expertise was not in apprehending criminals or even faulty security systems. So, I simply did as Tyson asked and waited.

Watched and waited.

I'd lost sight of Tyson at some point and grew restless.

I figured I'd do something to occupy my mind. Pulling out my phone, I sent a text to my sister.

Did Kyle tell you what's going on?

Cassie: No. Are you okay?

Me: Physically, yes. I'm still sitting in Tyson's truck. He told me to wait here.

Cassie: You've got more patience than I do.

Me: I don't want him to have to worry about me if there's something really wrong. I'd rather be right where he expects to find me.

Cassie: You've always been a smart girl.

Me: Mom and Dad will be expecting a call. You should let them know we're back in town. Don't tell them about this, though.

Cassie: Got it. Keep me updated. I want to know you're okay.

Me: I will.

Just then, there was a tap on my window. I practically jumped out of my seat at the sound. Tyson stood on the other side of the glass, so I unlocked the doors. Once he opened it, I asked, "Will you please tell me what's happening?"

"Someone broke into your house," he deadpanned.

I looked behind him to my house. While it was dark out, the lights from all the officers' vehicles lit up the front of my home. Nothing seemed out of the ordinary, and there wasn't anything that indicated to me that someone broke in.

When I returned my attention to Tyson, I asked, "How do you know?"

"I installed a security system in your house, Quinn," he began. "That alarm was tripped and sent a signal to the police as well as the Cunningham Security office."

That caught me off guard. While I knew that I hadn't really asked many questions about my security system, it dawned on me then that I hadn't actually asked him about monitoring.

"I didn't realize you guys did installations and monitoring," I shared.

"Typically, we don't," he confirmed. Then, he added, "Unless there's a reason to or a client specifically requests it."

Knowing that I didn't make any special requests, I asked "What was the reason to do that with mine then?"

His head tipped to the side and he stared at me, but he didn't respond.

When too much time passed without a reply, I called, "Tyson?"

"I did it because I wanted to make sure that if you were ever in trouble out here that my team and I would know.

Officer Kelley made a call to our office the day after your system malfunctioned weeks ago and told us what happened that night. He expressed how terrified you were, and once I saw you, I knew I wanted to make sure you felt safe. So, feeling uncomfortable with you being a single woman living alone without the monitoring on our end, I made it so I was no longer uncomfortable."

Wow.

I hadn't expected that.

"Oh," I whispered. Then, realizing I still didn't understand how he knew someone tried to break in, I asked, "Was someone inside?"

He shook his head.

"I don't understand then. How do you know someone tried to break in? The house looks fine. Did the alarm malfunction again?"

Tyson looked a bit insulted at the last question, but pushed past that and corrected, "Someone didn't try to break in, Quinn. They did break in."

Then, he held his hand out to me. I placed my hand in his and allowed him to walk me up to my house. We walked around the side of it and made it to the back. That's when I saw the proof that someone had broken in.

There were a few officers standing out on my deck, but I wasn't paying attention to them. Instead, I was staring at the gaping hole where the French doors that led from my home to the deck used to be. Technically, the doors were still there. But the windows had been smashed.

"Oh my God," I whispered.

Tyson put his arm around me and held me tight to his side. Before I could pull myself together enough to ask any questions, I saw someone approaching us from the corner of my eye. I looked to my right and saw Officer Kelley walking toward Tyson and me.

He dipped his chin to Tyson before he turned his attention to me and greeted, "Hi, Quinn."

"Officer Kelley," I returned.

"I'm sorry about what happened here tonight," he began. "But I want to let you know that we're going to do everything we can to find the people who did this."

"People?" I repeated.

Tyson's arm squeezed me a little tighter.

Nodding, Officer Kelley explained, "Yes, we believe there were at least two individuals involved."

"Evidence?" Tyson asked.

"Nothing tangible, but the fact that they came through the back here is a huge help. They walked up through the snow, so their shoes were wet. We can see two distinct sets of footprints on the hardwood floors. Detective Baines is on his way here, but we're photographing and collecting the evidence we can."

"Can I go inside?" I asked.

He shook his head. "I understand you want to go in your home, Quinn, but in order for us to have the best chance to catch the suspects, we don't want anyone in there right now who doesn't need to be."

My shoulders fell.

"Indication this was random?" That question came from Tyson.

But Officer Kelley didn't answer as our attention was drawn to the sound of approaching footsteps. I looked toward the front of the house, in the direction Tyson and I had come from, and saw Levi and Gunner approaching. After acknowledging everyone there, Levi asked, "What do we know?"

Officer Kelley insisted, "We've got this under control."

"Due respect, Officer," Levi returned. His eyes shifted to Tyson before they came to mine. After holding my gaze momentarily, he looked back to the officer and stated, "You know, as does Detective Baines, that we won't do anything to jeopardize the investigation. But she's ours. So, we're not sitting back on this one."

She's ours.

I didn't know exactly what that meant, but I knew I liked the way it made me feel.

Levi's words must have penetrated, because Officer Kelley finally acquiesced, "As I just mentioned to Quinn and Tyson, we know there are at least two suspects. Preliminarily, we're guessing this wasn't random. There haven't been any other similar break-ins over the last few weeks that would indicate this is linked to one of them."

Gunner looked over at my house and back to the group. "Someone possibly looking for a payoff?"

"What?" I asked.

Gunner explained, "If somebody was looking to burglarize a house that might net them the most amount of expensive goods, they'd presume your home was a good option. The cost of the home and the size of it tell someone that you might have something inside that's worth stealing."

That made sense. I didn't like hearing it, but it at least provided me with some explanation as to why someone would do this.

Or at least, it did. Until Officer Kelley spoke.

"That was our initial thought, but evidence suggests otherwise."

Now I was thoroughly confused.

Officer Kelley looked at Tyson momentarily before he

looked at me and asked, "Quinn, is there anything you believe someone would want to take from you?"

I felt Tyson's fingers press into my shoulder a little harder. He wasn't hurting me, but his reaction to that question made me nervous.

"No," I answered honestly.

"They didn't take anything, did they?" Tyson guessed.

"I obviously can't answer that conclusively, but that would be my guess. The obvious things usually taken during a random robbery attempt are still there. The laptop and electronics… they're all still there. If someone was looking for some quick cash, they'd have taken the valuable things in the house. That makes me believe that these people were looking for something specific."

What was going on?

Levi pressed, "Quinn, really think about this. Is there anything of yours that someone has ever expressed interest in?"

I thought about it. My home was probably the most valuable thing I owned. I didn't live a flashy lifestyle. I was smart with money and preferred to invest it wisely so that I could live comfortably.

Shaking my head, I insisted, "Beyond the actual house itself, I really don't own anything of substantial value. I invest my money. I'm not a huge spender. I buy what I need and little extras. Nothing extravagant. I honestly have no idea what someone would be looking for."

"Alright," Officer Kelley chimed in. "It's cold out here. Why don't you go and wait in your car, and as soon as Detective Baines arrives and we update him, we'll see what we're going to do. You know your house, you know what's inside. Maybe we'll have you walk through and see if there's anything missing. There's something we're overlooking here."

"Come on," Tyson urged me.

He led us back toward the front of the house while Levi and Gunner stayed with the officers behind the house.

Once we were inside the truck, Tyson took my hand in his.

"Are you okay?" he asked.

I shook my head. "I don't understand why this is happening," I admitted. "What am I going to do? I have a huge hole in the back of my house."

"I'll take care of it," Tyson assured me. "Once they're done here tonight, I'll board the place up. Then, I'll have Kyle come and help me repair everything."

I looked out the window at my home. Looking at it, I remember the day I signed on the dotted line. This home was supposed to be the beginning of my new life. If that new life involved getting burglarized for something I couldn't even figure out, it worried me to think what else was ahead.

"If I walk back in that house and don't see anything missing," I started. "What do we do next?"

"The first thing that's going to happen is I'm going to install cameras in there immediately. Once we fix the door and you're back in the house, you will always have your security system armed, even after we find whoever's behind this. That's all you'll need to worry about, though. Between the WPD and my guys at the office, we'll handle the rest."

I nodded because I think I was too emotionally drained to put up a fight.

But I couldn't stop thinking about something.

My body tensed, Tyson felt it, and called, "Quinn? Did you think of something?"

"Yeah. Why were all of you giving each other those looks back there? Everyone kept asking me if I owned something that someone would want to take. And it's hitting me now that regardless of the fact that I was asked that question and answered it once, I was asked that same question in a different way by someone else."

"Yeah," he agreed. "That's not uncommon. Sometimes, if you hear a question asked a different way, it might make you think differently."

"Right. I get that. But every time I said that there wasn't something specific that I owned that someone had expressed interest in or that would be of value to someone, you all looked at each other. Levi even pressed me to really think about it before I answered again. Why?" I demanded to know.

Tyson took in a deep breath before he confessed, "It's because we want you to come up with something, Quinn."

I shook my head. "I don't understand."

"We're hoping there's something because we don't want it to be the alternative," he explained.

"What's the alternative?" I wondered.

"If these people broke into your house and weren't looking for something specific, it might mean they were looking for someone specific."

"But I'm the only—" I stopped myself from finishing that statement and began to panic.

Before I could say anything, Tyson promised me, "Gorgeous, nobody is going to lay a hand on you."

My eyes filled with tears. "Somebody was looking for me?" I began to fret.

"Quinn, honey, listen to me," Tyson ordered. "I'm not going to let anything happen to you. I promise you that you'll be safe. But you've got to do what I say so that I can make sure you stay that way. Okay?"

I nodded.

"Good. Now that you're looking at this from a different perspective, is there anyone you can think of that would want to harm you or even just scare you?"

I shook my head. "No," I rasped.

Tyson put his hands under my arms and lifted me over the center console into his lap. "I'll keep you safe, Quinn. Do you trust me?"

"Yeah," I said softly before burying my face in his neck.

After that, Tyson and I didn't say anything else. He simply held me tight and pressed the occasional kiss to my forehead.

I wasn't sure how much time had passed when there was finally a tap on the window. I sat up and saw Gunner standing there. When Tyson opened the door, Gunner said, "They want to take her through the house now."

Tyson brought his gaze to mine. "Ready?"

I dipped my chin in response.

When we made it to the back of the house, I climbed the stairs to my deck and was carefully ushered through the opening in the doorway over the shattered glass. I had gone in expecting to see the worst, but other than the broken glass and the few wet spots on the floor, the rest of the house looked just as I left it.

I was carefully escorted through the house by Detective Baines and Officer Kelley while Tyson followed closely behind us. We went through each room and I took a quick visual inventory. Nothing jumped out at me as being out of place or missing.

As much as I should have been relieved to see that everything was as it should have been, I wasn't. Because with every room I entered being as I left it before I went home to Montana, I realized that what Tyson said in the truck was probably the case.

Whoever broke into my house wasn't looking for something specific. They were looking for someone. They were looking for me.

"It's all here," I stated.

Then I watched as the jaws of the three men in front of me clenched. Detective Baines was the first to recover.

"Thank you, Quinn, for coming in to check it out."

"If you don't need anything else right now, I'm going to get her out of here," Tyson announced.

"Sure."

Tyson held his hand out to me. I took it, and he led us back through the house. We found Levi and Gunner at the back entrance.

"I'm going to call Beau," he said to them. "Kyle's got Quinn's sister with him, so I'm going to have Beau come over and board the place up temporarily. Can you guys help him out when Detective Baines and his crew are done? I want to get Quinn out of here."

Levi and Gunner both nodded. Levi assured him, "We'll take care of it. I'll reach out tomorrow, and we'll figure out a game plan."

Tyson dipped his chin and replied, "Thanks."

When we were back in the truck, Tyson turned it on and started to back up so he could turn around.

"Would you mind taking me to the store real quick?" I asked.

"The store?" he repeated.

"Yeah, I need to get a set of bedsheets."

Tyson was about halfway down my driveway and stopped right in the middle of it. "What do you need bedsheets for?" he wondered.

"Well, I took everything out of my rental apartment a few

weeks ago when you helped me. There's still a bed there, but I don't have any sheets on it."

Tyson gave me a look of disbelief and declared, "It's official. You're crazy."

"What?"

"You're not staying at your apartment complex, Quinn," he instructed, but his tone left no room for debate. "You're coming home with me."

Given the seriousness of his tone, I pressed my lips together. I wasn't going to fight him on it partly because he was so serious, but mostly because I didn't want to be alone.

"You're good with that, I see," he noted.

I just nodded in return.

Then, Tyson turned his attention out the front window before he started driving.

And by the time he got us back to his place, he had managed to call both of his brothers to let them know what had happened and what he needed them to help him do that night and over the coming days. Hearing him talk with them calmly and without any fear in his voice helped to make me feel better. But it wasn't until we were in his bed and his arms were tucked tight around me that I truly settled into the fact that I knew that Tyson would do anything to keep me safe.

CHAPTER 18

Quinn
Two weeks later

"Okay, I've got everything all boxed up and ready to go," I declared.

"And I have all the paperwork ready for him," Cassie assured me. "Did Tyson get back yet?"

I shook my head. "No, but he called me a few minutes ago and let me know he was on his way," I told her.

Today I was going to be meeting with Patrick to deliver the necklace, earrings, and engagement ring I'd designed and made for him so that he could finally get to work on putting his plan into motion. It felt like it had taken forever to get to this point, especially when I was also dealing with everything else that had happened lately.

Three days after I returned from Montana with Tyson, my sister, and Kyle, I was finally able to move back into my house. I had been staying with Tyson at his place, which I actually enjoyed, but I was excited to go back home.

I loved my house. It symbolized the start of my new life after heartbreak. I'd been able to heal and find love again in this house. Literally.

So, being able to return meant a lot to me.

Of course, Tyson refused to let me go back until he was convinced that my home was secure. So, he enlisted the help of Kyle and Beau to get the repair and replacement of my French doors expedited. And while his brothers worked on that, Tyson installed a surveillance system in the house.

I tried not to think too much about the break-in. While the perpetrators still hadn't been caught, I knew the WPD, Tyson, and his team at Cunningham Security were doing everything they could to solve the case. And until they had a better idea of who was behind it, Tyson was being diligent about my safety. I told him I trusted him; I was going to prove that.

He'd been spending every night with me, and I couldn't say that I minded that because I loved waking up with him in the morning. Plus, going to bed every night after he made love to me wasn't something about which to complain.

So, I did my best to focus on the positives since the break-in, and that helped to distract me from the harsh reality of the whole situation.

Aside from the fact that Tyson was basically living with me for the time being, I had quite a few other things that consumed my thoughts. Most of those things were with regard to my business.

First and foremost, Cassie was officially working with me. As my new, first, and only employee, she was the best decision I'd made. I was thankful every day that she decided to move here because having her physically present was even more beneficial than when she'd been helping me out from a distance those two weeks before she moved.

She focused her efforts on cleaning up my website by getting my jewelry listed there and showcasing some of the custom pieces I'd made in a gallery there. In addition, she handled nearly all of my client communications. Unless an individual was looking for a custom piece, I didn't typically get involved. Cassie was just as much of an accessories junkie as me, so she knew enough about the pieces I was building to get by. When she was unsure of something, she came and asked about it. As time went on, I had no doubt that she'd learn more, and it'd be even easier for her. Essentially, if it wasn't the actual designing or building of the jewelry, and it was related to my business, my sister was handling it for me. I honestly had no idea how I'd ever managed to do it without her.

The best thing that happened over the last two weeks was that the diamond for the engagement ring I'd designed for Patrick was delivered. As soon as it arrived, I got to work and finished the ring. I emailed Patrick when it arrived and told him that I hoped to have it done by the end of this week. He told me to keep him posted because he wanted to make a trip out to see everything and pick it up.

Getting down to it, I spent my time doing nothing else but the ring. I managed to finish everything two days ago and called him right away. I figured it was the kind of thing that warranted a phone call and not an email.

Patrick was overjoyed at the news. He planned a trip out to Windsor and called me back to confirm the details.

Today was that day.

And while I'd managed to have some other big things happen over the last few weeks, such as Lily Mack wearing my jewelry at her red-carpet event, this one felt different to me. I didn't know if it was because it was my first big project that had essentially launched my career into overdrive, or if it was because this particular project was about someone else's new beginning. Either way, I was extremely proud.

In fact, I was so proud and thankful, that I wanted to celebrate it in a meaningful way with my sister.

So, now that we had everything ready for Patrick's arrival, I said, "Since we have a little bit of time before Patrick arrives, I want to show you something I made."

"When did you make something else?" she asked. "You've been working on the ring all week."

I smiled and agreed, "Yeah, but I had an idea for this when you took over my emails and other stuff back when you were in Montana. I started it then and finished it up after I got the ring done. Let me go grab it."

When I returned a few minutes later, I held the jewelry box out to her. Cassie took it from my hand and opened it.

Her eyes widened as she marveled, "Wow, Quinn. This is beautiful."

"Really? Do you like it?"

"It's gorgeous," she expressed. "I have no doubt that this one isn't going to last long once I add it to the website."

"I don't want it on the website," I stated.

She tore her eyes from the delicate, feminine diamond necklace featuring a cluster of hearts that I'd crafted and looked at me, utterly astounded. "Why not?" she asked. "This is my favorite piece you've ever made."

Hearing that made what I was about to do even more special. "I made it for you, Cass," I finally shared.

"What?" she questioned me, her shock clear as day.

Not wanting to get emotional, but knowing I wouldn't be able to hold back how I felt about her, I rasped, "You've always been there for me since day one. But I know I wouldn't have survived the last year if it weren't for you. And I wanted to do something to show you how much I appreciate all your love, support, and loyalty. I couldn't have asked for a better sister, Cassidy."

Her eyes filled with tears. "Quinn…" She trailed off.

"I don't know what I'd do without you," I whispered.

Cassie moved toward me and threw her arms around my neck. She hugged me tight for a long time, her tears soaking through the fabric at the shoulder of my shirt.

"Cass," I eventually called.

She pulled away and swiped at her cheeks.

"I love you, Quinn. I'd do anything for you," she murmured.

"I know. That's why I wanted to do something special for you."

My sister looked back down at the necklace one more time. When she looked at me again, she asked, "Will you put it on me?"

I nodded and took it from her. I hooked the necklace around her neck and watched as she marveled at it in the mirror on my wall.

"It's so pretty and feminine," she started. "I love that you made something that I can wear every day. It's the perfect piece for everyday wear or for dressing up. I love it."

"I'm so glad," I told her.

"Sometime this weekend, I'll take really good pictures of it, and then we'll get it up on the site for you to sell. You'll make a fortune off these, Quinn."

I took in a deep breath before I insisted, "I'm not making any more of those."

"Why not?" she asked as she spun around to look at me.

"It's a custom piece that I made specifically for you, Cassie. You're the only one who's going to have one. Well, besides me. I want them to be just for us. I know they would sell well, but I'm not interested in the money. What matters to me is you."

Cassie held her hand up and gently touched one of the hearts on the necklace.

Before she could say anything, there was a knock at the door.

"That's got to be Tyson," I announced as I walked out of the room toward the front door.

As soon as I opened the door, Tyson took one look at me, jerked his head to my shoulder, and asked, "What happened to your shirt?"

I glanced down at it and explained, "Cassie was crying."

"What's wrong?" he wondered as he closed the door behind him.

"I gave her the present I made for her. Remember that necklace I showed you with the cluster of hearts?" I reminded him.

He raised his brows and nodded. "And that made her cry?" he asked.

I shrugged and smiled. "She's crazy. What can I say?"

Tyson let out a laugh. "I don't know anyone else like that," he teased as he pulled me into a hug.

I tipped my head back so he could kiss me.

When he pulled back, he asked, "Have you heard from Patrick?"

Shaking my head, I replied, "No, so I'm guessing he's on his way and will be here shortly."

Tyson didn't want to interfere with my work, but given the fact that my home had been broken into two weeks ago, he wasn't real keen on having a man I didn't personally know in my home without him there.

I didn't have any concerns about Patrick, but I knew how important it was to Tyson that Cassie and I weren't left alone. So, I agreed to having him there. He wasn't going to be sitting on top of us, but he would be visible.

About ten minutes after Tyson arrived, the doorbell rang.

Patrick Dane was here.

I opened the door and greeted him by extending my hand to him. "Hi, Patrick. I'm Quinn. It's so nice to finally meet you in person."

"Likewise," he returned as he took my hand in his with a firm grip.

"Come on in," I urged after he let go.

Once he was in the house, my sister walked out into the foyer. "Patrick, this is my sister, Cassidy," I introduced them. "She's been working with me for the last month and is the reason I was able to get the ring finished up so quickly after the diamond was delivered."

"It's a pleasure to meet you," Patrick said to her.

"If you want, I'll take your coat," I offered. "Cassie can take you inside and get you a drink while I hang it up."

Patrick gave me his coat and followed Cassie out of the foyer. I hung his coat and moved to join them. When I did, I found that Tyson had already walked up and introduced himself. He quickly excused himself so that he was far enough away to give us privacy, but close enough that he could still see us.

Wanting to waste no time, I pulled out the necklace, bracelet, earring, and ring boxes. I opened each individually starting with the necklace.

Patrick lifted it from the table, analyzed it, and said, "It's stunning."

I smiled at him and held the open earring box out to him. He studied them much the same way he did the necklace before he shared, "They're perfect."

After I'd opened and shown him the bracelet, which he also loved, I opened the ring box, turned it around, and handed it to him. He stared at it a moment before he even took it from my hands. When he finally did, I watched his face. His throat bobbed up and down as he swallowed hard. He clenched his jaw several times, and his eyes got glassy. I saw him quickly blink away the emotion before he spoke. And when he did, he did it continuing to stare at the ring. "This is her ring," he rasped. He cleared his throat and went on, "It's exquisite. Just like her."

"I'm guessing you like it all?"

He set the ring box down in front of him and brought his attention to me. "I know I saw the sketches you did and the pictures you sent when you finished the necklace, bracelet, and the earrings, but there's something about seeing them all in person. And the ring is just… I can't believe I'm going to see this on her finger for the rest of our lives. Thank you so much, Quinn. You've done a phenomenal job."

I was so relieved to hear his compliments. Even though he'd approved the designs and insisted I'd captured his girlfriend's style right off the bat, it was still nerve-wracking to watch his initial reaction. Getting the praise from him in person helped solidify my confidence in what I was doing.

"Thank you, Patrick. I'm so thrilled that you like everything. This was truly a wonderful experience for me, and I'm so honored you trusted me with it," I informed him.

"Well, you're certainly worthy of it. And I hope the referrals I've sent your way have all panned out. I know that I saw a couple of your pieces on Lily Mack at her event recently," he offered.

"Yes. I had a feeling that you were the reason they found me," I stated. "Ever since Lily's event, I've been so busy. That's why I'm so relieved my sister finally decided to move here and join me in this."

Patrick looked at Cassie and noted, "Your sister is a talented woman."

Cassie smiled genuinely and replied, "I know. She's the best. Look at this necklace she made for me."

Cassie brushed her hair away from her neck, so Patrick had a clear view of it. "It's gorgeous," he affirmed.

For the next hour or so, Cassie and I sat and talked with Patrick about his plans for the proposal. He was planning to ask his girlfriend within the next month, so the jewelry being complete was perfect timing.

After we visited for a bit with each other, Patrick transferred the final payment to me electronically, signed a few documents acknowledging his receipt of the jewelry, and gathered up his purchase so he could leave.

Cassie and I both walked him to the door, thanked him again, and waved as he pulled away.

"Well, that's it," I declared as we leaned our backs against the door. "My first big custom project is complete."

"And he couldn't have been happier with it either," she added. "I'm so proud of you, Quinn. You deserve all the success in the world."

I tilted my head and rested it on her shoulder. "I meant what I said earlier, Cass," I started. "I never would have made it here without your support. It means everything to me to know that I can count on you."

"You'd do the same for me," she noted. "No matter what I need, I know you'd be there to help me in any way you could."

"Always."

"Good. How about we celebrate tonight with a game night? Since we're doing girls' night tomorrow with Kendra, Vera, and Josie, we should have dinner and game night with Kyle and Tyson tonight," she suggested.

I lifted my head from her shoulder, looked at her, and

grinned. "That's a great idea!" I exclaimed. "You call Kyle, and I'll run out to the kitchen and tell Tyson our plans."

"Perfect."

We did just that.

And we all ended up having such a great night filled with fun, food, and family. By the time Tyson and I went to bed hours later, after we'd made love, thoughts of someone attempting to burglarize my home were long gone.

At that point, there wasn't anything that could ruin all the good that I'd experienced all day. I had just finished my first big custom project, delivered that project to my client, spent time with family and friends, and ended my night wrapped up in the arms of a man who'd made me feel like I was the most precious thing in the world.

Yeah.

I definitely didn't have any reason to complain.

CHAPTER 19

Quinn

TYSON'S GROANS FILLED THE AIR IN THE SHOWER.

"I love your mouth, gorgeous," he said, his voice husky.

"Mmm."

That was the only response I could give him since I was squatting down in front of him in my huge shower with his penis filling my mouth. I looked up at him, and the moment his eyes connected with mine, I couldn't miss the fire burning in them.

Tyson made it clear that he not only liked the feel of my mouth on him, but that he also thoroughly enjoyed watching me take him in my mouth. Always seeking to give him even just a small fraction of what he gave me on an almost daily basis when we were intimate, I tried to make sure I put forth my best effort. I was never sure if he ever got out of it the same thing I did when he had his mouth on me, but he never gave me any complaints. So, I took that to mean good things.

I had one of my hands curled around his thick, muscled thigh while the other was at the root of his cock. I had been alternating between swirling my tongue around the tip of him and taking just the head into my mouth. Occasionally, I'd mix it up and suck all of him in. But I mostly focused my attention on the head because I wanted to drive him crazy.

Unfortunately, in doing so, I ended up driving myself crazy. Because I liked Tyson's penis. A lot. And once I'd had just a bit of it, I always wanted more. So, it was just as torturous for me to tease Tyson as I knew it had to be for him.

When I finally reached the point that I could no longer hold back, I didn't. I gave him all of it. I took him in my mouth as far as I could, feeling him start to go down the back of my throat. And when I did it, I wasn't slow or gentle. I was all about feeding my desire to please him. That was my only concern. Making sure Tyson wasn't disappointed with what I delivered.

His hand was in my hair, gently cupping the back of my head. He never forced me to move faster or take more of him; he allowed me to set the pace and took whatever I gave. Until, he didn't.

Until he decided he needed to give to me.

Tyson pulled his hips back, lifted me up, and pressed my back against the wall. Not even a second later, I had his cock back. Only this time, it was between my legs.

"Tyson," I moaned.

"Love your mouth, Quinn," he grunted as he powered into me. "Love you."

Then, before I could return the sentiment, he captured my mouth and kissed me hard. He didn't stop until he'd given me far more than I gave him. He didn't stop until I was a mess of quivering, trembling limbs. And it was only then that he allowed himself to have what I'd wanted to give him from the start.

That was Tyson.

My unselfish, generous lover.

Later, after we'd gotten out of the shower, Tyson and I were downstairs having breakfast discussing our plans for the day.

"So, I get you this morning," I began. "Then, Kyle brings my sister here, takes you, and I'll have her, Kendra, Vera, and Josie tonight. Right?"

Tyson shook his head. "No. You get me this morning and afternoon. And once girls' night has concluded, you'll have me tonight, too."

I smiled through a mouthful of eggs. "Sounds like I'm the one who gets to have all the fun today."

Tyson took a few bites of his bacon before he asked, "So, what's on the agenda for girls' night?"

I shrugged. "You just never know what craziness we'll get up to, but I will say that complaining about men is probably going to be in there for sure."

"And what exactly is it that you have to complain about?" he wondered.

I cocked an eyebrow and answered, "Lots of things actually. But my biggest complaint might be the fact that you don't ever seem to want to let me see you through to the end."

Tyson put his fork down and stared at me. "Are you serious?"

"Um, a little."

"You're upset about the fact that I want to see to you first and that I'm not just concerned with myself?"

I looked down at my plate and murmured, "I want to make you feel good."

"Quinn, gorgeous, look at me," he demanded.

When he had my gaze, he promised, "You do make me feel good. You make me feel fucking amazing. But you'll always be the priority. I don't come in your mouth, or anywhere else for that matter, if I haven't taken care of you first."

"But there are times when you make it just about me," I pointed out. "Or there are times when I have several orgasms to your one."

"And?"

"And I'm saying that it wouldn't be a problem if I was able to give to you every now and then," I explained.

"You want it to just be all about me?" he asked incredulously.

"I mean, not every time. But here and there might be nice," I suggested.

He pondered this for a minute before he took another bite of his bacon. After he chewed and swallowed, he decided, "Fine. You can make it all about me on my birthday."

"When's that?" I asked.

"September twentieth."

"That's so far away!" I cried.

He grinned and teased, "Looks like I've got a long time to get you all stocked up then."

"I'm so far in the black, Tyson. There's no chance I'm going to go through my reserve."

Tyson simply shook his head and continued eating. After a bit of silence stretched between us, he asked, "When's yours?"

"When's mine?"

"Your birthday," he clarified.

"May second."

"Soon," he declared.

I huffed. "Don't remind me. Pretty soon I'm going to be as old as you."

"You're not old," he assured me.

"I never said I was old. I said you were," I corrected him.

Tyson set his fork down, pushed his plate away, and leaned over to kiss me on the temple. After he did, he whispered, "I love my crazy girl."

Then, he got up, rounded the island, and loaded the dishes in the dishwasher.

It was early evening by the time Kyle arrived with Cassie. While she had her own car and could have easily driven herself to my place, Kyle insisted on bringing her. It was likely that there'd be consumption of wine tonight, so she wasn't going to be driving. Given that Tyson had spent the better part of the day with me, we decided that when Kyle dropped Cassie off, he'd pick Tyson up.

And since Josie was pregnant, she was the designated driver who'd be responsible for transporting not only herself but also Kendra and Vera.

I was excited for girls' night. Prior to my divorce, Alicia had really been the only person outside of my husband with whom I spent my time. It didn't bother me that I only had her. She was my best friend, and I truly believed that it was never about the quantity but rather about the quality of the people. Of course, it sadly turned out that she wasn't exactly the high-caliber friend I'd imagined for myself.

So, now that I had my sister close by again, I knew I had more than I'd ever need. But the addition of Kendra, Vera, and Josie was a huge bonus. While I still had some nerves about the size of Tyson's family, a small gathering like this didn't give me the same anxiety.

I was in the kitchen putting together my charcuterie and cheese board when Cassie walked in followed by Tyson and Kyle.

"Hey, Cass," I greeted, barely glancing up at her.

"Oh, you're the best," she returned. "I'm starving."

Not caring in the least that I wasn't finished, Cassie walked right over and stole a few crackers, some meat, and a couple cubes of cheese from the board.

"Hi, Kyle," I said, trying to ignore the fact that she'd just created more work for me.

He chuckled and returned, "Quinn."

"Are you starving, too?" I asked. "Would you like an appetizer?"

He shook his head. "No, thanks, I'm good."

When I returned my attention back to what I was doing, Cassie reached over and grabbed more food.

"Stop taking them from the board," I scolded her. "You could at least take the block of cheese over there and cut yourself a piece."

"That will delay the food getting to my belly, Quinn. I'm famished and can't be bothered right now with that. Besides, you offered Kyle some food."

I sent a death glare her way and explained, "He's a guest."

"And what am I?" she challenged. "Besides, he's technically not a guest. He's not staying."

I rolled my eyes and shook my head just as the doorbell rang.

"I'll get it," Tyson declared, clearly not wanting to be involved in the sibling dispute.

Once he walked away, I looked at my sister and asked, "Can you peel yourself off that stool and grab my stemless wine glasses?"

Cassie grumbled about it but still did what I asked.

Seconds later, Kendra, Vera, and Josie entered the kitchen with Tyson following close behind them.

"Hi, ladies," I greeted them.

"Hi, Quinn," Vera returned. "Hey, Cassie."

"Hey, girls," Kendra greeted us.

"Quinn, this house is magnificent," Josie marveled. "Hi, Cass."

"Thank you. I'll give you all the grand tour later."

Kendra turned toward her brothers. "So, what's on the agenda for you two tonight?" she asked. "Because you're not staying here."

I pressed my lips together to stop myself from laughing. No matter what the situation was, Kendra's personality was always the same. She cut to the chase and being in someone else's home wasn't going to change that about her.

"Heading to Beau and Josie's. Tony and Dave are coming with the kids, and we promised to deliver on our duties as the fun uncles," Tyson shared.

Kendra spun around and looked at Vera and Josie. "Did you two know about this?" she asked. "Tony never mentioned it to me."

"I knew," Josie confirmed. "I think Beau knew it'd be hard to cover up the fact that there were eight kids and five adults in the house."

"Dave told me last night," Vera added. "I told him I didn't care what he did. The only rule was that he had to keep himself and the kids alive."

Cassie burst out laughing.

"Everyone will be alive, Vera," Kyle assured her. "We should head out."

"Yes," Kendra agreed. "Go and spend time with your nieces and nephews so that hopefully you'll be inspired one day very soon to help us grow this family."

I bit my lip as Tyson's eyes came to mine.

The girls didn't miss it.

"What was that?" Josie asked.

I shook my head.

"Nothing," Tyson insisted.

Vera wasn't buying it. In fact, I was convinced that none of them were, but Vera was the one who decided to push it. "That wasn't nothing. There was definitely a look there. What was that all about?"

"Vera," Tyson called.

When her eyes went to his, he repeated, "It's nothing." There was an edge to his tone that clearly indicated the discussion was over.

She noted how serious he was, her expression changed, and she gave him a slight nod.

Cassie moved to Kyle, gave him a quick kiss, and said goodbye. The rest of us did the same, minus the kiss. Kyle started walking to the front door.

Then, Tyson looked at me and urged, "Walk me to the door."

I stopped what I was doing, rounded the island, and walked with him. By the time we made it to the door, Kyle had already walked out. Tyson stood at the entrance, curled his fingers behind my neck, and lowered his mouth to mine. He gave me several soft touches with his lips against mine before he completely captured my mouth and seriously kissed me. When he pulled back, he said, "If you want to discuss it, I have no problems at all with that. But if you don't want to talk about it, don't let them force you. The talk of children and having a family is between me and you. And it's okay if you want to keep it that way."

"I appreciate that, Tyson. They don't mean any harm, though," I assured him.

"I know they don't," he insisted. "But that doesn't mean you should have to feel uncomfortable."

"I understand. I'll only discuss what I'm comfortable with sharing."

He gave me a nod of approval and ordered, "Lock the door and set the alarm after I'm out, okay?"

"I will," I promised.

After giving me one more kiss, Tyson whispered against my lips. "I love you."

I smiled against his and returned, "I love you, too."

"Have fun."

"You too!"

With that, he turned and walked out. I did as I promised him by locking the door and setting the alarm.

When I walked back into the kitchen, I was relieved to find the girls talking amongst themselves.

"Okay, ladies," I interrupted the conversation. "Do you want me to order something special in?"

"I could totally go for a pizza from Sal's," Josie announced.

"The pregnant lady has spoken," I began. "Anybody want anything else from there?"

The girls all chimed in with their food requests, and I called the order in for delivery. Given that it was a Saturday night, I shouldn't have been surprised that they said it'd take closer to an hour for the delivery. It wasn't a huge deal, though, because I had plenty of finger foods to hold us over until it arrived.

Thirty minutes after I'd ordered it, the doorbell rang.

"Wow," I marveled, noting the time. "Apparently, Sal's is the epitome of under promise and over deliver."

I grabbed the money I'd pulled out after I placed the order and moved to the door. After disabling the alarm and unlocking the door, I opened it and realized Sal's wasn't over delivering.

Because instead of finding the delivery driver standing there, I found myself staring down the barrel of a gun.

And the person holding it was my former best friend.

CHAPTER 20

Quinn

"Where is it?"

Just over a year ago, I looked into the eyes of the woman standing in front of me, as she pretended to feel sorry about the fact that she was having an affair with my husband. I didn't believe then that Alicia was sorry for what she'd done to betray my trust and our friendship. Now that I was seeing her for the first time since then and she had a gun pointed at me, there was no doubt she was pure evil.

"What?" I nervously asked.

As much as I wanted to scream and yell at her, the firearm aimed at my head had me holding myself back. Tyson may have called me crazy from time to time. Maybe he was right about that in some cases. But I knew my limits on crazy. And this was one of those situations where I'd definitely get a hold on it.

"The diamond," she seethed. "Where is the diamond?"

"Hey, Quinn, do you need any hel—" Josie stopped dead in her tracks. I never turned around to see her because I refused to take my eyes off of what was right in front of me.

"Go back to the kitchen, Josie," I instructed.

"Don't move," Alicia ordered. I never heard any

movement, so I assumed Josie stayed put. Alicia brought her attention to me again. "Talk."

I didn't say anything.

Instead, I stood there trying to figure out how it was possible that I never saw her for the kind of woman that she was. I'd known her for years, shared my joys and triumphs with her and allowed her to comfort me in my times of tragedy and sorrow.

Until, of course, she became one half of the equation in what was probably the worst thing I'd ever experienced in my life.

That is, until this very moment.

Having a gun pointed at me made me realize that learning that my ex-husband and my ex-best friend were liars and cheaters wasn't the worst thing that could happen to me.

No.

Not at all.

The worst thing that could happen to me would be getting shot in the face and killed by said ex-best friend after I'd managed to pick myself up and put myself back together. After I'd found someone who loved and honored what I had with him. That would be tragic.

When I made no attempt to honor Alicia's request, she stepped inside the house. What happened next wasn't what I expected either. Instead of closing the door, she moved to the side and allowed someone to walk in behind her. A large masked man dressed in black. Based on his build, I knew he wasn't Chris.

Suddenly, this situation went from bad to worse.

Because following our separation, Chris had shown a shred of decency as we worked through the divorce. Maybe he regretted what he'd done and that was his way of communicating his apology. Or maybe he was happy to finally have the betrayal out in the open so he could take the steps to be finished with me. Either way, I didn't have to deal with a lot of strife to completely dissolve our marriage.

So, seeing this other man now made me curious about what was happening. Part of me wondered how and if Chris was involved in this.

I hated to think that I'd been *that* bad a judge of character. Because if I was, what did I stand to deal with moving forward in my life? Assuming, obviously, that I survived this.

The second the man closed the door, I tensed.

And the reason I tensed was because another person was about to be put at risk. I heard Kendra's voice before she was visible to anyone.

"What is the holdup out here?" she asked. "We're hungry."

When her footsteps suddenly stopped, I knew she'd seen what the holdup was.

"Oh, no," she started, sounding irritated that her evening had been interrupted by a gun-wielding bitch and her muscle. "What is this all about?"

I was fond of Kendra. Really, I was. But I didn't think her sassy personality would bode well in this situation.

"Where is the diamond?" Alicia repeated.

"What diamond?" I asked, playing stupid.

"The one for the engagement ring you designed for Patrick Dane," she clarified. "Where are you hiding it?"

Shaking my head, I answered, "I don't have it."

"Bullshit," she shouted. "I saw the emails. I know it was supposed to be delivered to you a little over two weeks ago."

She saw my emails? How did she see my emails?

Before I could respond, Kendra stepped in. "Why do you want a diamond that's not yours?" she asked.

I figured there was a pretty obvious answer to that question but didn't think now was the right time to point that out.

"Kendra," I called, hoping my tone indicated that I was warning her not to get involved.

Kendra ignored me and pressed, "I'm serious. Why do you want something that clearly does not belong to you?"

Alicia's eyes darted back and forth between me and Kendra.

"Alicia, I don't have it. The ring was completed and picked up yesterday."

She narrowed her eyes at me and hissed, "I don't believe you."

"It's true," Cassie's voice confirmed from behind me.

I closed my eyes, feeling fear come over me. It was bad enough I had a pregnant Josie and the exuberant Kendra standing here with me. Now, my sister was involved. And on a scale of Josie to Kendra, she definitely leaned more toward Kendra. I had no doubt she'd get involved beyond what was safe, and she'd be very vocal about it.

"Cass," I whispered.

"You think I'm going to take your word for it, Cassidy?" Alicia bit out. "I know you're lying. You never emailed Patrick with pictures of the completed ring. You never even emailed him to tell him it was finished."

"How did you even get into her emails?" Kendra asked.

"I've known Quinn for years," she started. "It wasn't hard to figure out her password."

I made a mental note at that point that once I got out of this mess that I was going to change every password for all of my online accounts, emails, banking, and the like.

"I called him," I explained. "He was here yesterday afternoon, and he picked up everything."

"You're lying," she insisted.

"I'm not."

"Where was it two weeks ago then? If it was just picked up yesterday, why couldn't I find it here then?"

I tried to ignore the fact that she'd just admitted she was one of the two people who'd broken into my house and the fact that it was probably the man standing next to her that was the other and shared, "It wasn't delivered until a few days after I got back from Montana. Delivery was delayed, and so I told them to wait until I returned."

"You had the necklace and earrings done before that," she shot back. "I saw the pictures of them. Where were they?"

"They were here in the house," I admitted.

"We searched this place," she confessed. "There was nothing here that even indicated you did jewelry. You need to stop messing with me and start telling the truth. I want that diamond."

Cassie cut in and offered, "I can get you the paperwork Patrick signed indicating he picked it up yesterday."

Alicia's eyes shot to my sister. While it was evident she wanted the proof, I had a feeling part of her was nervous about the fact that we were actually telling the truth. And even though I understood the value behind the diamond, I just didn't understand why she was willing to go to these lengths to get this diamond.

"I'll just go get it right now," Cassie decided.

I heard her movement before Alicia shifted and pointed the gun at Cassie. "Stop."

My eyes flew to my sister and silently pleaded with her to listen to what Alicia was ordering her to do. Thankfully, she did as she was demanded to do.

"Go with her," Alicia ordered the man next to her. "She's

not leaving here and running off to call the police. She gets the proof, and then she's right back here."

I watched as the man moved toward my sister, prayed that he'd only escort her to my office where the paperwork was, and follow her back.

I was actually surprised that while Cassie and this man were gone, nobody said anything. I was also acutely aware of the fact that Vera hadn't come out to see where we'd all gone. It was my hope that she realized something was wrong and called somebody for help.

When Cassie returned, she started walking toward Alicia.

"Not another step," Alicia ordered. "Give the paper to him."

Cassie stopped and handed it off. He brought it over and gave it to Alicia. She looked at it, and I immediately saw the change in her features. She thought we were bluffing.

"Seems like you're not going to get what you came here for," Kendra taunted her. My gaze went to her, but she wasn't paying any attention to me. Instead, Kendra asked, "How do you two even know each other?"

That's when I didn't hesitate to respond. "Alicia and I used to be friends. But then she slept with my husband, who's obviously now my ex-husband."

Saying the words out loud made me grow angry. I directed my attention to Alicia and asked, "What are you doing here? Why were you even trying to get this diamond?"

She remained silent a long time with the gun still trained on me. Her voice broke when she shared, "He's always working."

I was completely caught off guard by her admission. It wasn't that I was surprised by what she said; I was simply not expecting her to tell me about it.

I was even more astounded when she continued to provide details. "If he's not working, he's hanging out with his buddies or sitting on the couch watching a game. He used to be so attentive. We made all these plans about what we'd do once you were no longer in the picture. He promised me vacations, shopping trips, massages, and facials. The divorce wiped him out, but you seem to be doing alright."

"Alicia, the divorce was not tilted in my favor. You should know this," I reasoned. "He pushed to keep the apartment complexes. That's what he wanted, probably because he knew there was far more income potential from them. But you should be smart enough to figure out that that means more maintenance. Chris always worked a lot. I'm not even sure how he managed to find the time to hook up with you. Either way, this has nothing to do with me."

"I want what I was promised," she tossed out.

Kendra jumped in and advised, "Well, then maybe you want to turn around and walk your butt back out that door to get it from the man who promised it to you."

Alicia ignored her and said, "You and I were supposed to run the jewelry business together."

"We were," I agreed. "But you were too busy sleeping with my husband instead of putting in the work to make it a success. So now, I'm reaping the benefits of my hard work and I'm doing it with my sister at my side."

Alicia's eyes shifted again between Cassie and me. When they settled on me, she demanded, "Take off your necklace."

I blinked at her. "What?" I asked, putting my hand up to touch the necklace I'd made and shared with my sister.

"I want the necklace," she ordered before looking at Cassie. "Both of them."

"You've got to be kidding me," Kendra scoffed. When

Alicia directed her attention to Tyson's sister, Kendra scolded her. "Are you seriously standing here demanding something else from this woman who used to be your best friend after you've done the lowest of the low by sleeping with her husband?"

"Kendra—" I got out before she cut me off.

"No," she clipped. "This is not okay. What kind of woman are you? You do not go and sleep with another woman's husband, especially not your best friend's husband, and then come complaining to her when things didn't turn out the way you had hoped. Newsflash, sister. He cheated on a diamond to be with the likes of you. I'm sorry, but I'm not surprised he's no longer interested. He probably realizes the gem that he lost and never stands a chance to get back. Honestly, it's just sad that you didn't see this coming all along."

Wow.

I had considered myself to be fond of Kendra, but hearing everything she'd just said, I suddenly decided I loved her. In this moment, when she should have been terrified for her life, she was standing up to a woman who was holding us at gunpoint. That was a level of loyalty I hadn't ever expected from someone who wasn't my blood relative.

How Alicia managed not to react, at least not verbally, to Kendra's insult was beyond me. Instead, she repeated, "Take off the necklaces."

"No way," Cassie ordered. "You're not taking this from me."

I could make another one for each of us. Sure, I'd taken some of the money I'd made from Patrick's project to get the diamonds I used for these necklaces because I wanted to celebrate it a bit, but this wasn't worth risking our lives over either.

"Cass," I called. Her eyes came to mine. "It's okay."

I was hoping my sister would heed my warning and know that I would make us new necklaces. My hopes were dashed when she stuck to her guns. "No."

"Fine," Alicia said. "You don't want to give them to me, I'll take something more valuable. The price I can get for two is far more than just one."

She pointed the gun at Josie and ordered, "You. Come here."

When Josie didn't move, Alicia gave a jerk of her head in her direction at the man next to her.

No way. There was no way I was letting her take my pregnant friend. Tyson's pregnant sister-in-law. The woman carrying his nephew.

The moment he took one step toward Josie, I begged, "No. Please stop."

Before I did what I was about to do I said, "I'll give it to you. Cassie will, too. You want my used necklace? You want Cassie's used necklace? Take them. You wanted my husband, and you took him. That obviously hasn't gone well for you. You want a piece of what I've worked hard for, you can have it. And every time you put this on, you can think of me. You can think about the fact that all you'll ever have in life is what you've stolen from me. You won't ever know what it's like to truly work hard for something and see the fruits of your labor. All you'll ever be is a sad, bitter woman who never gave herself the chance to be something better. You can take the jewelry, but you're not leaving here with any of these women. They're honest and loyal and they belong to me in a way that no matter what you do, you'll never succeed in taking them away. Chris was weak and succumbed to you. These ladies aren't."

With that, I lifted my hands to slide them around to the

clasp behind my neck. I removed the necklace and held it out to her. Alicia grabbed it from my hand and looked at my sister.

Cassie was staring at her like she wanted to kill her. I understood her feelings, but my only concern was her safety.

"Cassie," I urged.

Just then, the doorbell rang.

"Looks like our food is finally here," Kendra noted.

"Nobody moves," Alicia seethed.

"Alicia, they aren't going to go away. We ordered delivery. I thought that's who I was opening the door to when you showed up," I explained.

She shifted her position and stood behind the door with the man, but didn't lower her gun.

"Open it," she ordered. "But if you make even one false move, I won't hesitate to pull the trigger."

I nodded at her and moved to the door.

But no sooner did I get the door opened when I was forcefully pulled through and heard the gun blasts.

Realizing I didn't feel any of the pain that I presumed I would have if I had a gunshot wound, I looked up and saw Tyson. He had a gun in his hand and tossed me back into someone else's arms while he went inside. I didn't even have a chance to say anything to him.

Horrified, I looked up to see Gunner lifting me up and moving me out toward one of the many cars in the driveway.

"Are you okay?" he shouted.

I nodded. "Yes, but my sister," I begged as he ran away from the house with me.

"The guys will get her out," he promised.

I had no idea what he was talking about considering Tyson was the only one who went inside.

Once we made it to the car, Gunner set me down. I looked

back at my house and saw Vera being escorted toward me by a man who resembled Levi, but had slightly longer hair that was a bit lighter.

Seconds later, Kendra was following behind her with the man I remembered as Dom guiding her. Relief swept through me when Cassie rounded the corner with Kyle. Levi was shielding them. And finally, Tyson emerged from behind the house carrying Josie in his arms.

My emotions over everything that had just happened consumed my mind and caused my legs to buckle. Gunner caught me in time before I fell to the ground.

"I told you they'd all be fine," he stressed quietly. "If we walked in there right now, I have no doubt that man and the woman with the gun will be on the ground in handcuffs with Lorenzo and Pierce keeping them company. Everyone is safe. You're safe."

I nodded, but couldn't take my eyes off Tyson. I vaguely noticed out of the corner of my eyes that some of the other guys were returning to the house. Tyson made it back to where we were all standing and set Josie down beside one of the open car doors.

"Get in and sit down," he ordered.

She didn't hesitate to do as she was told. Once he closed the door, he pulled his phone out, handed it to Kendra, and instructed, "Get in with Josie. Call Beau. Tell him you're all safe so he can let Tony and Dave know."

She took his phone and nodded.

Then Tyson turned and came toward me. The minute he was close enough and had a hand on me, Gunner let go and walked away. I threw my arms around his neck and held on. Tyson held me just as fiercely.

"Oh my God," I cried.

"You're okay," he assured me, his hands moving up and down my back at my sides.

He kissed me on the neck several times as he continued to move his fingers along my body.

And even though it took some time, slowly but surely, Tyson eventually made me see that I was, in fact, okay.

CHAPTER 21

Quinn
Six months later

TODAY WAS A BIG DAY.

Today was a day I'd been anticipating for months now.

Because it was Tyson's birthday.

And I'd planned something huge.

He deserved it, too.

I had just put the finishing touches on my makeup and was slipping into the new dress I'd purchased just for this occasion. As I did that, I thought about how happy I was to finally be able to do this for Tyson. Over the last several months, he had been there for me through so much. After he and his team saved me, my sister, and his family when Alicia showed up at my home, I questioned how he even knew we were in trouble.

As it turned out, when Alicia first raised her voice after both Kendra and Josie joined me in the foyer, Cassie and Vera knew something was wrong. Knowing that, Cassie couldn't sit and hide in the kitchen while her sister was in trouble. So, she joined the commotion while Vera called Tyson.

Tyson and his team quickly mobilized and came up with a plan. Since Vera explained that we had ordered delivery, while the rest of the team was going to go around the back of the house to enter it, Tyson was going to come to the front door and pretend to be the delivery driver.

Thankfully, Tyson and his team excelled at what they did and nobody was hurt. Police officers arrived on the scene minutes after we were rescued, and Alicia was taken into custody along with her accomplice.

They were both currently serving jail time.

I struggled for about a week after the whole thing went down. My issues weren't about the fact that my ex-best friend had attempted to betray me even more than she already had. I'd finally accepted that she had other deep-seated issues she needed to deal with as well. It was all on her. Mostly, I kept picturing the gun being pointed at my face. After a couple nights of waking up in a sweat, I finally moved on.

It also helped that every time I woke up, Tyson was right by my side. Sometimes, he'd talk to me if I needed it. Other times, he'd just hold me until I fell back asleep. About a week later, I no longer had any flashbacks.

The only other thing that had happened as a result of Alicia's actions occurred roughly two weeks later.

I was at home with Tyson. It was late morning on Saturday, and he had spent the night with me, as he often did on the weekends. We had just finished up with breakfast and I needed to use the bathroom. Tyson started cleaning up the kitchen.

After using the downstairs bathroom, I stepped out and prepared to go help Tyson with cleaning up from breakfast when there was a knock at the door.

I hadn't been expecting anyone, but thought my sister was dropping by unannounced. She'd done that a few times since everything happened with Alicia. It didn't bother me, and I appreciated the concern she'd shown me.

Not thinking twice about it, I went to the door and opened it.

I never expected to see who I saw.

My ex-husband.

And the look on his face was filled with nothing but regret.

Before I had the chance to slam the door in his face or tell him to leave, he spoke. "I'm so sorry, Quinn."

That was a surprise.

"What?"

Shaking his head, Chris mumbled, "I'm sorry. I heard about what Alicia did to you two weeks ago."

I shrugged. "Yeah. Well, I learned a long time ago what kind of person she is."

Chris winced. "I'm sorry about that, too," he declared. His eyes shifted to the side as he looked behind me. I had no doubt Tyson had appeared. With a nod of understanding as regret lined his face, Chris returned his attention to me. "It was the biggest mistake of my life."

It seemed everyone was right. They believed Chris was eventually going to realize his mistake. I didn't feel bad for him. Yes, I'd loved him at one time, but he destroyed that all on his own when he stepped outside of our marriage.

Maybe it shouldn't have mattered to me anymore since I'd moved on and was happy, but I couldn't stop myself from asking, "Why did you do it, Chris?"

"Because I was a fool," he admitted. "It had nothing to do with you, Quinn. It was nothing you did. I did it because it was there and I could." He shrugged his shoulders before he added, "It was stupid and selfish of me."

I didn't know if that helped me in any way, but I was happy to now know his reason. I gave him a nod. "Thank you for telling me that."

Dipping his chin, he replied, "Yeah."

His voice was filled with remorse and sorrow. It was a shame. He threw away something really good for no good reason at all.

"I know you probably don't care what I think or say, Quinn, but I do hope that you're happy now," he said. "You deserve it."

I took my eyes from Chris and looked back to Tyson. Smiling, I said softly, "I am. I'm really happy now."

Tyson's face softened.

When I looked back at Chris, I could see the disappointment in his eyes. "Right," he started. "Well, I'm going to go. I just wanted to come out here and do the right thing for once. I wanted to see that you were really okay. Take care of yourself, Quinn."

"I will. I appreciate you coming out to apologize," I replied.

After holding my eyes a moment, Chris turned and started to walk away.

"Chris," I called.

He stopped and looked back at me. "Yeah?" he answered.

After a moment of hesitation, I advised, "If you get another chance to fall in love, take it and don't screw it up."

He gave me a small smile before he jerked his chin down in acknowledgment. Without another word, he looked away and left.

The minute I closed the door behind him, I turned and saw Tyson had closed the distance between us. I appreciated and loved the fact that he gave me the distance when Chris was standing there, but knew I'd want him right next to me as soon as Chris was gone.

Taking me in his arms, he asked, "Are you alright?"

Squeezing him around his middle, I inhaled before I sighed, "Yeah. I am."

"That man is going to regret what he did to you for the rest of his life," Tyson noted.

When I tipped my head back to look up at him, I said, "Maybe. At the time it happened, I thought my world had ended. But Chris cheating on me turned out to be a blessing. It led me to you, and I've never been this happy."

Tyson lowered his mouth to mine and kissed me.

From that point forward, I never heard from Chris again.

Now, months later, I had prepared a huge surprise for the man who helped heal my heart and took care of it from the moment I put it in his hands.

Initially, I had been worried about my ability to pull off something so big, but I quickly realized that I had an arsenal of people willing to help.

With it finally here, I could sit back, relax, and know that everything had been taken care of to make this day everything I wanted it to be for Tyson.

I'd been trying to play it cool around Tyson since I first told him about celebrating his birthday. Of course, I didn't give him the full details of what to expect. In fact, all I had said was that I wanted to take him out for his birthday. Unless he'd somehow found out my plan and hadn't said anything to me, Tyson was currently under the impression that tonight was simply going to be a quiet dinner out for the two of us.

Having slipped my foot into my second shoe, I took one last look at myself in the full-length mirror.

"It's the best birthday already," Tyson's voice filled the room.

I spun around and saw him looking at me like I was his first meal in months. "Do you like it?" I asked.

Tyson moved toward me, slipped a hand around my waist, and tugged me toward him. He brought his mouth to mine, his lips barely brushing up against mine, and his voice dipped low. "I love it. You look gorgeous. So gorgeous that I'm convinced I'll be inhaling my dinner just so I can get you back here and have the rest of the night to do things with you out of this dress."

Wanting to tease him, I pressed my body closer to his and warned, "I have things planned for you tonight when we get back."

"As long as it involves you and me with no clothes on, I'll be up for it," he assured me.

I cocked an eyebrow and asserted, "Oh you'll be up for it alright."

Then, I touched my lips to his and strutted away.

Tyson growled as he followed behind me.

Twenty minutes later, we pulled up at the restaurant. When we walked in and were greeted by the hostess, I said, "Reservation for Quinn Jacobs."

Understanding flashed in her face. She shot me a knowing look and replied, "Yes, of course. Right this way."

Tyson and I followed behind the hostess as she walked through the restaurant. "We're going to have to talk about that," he warned.

Glancing up at him, I asked, "Talk about what?"

I didn't know what he was referring to, but I was grateful he was distracted. Luckily, he was so sidetracked that by the time he was about to answer my question, the hostess said, "Right through here."

Tyson's brows pulled together as he watched the hostess pull open the doors that led into the event room.

He urged me in ahead of him. No sooner did I step inside when I turned around to look at him and shouted, *"Surprise!!"*

Visibly stunned, Tyson stood there looking around the room at the many familiar faces.

"Happy birthday, Uncle Tyson!" Jordyn shouted as she ran right for him.

Tyson squatted down and caught her. "Thanks, princess," he said before he stood up and looked at me.

Beaming up at him, I asked, "Are you surprised?"

"You planned this?"

I dipped my chin.

Tyson held my eyes a few moments as he curled his arm around my back. Then, he looked toward his family, friends, and co-workers and thanked them all for coming.

After he finished speaking, everyone got back to their conversations. Tyson and I made our way around the room so he could say hello to everyone.

Ultimately, we ended up sitting down at a table where a bunch of his friends from work were sitting. The tables his family members were sitting at were already filled up. Truthfully, I didn't think it mattered where we sat because it was clear that every single person in the room was there for the right reason.

Tyson.

He was their brother, friend, and confidant.

And I had a pretty good feeling that it was just the nature of who he was and the way he was raised that resulted in him having that amount of people loyal to him.

Looking around the table, I realized there were only two people I recognized. Gunner and Levi. Tyson didn't hesitate to introduce me to everyone else.

"Quinn, you remember Gunner, right?" he asked.

I nodded.

"And I'm sure you recall meeting Levi, yeah?"

"I do," I confirmed.

"Right. Well, that's his wife, Elle, next to him. She's about to have their baby any day now," he offered.

My eyes widened. "Wow. Congratulations."

"Thanks," Elle replied. "It's nice to meet you, Quinn."

"You too."

"Next to Elle is Pierce and his woman, Zara," Tyson went on. "And next to Zara is Leni and her man, Holden."

"Hi," I said to all of them. "Thank you so much for coming tonight. I'm so happy I finally get to meet all of you."

They all replied with the same sentiments or nods of their heads.

Unfortunately, even though I'd met Gunner and Levi, I hadn't met any of Tyson's other co-workers. So, when I decided to plan the party, I wasn't sure who I should invite. That's when I enlisted the help of Kendra, Vera, and Josie. Not only did they know his co-workers, but they also were able to get me all of the contact information for Tyson's extended family and friends outside of work.

It wasn't much later when everyone had their food and was enjoying their dinner. Tyson leaned toward me and asked, "Are you okay?"

Confused at his question, I pulled my brows together and said, "Yes. Why wouldn't I be?"

Tyson looked around the room before bringing his eyes back to mine. "It's a lot of people in here," he stated. "I just want to make sure you aren't going to pass out on me."

I rolled my eyes at him. "I'm fine," I assured him.

"Thank you for this, gorgeous," he said, his voice husky.

"You're welcome," I replied. "I didn't want to only give you the one thing I have planned for later and realized that you were the kind of man who'd appreciate a big party with your family for your birthday."

Tyson cocked an eyebrow and asked, "What's planned for later?"

"You don't remember?"

The look on his face indicated he had no idea what I had planned. I was surprised he'd forgotten.

I moved closer to him, brought my mouth to his ear, and whispered, "I get to have fun with you tonight. You promised I could use my mouth on you tonight and make it all about you."

Tyson's hand, which had been resting on my thigh, squeezed into the flesh on my leg. He pulled back just a touch to look at me. "What time is this supposed to end?" he wondered, clearly ready to go home and get his present.

"Tyson? Quinn?" a female voice called.

We turned to see the girls and Holden standing around the table. The women who'd been sitting at the table beside ours and one of the men were also standing. Now, looking up at Elle, Zara, Leni, Holden, Lexi, Dom, Ekko, Jolie, and Delaney, I had no clue who had called my name.

Leni cleared up my confusion when she declared, "It's time to dance. Are you guys coming?"

I would have loved to dance. I looked at Tyson. "Are we dancing?" I asked.

He shook his head. "You're more than welcome, Quinn. It's not my thing, though."

My shoulders dropped. "Can you at least promise me a slow dance?" I asked.

Tyson let out a chuckle and promised, "Yeah, I can do that."

"Do you mind if I go dance with the girls?" I asked before looking back up at the group. Turning my attention to Tyson again, I corrected myself, "The girls, Dom, and Holden, that is."

"No, but you better grab Cassie, Kendra, Vera, and Josie," he noted.

I smiled before I leaned forward to touch my lips to his. Then, I gathered up Tyson's sisters, Josie, and Cassie before we made our way to the dance floor.

I had the best time.

Three songs later, Tyson joined me for a slow song.

As we danced, I looked around the room. If it hadn't been for the fact that she was nearly ready to have a baby, I had no doubt that Elle would have still been on the dance floor. Since she needed a break, she'd gone back to sit with Levi. The rest of the guys had joined their women for a dance.

And it was then I noticed that Gunner wasn't with anyone.

"Tyson?" I called.

"Yeah?"

"Is Gunner dating anyone?" I asked.

"Not at the moment," he answered. "Why?"

I shrugged. "I don't know. I just happened to notice that all of you guys who work together have a significant other. He doesn't and I feel bad. It seems like he's a little lonely."

"I'm not worried about him," Tyson declared. "It'll happen when the time is right."

"You believe that?"

Tyson dipped his chin. "Yeah, I do. I wasn't looking for you, but look where I am now. Found the love of my life when I was least expecting it."

Right there, in front of everyone, I was sure I was going to break down into tears. "The love of your life?" I rasped.

My chest was pulled tighter to Tyson's as he gave me a squeeze. "The love of my life," he confirmed.

There was nothing for me to do other than just stare at him. I knew we'd expressed our feelings for one another, but this seemed so surreal to me. It amazed me to think that years ago I thought I'd married the man of my dreams. Now, I was standing here with Tyson wondering how I ever lived my life without him in it.

My silence stretched on for too long, and Tyson used it as his opportunity to continue, "That reminds me."

"Reminds you of what?" I asked.

"Remember when we were walking in here and I said we needed to talk just before you revealed this surprise?"

I did. Actually, I hadn't remembered. I completely forgot all about it until he brought it up.

"I do now," I started. "What did you want to discuss?"

"You put this reservation under Quinn Jacobs," he remarked.

"Is there something wrong with that?" I wondered, unsure what issue he had with the reservation.

"I'm thinking I might like to see that name change from Jacobs to Reed," he shared.

Was he saying?

"What... do you... are you saying you want to marry me?" I stammered.

Tyson grinned but did not reply.

The weight of it all hit me hard. Just over a year ago I had reached the lowest point of my life when the two people I trusted with everything betrayed me in the worst way possible. At that time, it was hard to think I'd ever recover from that.

Now, I was beyond lucky to be standing in the arms of a man who took my battered heart and proved I was a woman who deserved unconditional, all-consuming love. Fortunate wasn't even close to describing how I felt.

Marriage never crossed my mind. After my divorce, I didn't think I'd get another chance.

Tyson gave that to me, and it meant the world to me.

I dropped my forehead to Tyson's chest and buried my face there. His arms tightened around me. I took a few deep, settling breaths. When I got myself together, I tipped my head back and looked up at the incredible man with whom I'd fallen head-over-heels in love.

"How did I get so lucky?" I whispered.

Tyson touched his mouth to mine before he returned, "I could say the same thing."

"If you want to stay longer, we can, but whenever you're ready, I'd love to get you home and have our private celebration," I told him.

"Let's go say goodbye," he suggested, the intensity in his eyes unmistakable.

With that, Tyson and I left the dance floor. We made our rounds again and thanked everyone who had come to the party. His family wasn't the least bit upset that we were heading out a little early. In fact, I wondered if they'd seen the emotional exchange between Tyson and me because they actually encouraged us to head out. I think they knew we wanted some time to ourselves to celebrate his birthday.

Once they assured us they had everything covered and we said goodbye to the remaining guests, Tyson and I left.

And later that night, when we got back to my place, I went all out. Not only had I been excited for months about what Tyson was going to let me do for him, but I also had more to be appreciative of now.

So, I wasted no time in giving him a gift with my mouth that he wouldn't soon forget.

But in true Tyson fashion, he couldn't be greedy and generously offered a gift of his own to me.

EPILOGUE

Tyson
Ten Months Later

"THIS IS THE BEST DAY OF MY LIFE."

I looked behind my reflection in the mirror to my brother-in-law, Tony. It was easy to see that he was happy. I expected that, but I was confused by his statement because he looked like he meant what he said.

Turning around, I asked, "Are you being serious?"

Tony dipped his chin. "Yep."

"Why is my wedding day the best day of your life?" I questioned him. "Shouldn't your wedding day or the day your kids were born be the best?"

Slowly shaking his head, Tony walked toward me. He put his hand on my shoulder, squeezed, and explained, "I love your sister. She's everything to me. So are my babies. But you don't understand what I've dealt with for the last four or five years."

My brows pulled together, and I started wondering if perhaps Levi should fire me. Were my sister and Tony having problems in their marriage that I had somehow missed? I would have thought I'd have picked up on something like that. But if they were, I wasn't sure how my wedding day played any role in that.

Tony didn't give me a chance to question him. He dropped his hand from my shoulder and started walking around the room as he explained, "You know Kendra. She doesn't rest until she finds a way to make something happen. For years now, she's been going on and on about how you weren't married. At least once a week I had to hear about it. Then, you met Quinn."

He paused and looked around the room at the rest of the men that would be standing by my side today. Beau, Kyle, and Dave.

When Tony brought his attention back to me, he continued, "I thought that was going to be it. Initially, she was talking so much, but it was all because she was so excited about the two of you. But after the first month or so, she settled and was just happy that you were with Quinn. It was great until my wife decided that her new concern was the possibility that you'd let Quinn get away."

"You're not alone," Beau chimed in. "You would think with Josie having just been pregnant and then being a mom to a newborn boy and the toddler girls that she'd be too exhausted."

I looked at my brother as he closed his eyes and shook his head. "I love my kids to death, but I spend one full day with them and I'm done. It's unbelievable how these women have the energy to meddle as much as they do."

Dave joined the conversation and added, "I hear it from Vera a couple times a month too. It's never-ending. Or, at least, it was until you proposed. She settled down a bit since then."

I had to laugh.

I loved my family.

As crazy as they were, I couldn't be mad about what I was hearing. They always wanted the best for me. For that reason, I felt it prudent to make the guys aware of something.

"I don't mean to rain on your parade, but Kendra, Vera,

and Josie have all been like this from the start," I began. "If you think that Quinn and me getting married is going to make it stop, you're crazy. They'll just move on to either being concerned about when we're going to have kids or they'll start worrying about when Kyle is going to make it official."

Suddenly, the three men turned their attention to my younger brother. Not even five seconds passed before Tony begged, "Kyle, man, I'm telling you right now, do not wait. You and Cassie are good. Make it official. If not for you and her, do it for the men in your family."

Kyle just laughed at them.

Sadly, for my older brother and two men who were like brothers to me, they didn't get the answer they were hoping for and the discussion was brought to a halt. Because a moment later, my parents popped their heads inside the room and informed us it was time to head to the ceremony.

I couldn't believe it was finally happening.

I was going to marry Quinn today.

From the minute I first laid eyes on her until now, I knew she was something extraordinary. She was an incredible woman; one I was soon going to be honored to have the privilege of calling my wife.

Before I knew it, I was standing at the end of the aisle waiting for my bride. As the music played and my sisters, Josie, and Cassie each walked down the aisle before our flower girl, Jordyn, I couldn't help but let my thoughts wander to my gorgeous girl.

I'd known for a long time that I wanted to marry Quinn. It wasn't long after I first walked up to her the day I met her. At the time, I didn't think it was possible for it to be the real thing, but it didn't take Quinn long to prove otherwise.

She was, without a doubt, the woman for me. And even

though I hated to think of her ever feeling any anguish or pain, I couldn't have been happier that her ex-husband was a selfish man who cheated on her.

Because that led her to me.

Now, I was looking at her standing at the end of the aisle with her arm linked through her father's before they took that walk toward me. I felt nothing but love.

Quinn's eyes connected with mine. She smiled at me, and I knew she was struggling not to break down. My gorgeous bride kept her eyes glued to me the whole walk down the aisle. When her father took her arm and linked it with mine, I placed my opposite hand over hers.

"You look beautiful," I whispered giving her a squeeze.

It took everything in me not to gather her in my arms and kiss her right there. Somehow, I managed to restrain myself.

And for the next little while, I stood beside the woman of my dreams as we committed ourselves to one another. It was likely I wouldn't remember every word spoken at the ceremony, but I knew I'd never forget the most important ones we said to each other.

Our vows.

The ones I planned to uphold for the rest of my life. The words that told Quinn she'd always be my priority and that she'd never have to doubt my loyalty. I'd never betray her. I'd never betray us.

Before I knew it, I gave Quinn her first kiss as my wife through the cheers of our family and friends. The moment was pure perfection.

Following a break in the festivities to take some photos, Quinn and I were finally at our wedding reception.

"Before they get things started, I'm going to run back to the room and have Nikki do a quick touch-up on my face. She told me she'd meet me there. Emme told me she'd be getting photos all night, but we're going to be having our first dance soon. I want to look perfect for those," Quinn declared.

Emme was married to Levi's brother, Zane, and she was a photographer. Nikki was her best friend and a stylist and makeup artist. She was married to my co-worker, Cruz's, brother-in-law. No matter where we went in town, there always seemed to be a connection.

Tugging Quinn tight to my body, I insisted, "Gorgeous, you already look perfect."

Quinn beamed up at me. "I love that you think so," she said softly. "I feel beautiful, Tyson. Really. But a quick touch-up won't hurt anything. This is the last one of the night. I promise."

I touched my mouth to hers and acquiesced, "Alright. I'll wait here for you."

With that, Quinn took off in the opposite direction. I waited in the main area down the hall from where the reception was going to take place. Most guests came in through the doors at the entrance to the reception hall, but I was surprised at that moment to look up and see Levi and Elle walking from the reception hall toward me.

Levi was holding his baby, Kash.

"Hey," I greeted them. "Everything alright?"

Levi shook his head. "Yeah, we just needed to take a quick break before the reception gets started. Elle wants to feed the baby, and with her dress, it's just easier for her to do it somewhere quiet. We've got a room waiting."

I gave him a nod of understanding as I looked at Kash. He was one seriously cute kid.

"Congratulations, Tyson," Elle chimed in. "It was a beautiful ceremony."

"Thanks. That was all Quinn," I shared.

Levi noted, "Don't feel bad about that. It was the same for me with Elle."

Elle took her son from Levi and declared, "I'm going to take Kash and go to the room. You can meet me when you're finished."

Levi kissed his boy before putting him in his wife's arms. He watched her walk away.

That's when I stated, "You know this is all your fault, right?"

He turned his head in my direction. "What?" he responded.

"I'm a married man now, and it's all thanks to you," I began. "If you hadn't considered the fact that I'd enjoy waking up to sweet, satin nighties, I might not have ever met Quinn."

Levi grinned. "You would have met her," he assured me. "But she would have been with Gunner because he was the other option that day."

I narrowed my eyes at my boss and friend.

He laughed.

"Hey, it all worked out for everyone in the end, didn't it?" he asked.

It had. Even for Gunner. So, I couldn't complain.

Not waiting for a response because one wasn't needed, Levi shared, "I'm going to go catch up with Elle and Kash. Congratulations, Tyson. I'm really happy for you."

"Thanks, boss. You too."

Levi offered me a chin lift before he went in search of his wife and kid. I stayed there and waited for Quinn.

It wasn't much later when she returned, and her timing was perfect. The introductions had started and we were ready for the celebration to begin. After a dance with my bride, everyone was seated for dinner.

While we ate, I looked over at Quinn and saw her watching our nieces and nephews on the dance floor. The younger ones were running around and dancing. In addition, some of the guys I worked with had brought their children as well.

"It's madness," I said.

Quinn's shining eyes came to mine. "What?" she asked.

I took in her face a moment and ignored her question. "You're so gorgeous. You know I think that about you no matter what you're wearing. But today you look incredible."

Her head tilted to the side. "I love you," she rasped.

I leaned toward her and gave her a kiss. When I pulled back, she wondered, "What did you mean when you said it was madness?"

Jerking my head toward the kids on the dance floor, I explained, "All the kids."

Understanding dawned in her features. "Yeah, there certainly are a lot of them," she agreed as she looked back out and saw Josie and Kendra chasing after them.

We both laughed.

"Sooner or later, that's going to be us," I told Quinn.

"Sooner," Quinn said.

At that single word, my body locked. "What?" I asked.

Her eyes were no longer shining. They were wet with tears. I watched as my wife swallowed hard and admitted, "I'm pregnant."

My eyes widened.

"I thought I was just feeling nerves with the wedding and everything going on, but last night after you brought me back here following the rehearsal dinner, I had this nagging suspicion in the back of my mind. I went out and got a test. I took one last night. It was positive. I took the other this morning and confirmed it. We're having a baby, Tyson," Quinn declared.

My fork clattered to my plate. I framed Quinn's face in my hands and asked, "Are you sure?"

She nodded. "I didn't go back just to get my makeup touched up, Tyson. I was feeling a little queasy. I just needed to give myself a minute to pull it together."

Suddenly, I was worried. I knew Quinn wanted to have children, but maybe this was sooner than she had wanted them.

"Quinn, gorgeous, are you okay?" I worried. "Don't worry about anything. Everything will be fine. I promise."

She was silent for so long, I wasn't sure what she was thinking. To say that I was scared would have been an understatement.

"I never thought I'd be able to see anything good come out of my divorce," she started. "Obviously, I was wrong. Because I got you. And now, I've got this baby we made together and the family I know we're going to have so much fun building with one another. I'm more than okay, Tyson. I'm the best I've ever been in my life. It's all because of you."

"Quinn…" I trailed off.

"Thank you for loving me the way that you do," she murmured. "It comes with a devotion and loyalty that means the world to me. You're the best thing that's ever happened to me."

I couldn't take anymore of her sweet words, so I brought my mouth to hers and hoped I communicated precisely how I felt about her.

Quinn didn't seem to mind.

And more than eight months later, we welcomed our son, Camden Reed, to the world.

ACKNOWLEDGEMENTS

To my husband, Jeff—Thank you for never allowing me to regret handing you my heart after I was betrayed. It hasn't always been easy, but it's always been worth it. And every day with you just gets better and better. I love you.

To my boys, J&J—You'll never have to doubt where my loyalty lies. I'll always have your back. I love you both so much more than I could ever tell you.

To my loyal readers—I feel like I always have to keep the word loyal there because that's precisely what it feels like. I've been through a lot in my life that's taught me all about loyalty. I cherish it more than is probably healthy, but that's how much it means to me. Thank you for always being there to gobble up my words.

To S.H., S.B., & E.M.—This cover, these words, and the design of this book. It's one of my top favorites I've ever written, and the three of you have polished it to perfection. Thank you so much for nailing it every single time!

To the bloggers—There's a lot of authors out there hoping for that extra little push of our books into the world. I'm so grateful to every one of you that chooses to add my books to your list. I hope you love Betrayed.

CONNECT WITH A.K. EVANS

To stay connected with A.K. Evans and receive all the first looks at upcoming releases, latest news, or to simply follow along on her journey, be sure to add or follow her on social media. You can also get the scoop by signing up for the monthly newsletter, which includes a giveaway every month.

Newsletter: http://eepurl.com/dmeo6z

Website: www.authorakevans.com

Facebook: www.facebook.com/authorAKEvans

Facebook Reader Group: www.facebook.com/groups/1285069088272037

Instagram: www.instagram.com/authorakevans

Twitter: twitter.com/AuthorAKEvans

Goodreads Author Page: www.goodreads.com/user/show/64525877-a-k-evans

Subscribe on YouTube: http://bit.ly2w01yb7

Twitter: twitter.com/AuthorAKEvans

OTHER BOOKS BY A.K. EVANS

The Everything Series
Everything I Need
Everything I Have
Everything I Want
Everything I Love

The Cunningham Security Series
Obsessed
Overcome
Desperate
Solitude
Burned
Unworthy
Surrender
Betrayed

Revived (Coming June 16, 2020)

Road Trip Romance

Tip the Scales
Play the Part
One Wrong Turn

Just a Fling (Coming March 17, 2020)
Meant to Be (Coming May 2020)

ABOUT A.K. EVANS

A.K. Evans is a married mother of two boys residing in a small town in northeastern Pennsylvania, where she graduated from Lafayette College in 2004 with two degrees (one in English and one in Economics & Business). Following a brief stint in the insurance and financial services industry, Evans realized the career was not for her and went on to manage her husband's performance automotive business. She even drove the shop's race cars! Looking for more personal fulfillment after eleven years in the automotive industry, Andrea decided to pursue her dream of becoming a writer.

While Andrea continues to help administratively with her husband's businesses, she spends most of her time writing and homeschooling her two boys. When she finds scraps of spare time, Evans enjoys reading, doing yoga, watching NY Rangers hockey, dancing, and vacationing with her family. Andrea, her husband, and her children are currently working on taking road trips to visit all 50 states (though, Alaska and Hawaii might require flights).

Need more Quinn and Tyson? I've written a bonus epilogue for their story.

BONUS EPILOGUE

Quinn

"CAM! DYLAN! PLEASE KNOCK IT OFF AND JUST GET OUT OF the car."

"Boys, listen to your mother," Tyson ordered walking up beside me.

"Dylan thinks we should get a hamster or a gerbil," my six-year-old son, Camden, complained as he climbed out of the car. "I think we should get a snake. A snake would be so much cooler."

My four-year-old son, Dylan, reached out for his dad to help him out of the car. As he did, he argued, "We can play with a hamster. We can't play with a snake."

"Right now, we aren't getting any animals," I told them. "I've got enough to deal with between the two of you. The last thing I need is something else that's not a human to worry about."

It was just before lunch, and I was already exhausted. I turned to look at my husband and gave him a look that I hoped indicated that I needed him to take over. Without hesitating, Tyson backed me up.

"When the time comes to get a pet, we'll discuss it as a family," he started. "Today, we need to focus on celebrating your cousin's birthday. It wouldn't be nice for you to spend Grayson's birthday party fighting with each other. So, can we hold off on the arguing for the next couple of hours?"

"Okay, Dad," Camden agreed.

"What about you, Dylan?" Tyson asked.

"No more fighting," he mumbled.

Today was Josie and Beau's son's birthday party. His actual birthday wasn't until next Friday, but they wanted to do the party on the weekend. So, today was that day. Cam and Dylan adored their older cousin, Grayson. Truthfully, they adored all of their cousins.

After we closed the car doors, we heard a car pull up behind us. I turned around to see Kyle and Cassie had arrived. Four years ago, they'd gotten married. Seeing my sister so happy was all I could have ever wanted for her. Two years after they were married, they had my beautiful niece, Taylor. Six months ago, they had a little boy, Owen. For the longest time, Cassie had insisted that she only wanted one baby. After Taylor was born, she changed her mind. Kyle was more than willing to accommodate her request.

After waving at my sister and brother-in-law, I moved with my family toward the front door. It was hard not to considering Tyson had his hand at the small of my back ushering me forward.

When we made it to the door, Tyson looked over at me and asked, "Are you okay?"

"Yeah, but I'm exhausted," I replied. "I couldn't get comfortable last night."

"You could have stayed home and rested. I would have brought the boys on my own," Tyson offered.

"I know, but I wanted to make an appearance for Grayson. Besides, pretty soon I'm going to be stuck inside for a while. It's best if I get out while I can."

Tyson shook his head in mock disbelief. "You're having a baby, gorgeous. That doesn't mean you won't ever get out."

Yes, I was pregnant for the third time. Not long after Dylan was born, I decided I wanted to try for one more baby. I wanted a little girl. Unable to wait until I delivered, we found out at our twenty-week ultrasound that we'd done it.

We were having a girl.

And she was due in three days.

I'd gotten well beyond the point of being uncomfortable. My pregnancies had been relatively uneventful and smooth-sailing. But by the time I reached those last three or four weeks, I was ready to be done. I couldn't sleep well because it seemed like I was up using the bathroom every five minutes or I just couldn't get comfortable.

Even still, it was all so soon forgotten once I held my babies in my arms.

They were the lights of my life. I never imagined how rewarding and fulfilling of a job motherhood would be. Of course, I still had my business making jewelry, but it didn't compare to raising my kids.

I didn't get a chance to respond to Tyson because the door opened and Camden yelled out, "Uncle Beau!"

Scooping him up in his arm, Beau replied just as loudly, "Cam, my buddy. What's up, little dude?"

Cam didn't respond. He let his uncle give him a kiss and hug. Then, he was back on his feet and running into the house. Beau moved to Dylan next and did the same thing with him as he'd done with Cam.

After the kids tore off, Beau stepped back and let us inside. We exchanged greetings as Kyle, Cassie, Taylor, and Owen came in right behind us.

No sooner did Beau close the door when we were thrown

into a frenzy of chaos. Kids were shouting and running. Adults were talking and laughing. The house was filled with so much love and joy. It was everything I never knew I needed in my life.

But now I had it all.

Because Tyson gave it to me.

About two hours after we had arrived, I made my way through the kitchen toward the bathroom. I hadn't even gotten the door completely closed when it happened. A rush of fluid came out of me and soaked my pants.

Apparently, my daughter was ready to make her debut. I opened the door up again as Josie was passing by.

"Josie," I called.

"What's up, Quinn?" she asked. "I feel like I haven't had five seconds today to talk to you."

I looked down at my belly and back up at her. Josie's eyes traveled down my body where I'm sure she saw that I looked like I'd wet myself. When she brought her attention to my face again, she said, "I'm going to get Tyson. Are you okay?"

I nodded.

With that, Josie took off to get Tyson.

Seconds later, she returned with Tyson following close behind her. Before either of them could say anything, I declared, "I think there's going to be another little girl in this family in the next few hours."

Josie looked at Tyson and ordered, "Go. Take her to the hospital. Cam and Dylan will be fine here."

"Thanks, Josie," Tyson replied as he took me by the hand.

"Good luck!" she called to our departing backs.

On the way to the front door, we were stopped by Cassie and Kendra. "Why do you look like that?" Kendra asked her brother.

Cassie's eyes immediately dropped to my hand that was cradling my stomach and they widened.

"It's time?"

I nodded. "Baby girl is on her way," I told them. "Josie said they've got the boys covered. Can you guys help her out with them?"

"Quinn, get your butt out of here and get me a new niece," Kendra ordered. "There's like a million people here. Your boys are in good hands."

"Thank you!" I called out as Tyson continued to lead us out of the house.

Then he got me in the car and drove us to the hospital. He was the picture-perfect definition of calm and collected.

Hours later, not much had changed for Tyson. Well, except for the fact that he was now the proud father of a beautiful baby girl named Vanessa.

From the moment he took my hand at Josie and Beau's house until Vanessa was born, he was as calm as ever. Because he'd already done this with me twice, he knew just what to do.

I loved that I could count on him to take charge in a situation, any situation, and make it so that I never felt an ounce of worry or stress. He just always took care of it.

So, as I sat in the bed looking down at our precious baby girl, I knew I needed to share something with Tyson. I tipped my head back and saw that he was watching Vanessa as she nursed. He looked at her like he looked at our boys when they were born. His face was one filled with so much love and adoration and determination. Determination to live up to whatever idea he had in his head about the kind of father he wanted to be.

I knew what kind of father he was.

He was a father who would move mountains to provide, protect, and care for his children.

And that was even more of a reason why I was excited to tell him what I wanted to tell him.

"She's perfect," I said softly.

Smiling, Tyson brought a hand up to touch her head. As his thumb stroked over the fine hair on her scalp, he looked at me. "She's just like her mom," he started. "Absolutely gorgeous."

"Considering the boys both look like you, I think I deserve to have one of our babies look like me," I reasoned.

He shook his head. "Yeah, but I'm not sure I want to think about what that means for me down the road."

"What do you mean?"

"If she's got even a fraction of your beauty, which it's clear to see she already does, I have no doubts that boys will be calling and wanting to take her out on dates. I don't know if I can handle that."

I laughed. "Tyson, she's not even a day old yet," I pointed out.

"Doesn't matter," he argued, shaking his head. "I'm going to be terrified about it until I know she's in good hands."

Suddenly, I wondered if maybe I was making a mistake. Of course, I wore my expression on my face and Tyson worried, "What's wrong?"

I hesitated a moment, but eventually shared, "I've been thinking a lot since we found out we were having a girl, and I want her to have a sister."

Tyson took all of three seconds to let my words filter into his brain. When understanding dawned, his brows shot up.

"Are you telling me you want more than three kids after you just pushed Vanessa out of your body?" he asked.

I nervously bit my lip and nodded.

Tyson stared at me without words for what felt like hours. I couldn't stand the silence any longer, so I asked, "Could you be happy with one or two more?"

I watched as his whole body relaxed and he insisted, "Quinn, if you want five more kids, I'll give them to you."

My eyes widened. "That might be too many," I said.

Tyson laughed and brought his mouth to mine. He kissed me before he pulled back, his lips still brushing up against mine. There, he whispered, "Whenever you're healed and ready to put your body through it again, we'll work on giving Vanessa a sister."

"I love you, Tyson."

"Love you, gorgeous."

Tyson kissed me again.

Two years later, we gave Vanessa a sister. Peyton was the final missing piece to our family.

Made in the USA
Las Vegas, NV
13 March 2022